CRUSOE'S
DAUGHTER

Jane Gardam

CRUSOE'S DAUGHTER

Europa
editions

Europa Editions
214 West 29th Street
New York, N.Y. 10001
www.europaeditions.com
info@europaeditions.com

Library of Congress Cataloging in Publication Data is available
ISBN 978-1-60945-069-4

Gardam, Jane
Crusoe's Daughter

Book design by Emanuele Ragnisco
www.mekkanografici.com

Cover illustration by Margherita Barrera

Prepress by Grafica Punto Print – Rome

Printed in the USA

For my mother, Kathleen Helm.

'The pressure of life when one is fending
for oneself alone on a desert island is really no laughing matter.
It is no crying one either.'
VIRGINIA WOOLF, *The Common Reader*

PREFACE

This, by far the favourite of all my books, was written thirty years ago after the run of short novels I had rushed off in joyous release but a bit of a sense of sin, the minute the last of my children had gone to school. I knew that one day there would be one that mattered and sub-consciously I suppose I knew what it would be; and because I had become a popular novelist and won some prizes I hoped that it might find a publisher. I wanted to write a novel with more depth, less comic-sardonic, less self-congratulatory, less about my childhood adventures and passions: in fact I wanted to obliterate self and become a writer of substance and wisdom. It took me a while to realise that I was putting the cart before the horse. Without the horse the cart stands idle. It is something outside the critical consciousness that decides what a novel will be about. To my surprise and slight annoyance I found that there was nothing I wanted to write about so much as the old-fashioned north-east English world of my mother's childhood.

But it would not be a nostalgic, romantic or historical novel of bonnets and bustles and tea parties and endless summer days. I would show women of the early nineteenth century as I knew they had been—starved of money, employment, sex and the love of men who were not their 'class'. Their success in life in these immovable, unrelenting country places was judged by their ability to get married as soon as possible to a suitable man who could support them, to breed, to live chaste and never to think of working for their living. They must not show any hankering after intellectual knowledge—to hide it if they had it. To read the Bible and attend a place of worship, only whisper to a particular friend about bodily functions and tell their soul's secrets only in Confession to a priest. In our part of North Yorkshire Christianity was 'High Church' and the priests often unmarried. My mother went to Confession every week. What she had to confess I can't imagine. She used to come home singing to herself. The Priest loved her!

My mother had been removed from her convent school at twelve on account of her poor health. She was pushed along by the sea in a 'bath-chair' and not expected to live. Hypochondria governed the town. My mother lived, hale and hearty, until she was ninety. From the age of fourteen she ran her mother's house and brought up two delightful but spoilt little brothers while her parents were abroad. My grandfather was a merchant-navy sea-captain: a rogue and a hero and didn't like girls. My mother took her duties very seriously and was a woman of great love and kindness. There were very few men available— I remember how the world seemed full of women in the twenties and thirties after the four-year massacre of World War I. My mother married however at twenty-two, to a tiny, very attractive Mathematics and Physics teacher, highly intelligent but, it was thought, socially beneath her for he was the son of a farmer. It was not a very happy marriage. It took years for me to be conceived and the fact that I was a girl was a bitter disappointment to my father's family. Six years later when my brother was born there was huge rejoicing. But the six years of my mother's love and storytelling were wonderful.

And the place where I was born was wonderful. It had been in the eighteenth century a little fishing village where my mother's forebears had had a little school for the fishermen to learn to read and write. One of them had been a sailor on Lord Nelson's flagship, Victory, and he gave my great-aunt Nelson's corner cupboard, from his state-room,which now hangs in our sitting-room. The sea swished along beside the town and then a wonderful marsh stretched to the Cleveland Hills, full of rare flowers and buds and colours and strange people. Huge houses of the eighteenth century rich stood here and there, people with little money but half a dozen servants, lovely paintings, flimsy old furniture, threadbare silk curtains, who sat with their prayer books and folded hands. The women were very proud and totally uneducated (there was always money to educate the boys). These lovely buildings nearly all vanished in World War II and the marsh was covered up by a vast chemical works, which in its turn is now derelict. The best thing that probably ever happened to me was in 1936 when a small public library appeared in the town. My school was almost bookless and the town library made me. I became a scholar at the University of London and hardly went back. But I swore to bring my mother to better things and took her to the London theatre and opera and the ballet which she found very strange. All she did was write letters home about it. She wrote wonderful letters. They were her life-line. She once said of Robinson Crusoe 'He couldn't even write home'.

And so—what of this great universal novel I hoped to write? It became clear to me that I could write only of what I knew. The academic world I had longed to belong to grew pretty hollow after I married in London and had children. It was the elf-light of childhood that still hung about, the wonder of the marsh. The people still more real to me in the vanished place than most of the people I've met since.

Suppose I had stayed there—like my mother. Let me suppose a sort of castaway girl who lived there all her life like Robinson Crusoe. I'd give her a library—her dead grandfather's vicarage books. I'd give her a wonderful lover. I'd give her a nervous breakdown when he is taken from her. I'd give her alcoholism (my mother never drank!). I'd give her children and knowledge of the holiness of the heart's affections. And I'd show the power of her childhood landscape, the enfolding murmuring magical marsh so flooded with light, sunshine, silvery rain and mist, and the running sea. When I had finished I felt I needn't write any more books. Take it or leave it, *Crusoe's Daughter* says everything I have to say.

I did go on, and the later books were considered better. Became best sellers. Never mind.

Crusoe is talking to Polly Flint, my heroine, on the last pages of *Crusoe's Daughter*. He is being his usual magnificent but unromantic self. He is assessing her life, telling her she has lived only for books. 'I never loved you, Polly Flint. Characters in fiction are eunuchs. Frozen eunuchs. Your life, as a life—not bad. Marooned of course. But there's something to be said for islands'.

What my mother would have made of this book I don't know.

Jane Gardam
Sandwich, Kent, England
November 2011

CRUSOE'S
DAUGHTER

I am Polly Flint. I came to live at the yellow house when I was six years old. I stood on the steps in the wind, and the swirls of sand, and my father pulled the brass bell-knob beside the huge front door. Together we listened to the distant jangle and to footsteps padding nearer. My father did a little dance on his short legs, and whistled.

Then there followed sharp scenes of confusion and dismay. 'Shut the door. Shut the door. The sand, the sand!' and figures stood about the hall on coloured tiles.

We were not expected. My father was bringing me to live with my aunts—bleak Miss Mary, gentle Miss Frances. They were my young mother's elderly sisters. My mother was dead.

A fat maid led me away to drink tea in the kitchen and then I was led away again by the gentle aunt to a huge and vaulted chamber which must have been the little morning room. With the gentle aunt I did a jig-saw the size of a continent. I did not look up as high as the aunt's face but watched our four hands hover over the oceans of mahogany.

Now and then a door across the hall would open on incisive conversation and once a woman with a green face who carried black knitting and was dressed in black knitting came and glared round the morning room door at me. She said, 'She looks tubercular,' and put her handkerchief to her mouth and went away.

Perhaps my father stayed at the yellow house for a number of days. I remember an afternoon walking with him by the sea, dodging waves, and his figure dozing (disgracefully in the morning) in a button-back chair beside the catafalque of the drawing-room chimney-piece.

And one evening he sang. I knew that he sang very dreadfully but at the same time he danced, and I knew that he danced well—a heavy little man on dainty feet. Sailor's feet. He pirouetted and twirled about the room and Aunt Frances in a rabbity tippet played the piano. It was a sea song.

Aunt Mary sat apart. The little knitted woman retired to the other end of the room and bent to her needles in an arbour of potted ferns, and the maid coming in with coals for the fire put them down and hid her head in her apron at the singing. This I found out soon was very unlike her, for Charlotte was bland and nearly invisible. But she had once been in a choir.

I sat on a stool and knew that my father was having all these funny people on.

It was 1904 and my father died two months later on the bridge of his ship in the Irish Sea, on the coal-run to Belfast. They told me that he had rejected a place in the last life-boat and had stood in the traditional way—to attention in his merchant sea-captain's uniform—but holding and swigging a great stone bottle of gin. He had always been known as a droll man, said Aunt Frances.

The doorstep, the cold waves, the button-back chair were my only memories of my father—these and the journey that we had made together towards the yellow house. My mother had died just before I was one, and the following five years I had spent with various foster-mothers in sea-faring places where the Captain might possibly dock but more often did not. These people were hazy and the last of them the haziest of all, though she should not have been since she was a dipsomaniac who spent much of her life beneath the kitchen table. I spent much of my life on the kitchen floor, too, alongside the three or four—I think—other children in her care. I learned how not to fall in the fire and how to negotiate the locks on the larder door in order to eat. She hugged me sometimes.

Captain Flint, arriving unexpectedly one day, removed me to a first-class railway carriage (he was improvident) and in a series of these we made our way from Wales to the North East.

I remember light and shadow over pale fields—black towns, cold moors—stone walls swooping through rain and a night in what must have been a railway hotel, for there was a blackened glass roof below a window. Steam leaked up through this in spires. There were booms and echoing clanks. Fear and joy.

On the rich fur of the penultimate carriage seat, with its embroidered tray-cloth on which to rest the head—though far above my head—we sat, the Captain and I, side by side. On the rack above me was a very small suitcase. On the seat beside me was a Chinese work-box full of Chinese sewing things—my father's coming-home present: his last voyage had been long— and a scruffy doll or so, and a china mandarin.

The train lolloped between plum-coloured brick, the railway sheds of the North. Very noble. Then came high tin chimneys, centipedes of clattery trucks, serpents' nests of pipes, then mud-flats with whitish pools. There were furnaces, rolling and flapping out fire, and glimpses of diamond bars held fast in enormous fire-tongs in the heart of flames.

Out of the carriage window on the other side of the train, fields stretched out to colourless hills with a line of trees along the tops. The light showing through them made them look like loops of knitting pulled off the needles. The train rocked and my father whistled through his teeth.

The last train stopped at stations which were only wooden platforms. Gritty-faced men got on and off at these but nobody came near the first-class carriage. Whenever the train stopped it was quiet enough to hear the voices of the men talking through the carriage-walls and when they passed our window I saw sharp faces and bright eyes and heard the squeak of the battered tin tea-cans they all carried. All the men were black, but not black like the black seamen in Wales who sometimes came to the foster-mother's house and when they washed were black still. These men were only very dirty and trickly with sweat which left white marks. Those men in Wales used to throw me up in the air when I was little and catch me. Big white teeth.

The train ran out of the grit and the chimneys when the last of the men got out, and between high sand-hills. In between the sand-hills, far away, there were cold gleams of sea.

Then the Captain shared between us a huge meat pie. He took it out of an oily cardboard box and pulled it into two parts with his hands and laid the pieces carefully on the Chinese sewing box. I felt interesting contradictions in my father. 'This', he said, 'is a *great* pie. There are *good* meat pies. This is a *great* meat pie.'

It was Aunt Mary, the older sister, who told me he was dead, waiting very tall just inside my bedroom door until Aunt Frances had finished brushing and plaiting my hair. I don't remember the words, only the white starched bow beneath Aunt Mary's chin. Under her indoor hat her hair was silvery fair, and on her chin the bristles were silvery too. Behind her on a shelf was the Chinese work-box with the mandarin sitting on top. Its head slotted into a hole in its china shoulders and it nodded in rime to the up-and-down ribbon bow. A cold wind was blowing through the open bedroom window. A glassy, flashing, pitiless morning, the sea roaring.

I said (I think) 'Can I go out now and see the hens?' and ran past Aunt Mary into the yard. Through the diamonds of the chicken-wire the bow and the mandarin still bobbed and wagged. 'It is so,' they said. 'It has occurred. It must be borne.'

The chickens hopped on and off their perches and talked to each other in long rusty sentences and I wound my fingers about in the wire. Then Aunt Frances came and took me indoors and gave me lemon jelly on the kitchen table—in the middle of the morning. The little green-faced woman watched from the landing window as we crossed the yard.

It was the light at first that was troublesome—the light and the space of the yellow house. Light flowed in from all sides and down from the enormous sky. In Cardiff and Fishguard there had been little sky and the only light was reflected from the rainy slates of the terrace across the street.

Here the wind knocked the clouds about over the hills and the marsh and the dunes and the sea, until the house seemed to toss like a ship. I remember that I clutched on to things a good deal.

For to a head not much higher than the door-knobs, the ceilings and cornices of the yellow house might have been up in another atmosphere. The distance between the loose-tiled hall and the foot of the staircase was a landscape, and the newel-post and the banisters had to be held tight. The drawing-room was a jungle of tables and rugs and foot-stools and glass-topped cabinets, and the dining-room a terror. People sat there, silent, at great distances from one another, their mouths chewing slowly round and round. My eyes were on a level with heavy rows of forks and spoons. The knives were for giants. Doom was in the dining-room.

Solemn grace was said before and after the food, so solemn that the sun took notice and never shone in, as it did in the rest of the house, even when it could be seen outside flashing cheerfully to Jutland.

I knew I felt all this when I was six because of the height of the privet hedge outside the window, a poor thing, withered by salt. It never grew higher than three feet in all its years, but then it blocked the view.

All these early mysteries are very clear—forks and privet;

and looking through the side of the glass fruit-bowl and the tapping acorns high above the blinds.

Yet I cannot at all remember the day my father went away. Perhaps I never knew it, or perhaps he went away at night after I had gone to bed. Yet I remember very clearly indeed what happened the moment he had gone.

Bowls of water were placed on the kitchen table which had first been covered with newspapers and a lump of opaque soap like rancid butter was put out, and some black liquid in a bottle and a tremendous washing of hair began. I shrieked and Charlotte rubbed and poured and swirled about and said, "Well, she can shriek, anyway,' and Mrs Woods—the knitted green woman—stood watching at the kitchen door. She said 'Work it well into the roots.'

Then, after torrents of rinsing, I had to sit with my back to the table, the hair spread all over the newspapers—Charlotte began to tug and drag a comb through it, a comb with tiny teeth, like the backbone of a fish. A dover sole. I shrieked again and said some words from Cardiff. Charlotte made a gulping noise and Mrs Woods cried out like a parrot.

'Are there any?' asked Mrs Woods. 'There baint,' said Charlotte.

'Are you sure? The Welsh are very dirty.'

'Never a one.'

'Would you know one, Charlotte?'

'Aye, I would. They're running with them down the cottages.'

Mrs Woods then went quickly away and I sat on the fender while Charlotte rubbed the hair all dry.

'It's not bad hair,' she said. 'There's that to be said. It'll be the clothes next.'

I remember the clothes. They came out of dark shops far away in a black town which may have been Middlesborough. Two thin ladies made more of them, in a house built for princesses—it had a spire and was at the end of a white terrace somewhere along by the sea after a slow ride in a horse and trap.

Long, long afternoons, Aunt Frances sitting near me eating Sally Lunns, as I turned and turned about on a table and got pricked with hemming-pins. One of the sewing ladies had had complete circles of rosy paint on her cheeks and each wore a wig. Once one lady stroked me all over and purred at me like a cat when Aunt Frances was out of the room and I cried and kicked out and said the words from Wales again, and the lady went red outside the circles of paint, and that had to be the last visit.

Then, the bundles on the bed, the open clothes-presses with clean paper linings, the heavy woollen vests, the body-belts and bodices and long drawers and frilly bloomers and petticoats with harnesses over the back and flat linen buttons; and the stockings and the garters and the gaiters and the button-hooks; and the coats and the bonnets and mittens and tam-o-shanters and the Sunday brimmed hat; and the shoes for the house and the shoes for the open air, and the thick wool over-stockings and the goloshes and a pair of boots that seemed weighted with lead.

Charlotte said, 'Best not fall in the marsh in them. You'll sink like an anchor.' The boots were iron black. All the other clothes were dun.

When the drawers and the press and the wardrobe were full and I was completed in all my layers like a prime onion, 'That', said Charlotte, 'is something like!'

'I think she looks very pretty,' said Aunt Frances when I was produced in the drawing-room.

'It's the best we can do,' said Mrs Woods.

Aunt Mary said nothing for she seemed to notice nothing. 'It's odd,' she said. 'I can never get very excited about clothes.'

I felt that I understood. I felt uncomfortable and stout, and that there was a very great deal of me. I seemed to be looking down at a globe with two weighted sticks hanging below it. I sat on the button-back chair and swung these weights.

'Humpty Dumpty sat on a wall,' I sang.

'Don't dangle yourself about, Polly,' said Mrs Woods. 'Not in those beautiful boots.'

'I've not much of a neck, have I?' I asked Charlotte, looking in the glass at bedtime—another great mound of clothes waiting on the bed to set me up for the night.

Charlotte said, 'Well, maybe it'll come.'

Not once, not once ever, after the short cries of surprise on the first morning did it ever occur to my aunts—the Miss Younghusbands was their name—that I should not be there for ever.

There was no question. I was theirs. I had arrived and should stay. Never in all the years did they suggest that they had been good to me or that there was the least need for my gratitude, or that I had in any way disturbed their lives.

Very quickly in fact I became muddled about whether I had ever lived anywhere else, and the time before the arrival on the sandy step was very cloudy. I seemed to have been born at the yellow house, delivered there neat and complete without the embarrassments and messiness of conception or birth.

The total sureness of Aunts Mary and Frances about this was so great and so calm that it spread about the yellow house, and not even Mrs Woods made any demur, not even when I was with her on her own, which I managed to avoid as much as was possible. Charlotte appeared to accept all that came her way. Life simply proceeded.

There was no mention of loving me of course, nor of any particular affection, but that was nothing, for I wouldn't have known what to do with love had it been offered. 'She is a very *good* child,' they said. 'What a very *good* little girl she is,'—

and they said it in front of me, which I found very nice. After
the dark, ramshackle years, to be charged with goodness was
agreeable. It was like being tucked into bed, which Aunt
Frances sometimes did, and sat on the end of it, too, and
smiled at me and told holy stories about things called the
apostles and the saints as I drank my milk. 'Not a very *demon-
strative* child,' they said sometimes, and in front of me. 'Not
at all like her mother. But that may be just as well. We could
not cope with another Emma. A stolid little thing. But she is
good. And considering—'

I listened and watched and began to allow myself to be
taken charge of and was rather put out to find very quickly that
the goodness, though a gift from God, was something I had to
see after. For it appeared that I might lose it. I must hold tight
to it. I must clutch at it like the newel-post of the stairs, like the
string of a kite. I must examine it like my new clothes. As soon
as I saw signs of wear and tear it would be well to report.

Saturdays were the time for this, after the three ladies had
all been to church for their own confession. I was asked to sit
by Aunt Mary in her study window and we talked of sin. I
knew from the very beginning that these occasions were the
only ones when she was disappointed in me, and in herself, for
she saw in them her own failure. I dreaded them.

'Now Polly, is that all?'
'Yes, Aunt Mary.'
'You have really tried to remember?'
'Yes, Aunt Mary.'
'Don't kick the window-seat, Polly. Shall we sit in silence
for a moment?'

When we sat in silence all sorts of things welled up from
long ago, but I didn't know if they were exactly about sin.

'What are you thinking, Polly?'
'Nothing, Aunt Mary.'

But I had been seeing the dipsomaniac at the old and filthy stone sink suddenly up with her skirts and peeing into a basin.

'Shall we say a prayer, Polly?'

'Yes, Aunt Mary.'

And there was the man who used to come in the afternoons and do things to her in the kitchen. Lie on the saggy couch and roll on her and spread out her legs and make noises and be cruel to her but she didn't mind.

'I want to talk about angels,' said Aunt Mary. 'You do know, don't you, that there are angels? You believe in angels?'

'Yes, Aunt Mary.'

'If you are very good you may see one. They are invisible most of the time, but when you are *very* good—in a state of what we call "grace"—then you might catch sight of one. They can be known by their bright raiment. What is raiment, Polly?'

'Clothes.'

'You have raiment, Polly.'

I thought of my raiment. The mountains of vests.

'And if you keep it bright—?'

I thought of the body-belts. I thought of the man's trousers dropped on the kitchen floor.

'If you keep your raiment bright—the raiment of your soul—then you may even see your very own guardian angel. You may catch the gleam of a shining feather.'

'Where, Aunt Mary?'

'Anywhere, wherever you are.'

I had a vision of myself in several inappropriate settings—clinging for example to the enormous wooden curves of the seat of the water-closet, tightly in case of disappearing and being washed away to sea. One couldn't imagine an angel in the water-closet. But I should have liked to see one even there. It might be more possible perhaps out upon the marsh.

While my aunt spoke of hagiography and sin I let my gaze go wandering. The study shelves were filled with books. High up went the books. High up went the books into the shadows. The wooden window-blinds were kept down almost always to protect the books from the sea-light and the sun, and they were dusted twice a week, though seldom read, for they were valuable. The shelves were old dark-red paint and set at different levels to make the books comfortable, yet the shelves were the servants of the books, not the other way round. Every title could be seen. Nothing was squashed, or leaning or lying collapsed, or upside down, and the bindings were old and dark. When you pulled one out, the boards were brighter than the spine, with a bloom on them—rose and blue and chestnut and roof-lead green. They had the look of books that had once been greatly used and loved, and if my sins had not been too bad that week and if I had been able to think up a few more to get rid of, Aunt Mary would read to me from one of them for a little while.

Aunt Mary taught me my lessons every morning in the study and Aunt Frances taught me the piano every afternoon. Mrs Woods gave me half an hour of frightening French and later on some German, too, in the morning-room which was always out of the sun by tea-time. After tea I went usually to sit in the kitchen with Charlotte. Charlotte taught me nothing and went about the potato-peeling and pudding-beating as if she were alone. But I watched her.

I watched everyone. When Aunt Mary saw me watching she met the look with an austere one back. Aunt Frances would return the look with an immediate smile and a nod. Mrs Woods would turn away.

Charlotte just gazed. That is to say that her face did not change at all for she always kept what looked like a smile upon it—anyway a smile until you looked again, and then you saw that it was only a drawing back of pink lips that must once have been rosy, the result was an expression of aimless docility.

The face from a distance looked quite pretty and Charlotte

had a reputation for good nature, yet I knew quite early I think that what Charlotte carried about between nose and chin was something rather surprising. It was not a snarl exactly—but something like that. A disguise of some sort. A mask. As smiles went it was a dud.

I discovered soon, too, that there was some other mystery about Charlotte. One day, in perhaps the second year at the yellow house, I climbed the attic stairs to Charlotte's bedroom when she was out visiting her sister in the cottages in Fisherman's Square, and under her iron bedstead I found a sack full of old crusts. Crustless bread was Aunt Mary's only extravagance and thousands upon thousands of crusts were stuffed into the paper sack, the top ones turning green and curling into twists. I said nothing to anyone of this and made sure not to think of it again.

Charlotte herself was always washing and scrubbing and scouring—tearing down curtains, whipping off tablecloths, hanging heavy rugs on ropes across the yard and belabouring them with carpet-beaters. Clothes enough for an institution blew board-dry in the wind three times a week, terrible as an army with banners when you considered the ironing. 'Oh, we'll never get another Charlotte,' my aunts would say. 'We know how very lucky we are,' and Charlotte drew back her rosy lips in the non-smile.

Yet Charlotte never seemed clean. She wore her clothes in a bundled way. Her hair was always greasy, her cap held on with oily pins. There was something rather squashy-looking about her feet, and although she did not exactly smell, there was something.

I never felt she liked me—as I never felt that Mrs Woods liked me, although they both sang in a minor key the song about my general goodness—and Mrs Woods sometimes became a little animated when I felt out of sorts, for illness played some mystical part in her religion. Our Lord had suffered. We are told to do as He did. *Ipso facto*, to Mrs Woods; illness was blessed. For perhaps five or six years—perhaps many more—I thought that 'suffer the little children' meant that Jesus had been all for measles and mumps, and this made me thoughtful. In spite of all the care and generosity and approbation and the lovely security that breathed everywhere in the compelling yellow house, I became wary of God there. Oh very wary, indeed.

And time went by at the yellow house. One after another the years must have come and gone, summers flashing over the marsh and winters powdering it with snow. The house—it was called Oversands—was very tall and large and foreign-looking with deep roofs and two gable-ends which needed cypresses. It reflected my grandfather Younghusband's honeymoon in Siena for he had begun to build it on his return, supervising various Medici-like grilles on pantry windows and the panelling of the great front door which he had always longed to make a replica, in majolica, of the Baptistery doors of Florence. 'A joyful man,' Aunt Frances called him. Each morning, she said, he would burst from the yellow house and rush into the sea dressed in semi-deshabille—parson's stock and black old-fashioned dinner-plate hat—which he cast off as he ran. His were the books and his the huge photograph with beard of Jove that hung over the study mantelpiece. He had been a great singer of hymns and a student of old stones.

Oversands stared at the German Ocean and its back was turned towards the land. 'Grandfather was a sea-gull man,' said Aunt Mary, mystifyingly, until I realised that she meant he needed to watch the sea a great deal for the black-headed gull which was his speciality. Between its back-door and the Cleveland Hills was only the marsh.

On the marsh there were a few but surprising buildings set far apart: a church, a nunnery, an unfinished folly and away

over towards the hills in a drift of trees, a long, noble place—
The Hall. This had a little domed building beside it gleaming
gold when the sun shone.

Across the wide bay was the clutch of fisherman's cottages
sunk down almost into the sand, and inland from them some
sudden terrace houses—where the dressmakers lived—a terrace cut off in the prime of its life and looking as if it wanted
to be spirited off to Bath.

On the northern horizon there was a kind of bruise in the
sky which was the Iron-Works, the demon kitchens my father
and I had clattered through in the train, and when the wind
was from the north these made alarming roaring noises now
and then, and great surging sounds like tidal waves; but usually the marsh and everyone who lived on it was very quiet.

Only the North-East wind was disturbing and this blew
almost every day of the year. It piled up sand in front of
Fisherman's Square in a barrier reef which had to be dug away
as part of life, normal as washing day. It flung sand into the
transparent curls of the bread and butter in the white terraces
and in among the naked marble crevices of the incumbents of
the golden dome who were fortunately dead, for it was a mausoleum. It howled and bansheed on stormy nights around the
nunnery which was run partly as a convalescent home for the
poor from the Iron-Works villages over the dunes, giving the
patients headaches as they lay out on its healthy balconies; and
it blew hardest of all into and onto and through and round the
yellow house which was closest to the sea of all of them, shaking its window sashes, hurling pan-lids off Charlotte's shelves,
whisking and pulling at Aunt Mary's unusual clothes. Aunt
Mary wore Florence Nightingale veiling—the old nursing uniform from the Workers' Hospital—and looked like a black
bride. These garments were her statement and her pride, pro-
claiming that she was not only the daughter of a dead archdeacon, but had once been In Charge of Burns. The wind made

Mrs Woods shake her head and reach for her embrocation. It whined and snarled in the rafters of the huge unfinished folly, the house the millionaire-ironmaster had been building for years as one of his seaside retreats.

But when it dropped, the marsh was utterly still except for birds and bells. The birds swung about and cried, watching the sea and land and the few figures moving over them. The bells kept the time—the church bell with a sombre boom that turned each hour into a funeral (it was very High), the bells from the nunnery canonical and complex, and a bell from the Hall stables far-off and uncertain—clear and thin and old and lovely.

Sometimes the marsh dazzled. Sometimes it was so pale and unnoticeable that it seemed only an extension of the sea. The fishermen said that a hundred yards from land, it vanished completely and the waves heaved up over it and appeared to wash the hills. The church-spire stuck up out of the water and the bells chimed eerily from nowhere.

But living on the marsh it was visible enough and had great beauty. Blue-green salt-marsh grasses, shadowy fields of sea-lavender reflected and were reflected in the sky, and the build-ings between the salt and fresh-water flats and the rolling skies gave definition and authority to what otherwise would have seemed in the power of the haphazard. Nuns and fishermen went about their business—the fishermen sailing their boats on little wheels across the sand, the nuns, flickers of black and white along their balcony, moving between the scarlet blankets of the sick, or now and then about the beach where they could sometimes be seen laughing, wickedly holding their sandals in their hands. They pushed each other and squealed like bump-kins, though only in the shallowest pools.

Aunt Frances and I walked on the marsh and on the beach almost every day of my first seven years at the yellow house. Aunt Mary came with us on the marsh now and then, but did not seem aware of it. 'We've seen the sea,' she said one day. 'What shall we do now?' Charlotte walked abroad on it, but as little as possible, and Mrs Woods crossed it only to go to church. The news of the value of ozone had not reached us. 'Marshes kill,' said Mrs Woods. 'I have lived in Africa, I understand stagnant water.'

There were very few outings, very few occasions planned for a child. Even Christmas passed almost invisibly. But one day in spring when I was eight years old one great outing was announced. Aunt Mary and I were to go to tea at The Hall with Lady Vipont, Aunt Mary's old colleague. Not a nursing colleague exactly but someone very closely connected with nursing in a Christian sort of way. After that Lady Vipont had founded the curious nunnery on the marsh, The Rood, and then the convalescent home. At some very remote time she had been a young woman, Aunt Mary living not far from her. They had ridden ponies together. Lady Vipont had been greatly influenced by Grandfather Younghusband and listened often to him discussing stones. They had had holidays together at Danby Wiske at what sounded like the dawning of the world.

'You're for tea at The Hall,' said Charlotte.

'Who lives there?'

'One old lady. And one young child. Her grand-daughter. Not much older than you. Though she's usually at boarding school.'

'Is she an orphan?'

'She's something. Something queer. Her grandmother— Lady Vipont—has the handling of her. You're to go as a holiday friend.'

'What's her name? Is she like me?'

'Her name's something peculiar. She's eleven.'

'Is there to be a girl there?' I asked Aunt Mary in the hired barouche.

'A girl? Oh yes. A little girl. Lady Vipont's grand-daughter Delphi.'

We rattled up a weedy drive with tall trees drooping and came to an archway and through it a courtyard with a round building and a chapel beyond that. At the other end of the courtyard, between two broken urns on piers, were pale shallow steps. A young man in some sort of livery was standing there with his mouth open and poking about at his teeth with a twig.

When we got out—Aunt Mary in her nursing robes as usual—he stopped his work on his teeth but began scratching about at his behind, then ambled forward and stood, uncertain what to do, in his satin breeches. Aunt Mary said, 'Lady Vipont? Miss Younghusband and Miss Polly,' and while he thought what to do next there appeared round the corner of the chapel a great wheelbarrow, and two girls laughing. The wheelbarrow was full of hymn-books. The girls stopped when they saw us and dropped the handles of the barrow and turned to each other. Face to face they both exploded and spat out laughter again and I knew that they were laughing at us.

'Will you come on this way?' said the tooth-picker with a sketchy dip of the head, and Aunt Mary and I were removed into the house where, in the vastest and coldest of marble drawing-rooms, sat some semi-transparent bones with black silk hung on them. Lady Vipont sat looking out at the ashy terrace and the ashy sky.

'Mary dear—and the little one. Polly—Emma's Polly!'

Aunt Mary sat on a gold chair covered in gold satin, shredding here and there. From between the shreds bulged grubby stuffing originally placed there by eighteenth-century fingers. I stood behind this chair.

'May Polly join the children, Lavinia?'

'Children?'

'There were children in the courtyard. With a barrow full of hymn-books.'

'Oh my dear Mary, no! Not hymn-books!'

'They were unmistakable.'

'Not *hymn*-books,' said the upright glassy little lady to the two girls who then came in to the room—a bronzy girl and a silvery girl. Behind them there seemed to be the shadow of a boy. A gawk.

'Delphi—what is this about the wheelbarrow?'

'It's for fires. They're no use. They're all mouldering. They've got mushroom-spores flying out of them. They make you wheeze.'

'Now Delphi, *who* told you to take the hymn-books?'

'Commonsense did. If we don't use them for fires we've got nothing. Nothing till the trees are felled and who's to do that? We'll wait till they fall. You'll freeze this winter. And they're foul hymn-books. We never use them.'

'This is Polly. Polly Flint. This is Delphi and her two little friends from er. Off you all go and play.'

I went in my draggle of heavy clothes, my regimental gaiters and weighted boots, slowly, one step at a time behind the big girls who ran ahead of me, laughing.

The shadowy boy in the background seemed to give off a sort of friendliness, but outside he called, 'I have to go now,' and disappeared. 'We'll be in the mausoleum,' called one of the girls—the bronzy one with red hair, 'after we've got another load.' She had strong, short arms and she bent to the wheelbarrow in which the silvery girl was sitting holding its sides and they ran shrieking over the cobbles, past all the stable-doors with their rickety hinges. 'Stop,' called the girl in the barrow at the steps of the round building and rose carefully, gracefully to her feet. She was tall and narrow. She stepped deftly out.

'She's Delphi, I'm Rebecca. Rebecca Zeit,' said the bronzy one. 'Hello, child. We're stealing hymn-books from the chapel.'

'The awful chapel,' said Delphi. 'Grandmother's chapel. Full of dead birds and coffin-stools and terrible echoes and broken stoves.'

'We're going to light the stoves. And we're going to look at dead ancestors. Do you want to come and look at dead ancestors? Delphi—could we bring our tea out here? To the mausoleum?'

'If you like.'

'Would they let us?'

'If I say so. I'll go and tell them.' She was gone.

'What's a—what you said?' I asked the red-haired girl Rebecca.

'Mausoleum? It's where dead people are put if they're important enough and all in the same family. Come and see.'

'I don't want to see dead people.'

'It's only statues. The skeletons are all under the floor. Come on—it's very unusual.'

'No, I'd rather just look about outside.'

'Look about inside. Don't you want to have a new experience?'

'No.'

'Delphi—she daren't come in. Make her come in.'

Delphi, coming back, passed me however without a glance. She was a tall girl, very spare, white-blonde, not exactly smiling. Her hair and legs were very long and she had no eyebrows or lashes but a heavy mouth and broad, shiny eyelids. There was a flimsy, brittle look about her as if she never went into the sun. She was like a pressed flower.

As she went by and up the mausoleum steps with her hands full of food she turned funny flat eyes on me—huge. She laughed but did nothing to urge me to follow her.

'Why is there no tea? Tea to drink?' the Rebecca girl was complaining, and I looked in through the doors, then leaned, awkward against the door-post and saw Delphi arranging hefty jam-sandwiches and slabs of seed-cake along the top of a tomb. I thought, 'A guest *ordering* things when she's out to tea!' I remember thinking how dreadful if they ever came to tea at Oversands.

'Too long,' said Delphi. 'Can't wait. We'll have water. You—

what's your name? Polly—go and get some water out of that horse-trough.'

'What do I put it in?'

'Use your head.'

'I can't use my head—'

But the pale flat eyes did not smile, so I wandered off and found a bucket and dipped it in the trough and brought it into the mausoleum, totteringly.

'She's brought it—look,' I heard Rebecca say and Delphi turned round and stared. They both collapsed again with laughter. 'Clear spring-water for tea,' Delphi said. '*What* a clever little girl! But shouldn't she wash the floor with it?'

'No, stop it Delphi,' said Rebecca, and I wanted to cry because I was listening to a foreign language I couldn't understand and knew that they felt their power. 'Go on—wash the floor, wash the floor—see if she can bend in the—oh lor!—the *gaiters*.'

And that is all I remember of the visit. Just that—and a hateful memory of wetness and paddly black water running over marble. On one of the tombs I remember a bottle of horse liniment cocooned in cobwebs with some marble roses and the head of a cherub. I must have looked up above their heads because I heard, 'Oh my! We're very haughty,' and I think I saw a tall, high dome with heraldic emblems in the plaster dropping flakes of blue and gold and scarlet turned to old rose pink, like flakes of coloured snow. And the inside of the dome's plaster was woven with swallows' nests and droppings were splattered. Near a broken pane a clump of harebells flourished and in the dome itself was a great and horrible crack stuffed with dangles of roots from the greenery growing above on the roof. Quite a sizable, cobwebby silver-birch was sprouting behind a marble man dressed only in sheets.

'Did you have a nice time with the children?' Aunt Mary asked.

'Yes, thank you.'

'*What* a pretty girl, little Delphi. She'll be a great beauty. It's difficult for beauties.'

'She's not a beauty now,' I said. 'She's very ugly indeed.'

'What dear? Well, I'm sure you looked very nice, too. And *so* good.'

I came in off the salt-marsh one day soon after my twelfth birthday with my hands full of flowers and grasses. I had found some sea milkwort and Aunt Mary was delighted. We were making a *hortus siccus* and I think at that moment she felt I was her own. 'Oh Polly!' she said. 'How lovely! And soon you're to be Confirmed.'

'No.'

The word rang round the study and bounced off Archdeacon Younghusband's face. It left him with a stunned look, reflected in my aunt's and in my own.

'No?'

'No, Aunt Mary.'

'But my dear child, why?'

'I—Just no, thank you.'

'But whyever not?'

I did not know whyever not but I knew that the answer was no.

'Is it Father Pocock? Don't you like Father Pocock?'

I had not thought about it, but considering now I found that this was so. But it was not the reason.

'It's not Father Pocock,' I said. 'I'm awfully sorry. I don't want to be Confirmed.'

'Don't say awfully dear unless it is in the accurate sense which I fear it is not. Do you feel that you are too young? Father Pocock could speak to you about that. What's that?'

I looked at the carpet.

'I just said, "How? He couldn't change it."'

'Change it?'

'My age. Twelve's twelve.'

'Nearly thirteen. He could speak to you of Grace.'

I stared ahead at the books. The matter rested.

Every few months however it was dragged alive again, and each time not I but some other girl answered, 'No.'

'I'm sorry to be so rotten,' I said.

'Don't say rotten, Polly. It means decayed. Have you *truly* thought about this? About salvation? You have heard so many wonderful sermons. You have lived for six years in this house.'

'Yes. And it's no. I'm terribly sorry.'

I prickled with fear and triumph every time. I was like a new tennis-player facing a champion and whamming back the ball where she couldn't reach it.

'Confirmed, Polly—'

'No!'

'No. Aunt Mary, I'm terribly—'

'Don't say terribly dear. It is not appropriate to penitence unless you are using it in the Greek sense, meaning large, which is obsolete now. Come let us say a prayer together and then we'll read some Tennyson.'

Confirmed I would not be.

'Is it because of the smells?' asked Charlotte in the kitchen. The old ladies were all out visiting the nunnery. The Rood. The kitchen was hot and I was sleepy after being on the marsh all afternoon. Charlotte was boiling up her knickers in a big black pan on the fire and I was looking drowsily at the pan and thinking 'Holy Rude'—and feeling wicked. Guilt lurked all over the yellow house.

'Smells,' said Charlotte. 'Incense. Sundays.'

'Oh no. I love the incense.'

Sunday was the day of processions. The first one was at

seven-thirty in the morning when my aunts and Mrs Woods gathered silently in the hall and then over the marsh they went to church. At nine o'clock they processed back for the glory of the week—breakfast, for on Sunday we had coffee.

This coffee was the one glamorous event in our lives and it was excellent, for Mrs Woods' dead husband had been in coffee in Africa and she was very much a specialist. The coffee was sent by rail to her in person from London, and she paid for it. Perhaps it was her rent, for my aunts would have never thought of asking for any money from her, since she was, we were told, 'in total penury'.

Mrs Woods made the coffee herself and carried the pot from the kitchen herself and there was a great deal of stirring and pausing and peering and sniffing and sedate smacking of lips before the three other large cups of it were poured and passed.

I adored the coffee. It meant primary colours to me, and glorious sunshine, though how I knew it did I don't know, except that I suppose I had begun to learn something from the archdeacon's globes in the study, and of islands and tropical shores, and coral reefs from any sea-faring book I could find. Africa was beginning to sound desirably wild. 'Coffee is where Woods excelled,' said his widow as we kept a reverent silence.

Colour and heat.

Try as I might, I couldn't associate Mr Woods with colour and heat or with anything that was not decidedly pale and chill. Transparent, I imagined Mr Woods, an amoeba, an emergent tadpole. The darkness which surrounded Mrs Woods, one felt, must have soaked him up. She had taken me to see his grave once—very small and lonely in the superior part of the new church's graveyard. It was a particularly small grave decorated with an upturned glass blancmange-dish. Inside the dish was a wreath of everlasting roses made out of what seemed to be candle-grease. 'Woods,' she had said stoically, pointing at the dish, and I saw him small and helpless before the cutting edge of her will, comforted only by his coffee, longing for the gaudy forest. I hoped he'd found coffee in heaven.

After breakfast came procession number two—and hat, coat, gloves, prayer-book, gaiters, sober face. At half past ten away we went, with me following this time behind, for I was allowed to the eleven o'clock service as it was Sung, and only the very holiest of the priests—Mr Pocock—actually received the Communion. I sat as good as the rest, and to look at me you'd never have guessed that I was un-Confirmed.

Eleven o'clock.

Incense.

Greek and solemn music, an hour-long sermon and a sort of tribal dance in the wind at the church-door with Father Pocock bending about towards us all and all of us bending about towards him. Laughter and little hand-shakes. Big stupid smiles. Guilt at disdain. Then home over the marsh again—no guilt there. No guilt ever on the marsh, just joy. And then Sunday dinner.

And the great blast of it through the blue and red glass of the vestibule door: the beef and the minted potatoes, the riches of gravy, the knock-out blow of the cabbage.

Then the duff. Charlotte called it a duff, the aunts called it a steamed sponge. Mrs Woods called it 'very indigestible'. The duff held the shape of the basin and jam or sometimes chocolate sauce ran down its sides. It always came in the yellow jug with the dazzling parrots on it filled with yellow custard. The jug made me think of my father. I never knew why. I loved it.

After which we all retired to our rooms, though I don't think Aunt Mary slept. I think she knelt at her prie-dieu because I saw her there once through the door when Charlotte went round at four o'clock with the reviving cups of tea. Aunt Mary knelt tall, her skin waxy. She still wore her white cap with the ribbon under the chin. The room was always so cold that the drop on the end of her nose might well have been frozen there.

Then, at five-thirty, procession number three for Evensong, and I went to this, too, after a ceremonial locking of the house; for this service—it was the 'servants' service'—Charlotte also attended, leaving ten minutes ahead of us by the back door and sitting with some other maids in the gallery. She returned by herself, too, rather later than us, for she was allowed time off on Sunday evening, so long as she had put ready the supper properly on the sideboard—cold beef, cold duff, cold custard—and we helped ourselves, sometimes kindly carrying through the dishes for her to wash up.

Then I went to my room to do my preparation for Aunt Mary's and Mrs Woods' lessons tomorrow. And then I went to bed.

At nine I heard Charlotte creak up the attic stairs and cross the boarded floor above me and the bedsprings twang above the crusts. Then the three ladies came to bed—first Mrs Woods and Aunt Frances who often talked together at the turn of the stairs at the end of my little corridor—Mrs Woods sharply, and once or twice I heard Aunt Frances crying.

Then Aunt Mary's slow feet followed, and a clonking noise against the banisters because she always brought up as bedfellows the silver spoons. Burglars are not meant to take spoons out of bedrooms.

And then I watched the mandarin if it were light enough, and listened to the sea and the wind over the marsh until I fell asleep.

When I was still twelve, not yet quite thirteen, one particular Sunday in March, we had embarked upon our journey over the marsh for the eleven o'clock service when I saw an angel. It was a huge gold man looking at me from the tower on the unfinished house.

First there was the flash of light off its wings which were curved over its head like a boat and enclosed a halo which was translucent and rose-pink. Then the clouds flew across the sun and it was gone.

I turned from it and looked back towards the sea. 'Just ordinary,' I said; 'an ordinary morning,' and I held my arms out on either side and became a bird for a time. When I said that there wasn't a thing Father Pocock could do about my age I had spoken wisdom, for ages merge. Twelve is not too old to be a bird, and I knew that Mrs Woods who thought otherwise, stomping in front of me, would never turn her head once it was launched towards the Eucharist.

'I'm just playing about,' I told the marsh and walked backwards for a time and put my boot into a pool up to the ankle and felt it being sucked down in the rushes. I pulled it out and watched the hole it had made close over with a slap. 'Now there'll be a to-do,' I said to the boot—again aloud so that the angel upon the folly might take note that everyday things must go on.

Anyway it was probably a trick of the light.

I looked again at the unfinished house and there seemed only to be some sort of machine on its tower, probably a pulley for the new slates.

'Angels, how ridiculous!' I said and continued playing birds up to the lych-gate. I let all three of my earthly guardians vanish into the dark porch before I followed them because of the boot. The final quick bell was beating like a heart, saying hurry hurry, it's almost beginning. Then it stopped, which meant there—you've done it now! You're late.

An excited, wicked, pleasant feeling usually swept over me when this happened, which wasn't often—today there had been some serious matter about a leaky hot-water bottle in Mrs Woods's muff which had damped her. I heard the organ give its first cry and stepped in towards the dark, thinking 'Two hours—two whole hours of life going to waste,' and turned back again to say goodbye to the fresh air.

From the roof-top the angel regarded me again—huge and firm and gold. He shone with comprehension and strength and I knew that he loved me and was on my side.

So that at lunch-time later that day I said that I wouldn't be able to go to church in the evening. Or probably again. Ever.

We had reached the duff. It was what Charlotte called a nice marmalade and the custard was extra thick. 'Particularly delicious,' Aunt Mary had said of her three small saintly bites.

Six eyes looked at me over their helpings and Aunt Mary said, 'You are not well, Polly. You haven't eaten your pudding.' It happened that I did have rather a pain but I said, 'I am well. But I am afraid that I can't go to Evensong.'

'Please,' I said in the silence, 'I simply can't.'

'We could of course, Polly, *order* you to come.'

'Please—'

'My dear of course you'll come,' said Aunt Frances.

'She must come, and Father Pocock must speak to her afterwards,' said Mrs Woods. The tight veil of her morning hat had left diamonds all over her cheeks and these always lasted as far as the duff. Today they were looking very deeply ingrained under a flush such as I'd not seen before. 'This of course is because she is not Confirmed.'

'I can't come,' I said to Aunt Frances sadly. If we had been alone I would have told her then about the angel. 'I've a feeling—'

'You are ill,' said Aunt Mary, and Mrs Woods perked up.

'No. I'm not. It's just—'

'Yes?'

'The eleven o'clock all seemed so—'

'This morning was a little—long,' said Aunt Frances.

'No it all seemed so—I felt that I was being told that it was—well a bit of a waste of time.'

'Felt *told*?'

'Yes. That it was all—stupid, somehow.'

'Stupid!'

'Yes. All the dreary people dirging away. And the sad music. On such a lovely day. I've wanted to say for ages—.'

'Polly!'

'That awful giant crucifix with the dead body and the blood-drips all carved in wood. And that ghastly face with the thorns all hung over one eye.'

'Go to your room.'

I went, and Aunt Mary followed. 'You are to stay here until supper-time. After Evensong I will speak to Father Pocock.'

When she was gone there was a pause and then a creak in the passage and then Charlotte came in. I knew she had been listening downstairs—she often listened at the dining-room door. She said, 'Well, you've done it. Whatever's got into you?' and sat down on the end of my bed which sank beneath her. She scratched her thighs through her apron and regarded her fat feet and flexed them. She had not sat on my bed before. She felt that my rebellion had drawn us closer and I felt frightened a little.

'You don't look so well,' she said. 'Peaky. You're blue under the eyes. D'you want a drop of something?'

'No thank you, Charlotte.'

'Drop of gin.'

'Gin?'

'I keep a drop for my bad times. Wait on.'

She brought me an inch and a half of clear-looking water in a tumbler. 'Knock it down,' she said, so I did and gave a yell and began coughing until I thought I'd die. 'It's awful. It's poison. Is it a punishment?'

'Punishment? It is not. Who'd do you favours? My word—punishment.'

Warmth was tearing about inside me. I lay still. Joyful heat sprang down my veins until even my fingers and toes were delighted. 'Oh my! Charlotte!' I said.

'Nothing like it. Go to sleep.' She went off with the empty glass. At the door she said, 'Are you right?'

'Yes. Much better. I had a pain.'

'Thought as much. Why didn't you tell them?'

'It wasn't the pain. It was the angel. I saw an angel on the marsh.'

'Oh yes.'

'It told me—well, that I can't go on with them. With church and so on. It's silly. Now.'

'The angel said this, then?'

'In a way.'

'I'd angel it.'

'What?'

'I'd angel it. The idea! Go on, you must. You're twelve. As I must at near forty. Beggars can't choose. You mind your step. It's fine for angels.'

'But I don't believe in it. All the—oh please never tell them, but—all the church. I've found out you see. It's acting lies to go on. I have acted lies, Charlotte. For years and years.'

'Then you'll have to act lies more. What harm's it do? You'll never change them downstairs. Act along with them, poor souls. It's least return. You can't break with them at twelve. All they've got's God—and you.'

When she'd gone I drifted into a haze of gin, and thought about it. I knew that I did not like Charlotte. I knew that there was something she kept hidden and hostile inside her. At the same time I knew—though how?—that she had known a world outside Oversands, a bad uncertain complex knock-about world and the one I wanted.

I dozed and woke to the face of Aunt Frances looking down miserably at me. 'Come down, dear,' she said. 'We've sent for

Father Pocock now instead of after Evensong. He wants to have a little talk with you.'

'I can't.' I shut my eyes.

'Polly, please.' But I lay still and imagined the angel, huge, untroubled as he rose off the far roof-top and stood supreme in the fat clouds, smiling.

Aunt Mary and Mrs Woods came next, together. Mrs Woods as usual with her face a little turned away and keeping over near the door.

'Polly, at once please,' said Aunt Mary in her very rare Commander of Burns voice. 'Whatever do you smell of? Come along.'

'I've a pain.'

'You have *not!*' said Mrs Woods, her face flushing again the alarming red through the African sallow. 'Father Pocock is being kept waiting. A child to keep Father Pocock waiting!'

'This is presumably the mother,' she added, to the wall.

I looked at them both as the angel's ankle-wings and golden soles passed up into the clouds, staining them for a moment with radiance. Then I smiled at Mrs Woods, for I was suddenly unaccountably happy and quite without a sense of sin. And she did look so ridiculously dreadful.

I rolled sideways out of the bed—I was in all my clothes—and said, 'Oh well, all right then Mrs Woods, I'm coming,' and tumbled upright onto the white sheepskin-rug and found that blood was pouring all down my legs.

I don't know which of the three of us was more frightened. Mrs Woods was suddenly not with us any more. Aunt Mary in her nurse's drapes drew herself up to the height of the ceiling and said, 'I shall get Frances,' and vanished, too, and I stood drunk and shaking and thinking of the crucifixion. 'I'm bleeding to death,' I said to Aunt Frances as she tiptoed in. 'No, no dear, you're not,' she said. 'I'll get Charlotte.'

So I wrapped myself in a sheet and huddled on the rug and

lay down and heard my teeth chattering. I rocked myself and I caught the mandarin watching me. I knew that it was wrong that he should see. I hid my face in my knees.

But when I looked up again he was still staring with distaste so I crawled to his shelf to put him away out of sight and dropped him on the black hearth stone and he smashed to pieces.

Charlotte arrived with bandage things, looking important, and made the bed with fresh sheets and said, 'Well, it's a fine set-on, this. I wonder whatever they're telling the parson? I've had to take them all in a tray of sherry. Two o'clock in the afternoon! I suppose they'll say you're ill.'

'I am ill, Charlotte. I'm dying. There'll have to be a doctor.' I could hear my teeth knocking about in my jaw.

'Can I go back to bed? I've broken the mandarin.'

'I see that. But you're not dying. Don't you honestly know?'

'Know what?'

'About growing up?'

'Only about being Confirmed. Is it because I won't be Confirmed?'

'No. It happens to everyone. Christians too. But it's happened to you young.'

'Everyone? To everyone? To good people? To Father Pocock?'

'Not to men. To women.'

'All women? To you?'

'All women. Even to them downstairs once over, poor old faggots.'

I forgot that I was bleeding to death.

'Charlotte! Shut up.'

'You shut up yourself,' she said, 'great lady. If you want to know what's up with you get back into bed and I'll tell you,' and she began to go about the room picking up the shattered mandarin, rolling up the terrible shame of the sheepskin rug as she gave me her version of our common female doom. I listened with horror, not only at the obscenity she was telling me but because it was she who had been chosen to tell me; and because she knew the shock it was and that she was enjoying herself enormously and would enjoy the retelling in the Evensong gallery even more. 'Now', I thought, 'I shall always hate her and now she will always despise me.' I closed my eyes and pretended to sleep.

She crept to the door at last and uttered the last foulness. 'Keep yourself nice and warm now. At these times. That's my way anyhow. Nice and warm. Don't wash yourself too much and never take a bath. You're a lady now. Keep well wrapped up. I know I do.'

The idea of Charlotte. These bits of cloth. Where did she put hers? Oh unspeakable. Were they in the bag with the crusts? The house achieved its Sunday afternoon silence and I suppose I must have sunk into some sort of unconsciousness, too.

When I woke it seemed many days later, though the sun was still at afternoon. I was feeling very well—wide awake and tough and quite unlike myself. Perhaps I was still drunk. 'Angels,' I thought. 'Blood. It's dreams.'

'It didn't happen,' I thought, 'any of it,' and I went to the bathroom and noisily, with the door open, I filled the iron bath to the top from both taps. At that time of day it was almost cold but I undressed and jumped in. Still silence in the house, though I splashed tremendously. Sherry perhaps—and shock. I dried myself and left my clothes all over the floor, tied a towel about me and went back to my room and put on a completely new set—everything of the best, topping it all off with my velvet Christmas dress and indoor pumps rather than the stygian boots. I sang a bit and made plenty of noise going down the stairs and getting into my coat in the hall. I pulled down a wool tam-o-shanter over my head, arranged my pigtails over each shoulder and marched into the study. Canon Younghusband's eyebrows seemed to rise and fall as I pulled a great fat edition off one of his shelves, for no book was meant to leave his shrine, let alone the house—or indeed even the shelf it was on if it was a Sunday and it was a novel.

The book was *Robinson Crusoe,* a book that I knew very well. Today it was going where it and I would feel at home. I pushed it inside the front of my coat and set off, giving both inner and outer door a slam, for the wide sea-shore.

The wind was tremendous over the dunes but the beach was in full sunlight and I walked fast and then ran and then walked again until I began to be aware of my fingers and toes again after the bath.

The aches and pains of the past few days had gone and I felt springy. Rather pleased with myself. I considered my body and that it was taking decisions by itself as it must have done, and my mother's must have done when it got born, as presumably it would when I died. I felt excited. There was much less to fuss about in life than I had thought. The big things it seemed were to be taken out of my hands.

I wanted to kiss someone.

Robinson Crusoe hard against my chest, I climbed the sea-wall and jumped down and began to run across the huge white beach. The wind battered me, the sun shone on me and the sea was far away with a silver line along the edge of it. The horizon was broken, so broken and curved that it seemed strange it had taken everyone so long to know that the world was round—smoke then ship came sailing towards me, ship then smoke went sailing away.

But, perhaps we had always known really. Perhaps in some aspect of us, we all know everything. Perhaps in some sort of memory I had even known this business of the blood. Perhaps everything is arranged.

The bay disappeared in the direction of the fishermen's cottages and mist, and in the other direction it stretched to the Works standing along the estuary like a line of ironclads. Steam drifted from them in plumes and turned into cream and purple clouds which took charge of the sky. The Works were 'a disgrace', said Mrs Woods, 'against nature', but Aunt Mary said there would be starvation here without them. Aunt Frances said that they made for our wonderful sunsets. I thought only that they were a marvel.

The chimneys of them now stood out against the dropping sun and I sat down in the middle of the beach on some dry seaweed and dug my heels into it and opened *Robinson Crusoe*. 'Evil,' I read, as I had read before—

EVIL
I am cast upon a horrible desolate island, void of all hope of recovery. I am singled out and separated, as it were, from all the world to be miserable.

but

GOOD
. . . I am alive and not drowned . . . I am singled out . . . to be spared from death, and He that miraculously saved me from death can deliver me from this condition.

'I am singled out'. 'Separated'. Years of solemn sermons floating scarcely listened to over my head came floating back, striking warning chords. Pride. Beware Pride—But I always had felt separated, singled out. It was why she'd gone for me so in Wales. Why she'd thrown the chip-pan and hit me. Got me out of bed and screamed at me. 'Watching me all the time,' she had said, 'you in your separate place.' Then she would hug me.

I blinked then at the beautiful page of *Robinson Crusoe* because I had only just remembered the chip-pan and the screaming. That page would always now be her great face. I must be right. Somewhere inside we do know everything about ourselves. There is no real forgetting. Perhaps we know somewhere, too, about all that is to come.

I watched the wind send tremendous ribbons of sand snaking the beach like whips.

EVIL
I am divided from mankind, a
solitaire, one banished

but

GOOD
I am not starved and perishing
on a barren place, affording no
sustenance.

The sea's edge ruffled up now and then in a splash. I willed the day to grow even colder and tax me a bit more.

EVIL
I am without any defence or
means to resist

but

GOOD
I am cast on an island where
I see no wild beasts.

I should have liked him, I thought, Robinson. He liked to set things straight. To put down the hopeful things. So sensible and brave. So strong and handsome. He made a huge effort at self-respect. He was a man of course, so it would be easier. He didn't have blood pouring out of himself every four weeks until he was old. He would never feel disgusting.

EVIL
I have no soul to speak to or
relieve me . . .

Nobody much was about on my beach either. I saw a distant sea-coal gatherer with his hand-cart, then a far-away grasshopper sitting up on a high bicycle with small children grasshoppers following on theirs—fashionable people from the terraces, 'people we don't know socially', as the aunts said. Behind them was only the sea—the long, crocodile rocks.

The wind dropped and the beach was full of small blue scallops of light as the sun went lower in the sky, saucer-shaped dents. A million, and each one of them shone. 'Having now brought my mind a little to relish my condition,' I read, 'and given over looking at the sea . . .' and I looked up myself and saw, far away towards the works, a bouncing dark dot.

I thought it was a bird at first, but then at once knew that it was too big. Up and down it danced on the sand, growing all the time, and soon I could hear something—perhaps just the clatter from the foundries blowing across unevenly in the wind.

But the noise was not a clatter. It was a thudding, and quite soon it was a crying and calling. Head-on the small black triangle bounced and for seconds together seemed to get no nearer, but to be some little insistent machine or spring capering on the same spot.

Then it was quite near and it was a pony and trap, the trap polished very smart, with graceful shafts and a basketwork body slung between high wheels. Two people sat in it, a girl and a boy, the girl holding the reins and the boy with a long arm across the seat behind her. The girl was hatless and her hair was flying. The boy was watching how she did as the pony galloped, its head stiff and sideways and white froth blowing round its black mouth. Under the wheels the sand splattered out from all the blue saucers of light. It was a picture of joy.

When they came near the boy called out, 'Woah, Hey up!' and looked over in my direction, and called again, and the gallop slowed to a canter and then a trot and the pony made a circle and the trap came squeaking and bouncing near to me and stopped. It stopped, then started again. Stopped. Then came up within a few feet of the seaweed, crunching the sand, everyone gasping.

'Good afternoon,' said the boy. 'Are you a mermaid?' The girl said nothing but shook her dark red hair about and fussed over the reins.

'Freezing with a book,' said the boy. He behaved like a man. He was nearly a man. He looked as if everything in the world was well known to him and followed a good set of rules, which he kept and was happy. Yet there was wariness about him too, as if perhaps all he knew had been thought out only on the outside. When he smiled he looked as if he found ridiculous things very nice and when he didn't smile he looked serious and good. The girl who had bigger, less careful eyes and a beak of a nose looked as if she didn't smile very often. She was examining me slowly and I saw the eyes were green. I did not like her. I also remembered her, for it was Rebecca Zeit who had burned the hymn-books.

'What's the book?' asked the boy, looking down, tall and kind. They were far above me. I started reading again. He said, 'Oh I'm sorry. I'm Theo Zeit. My sister, Rebecca. We're from the new house. The one on the marsh that never gets finished. It's to be our holiday home. The one with a tower.'

After a while I found I had said—still looking at the book—that I was Polly Flint. From the yellow house. Oversands.

I read

but

GOOD

God hath wondrously sent . . .

'We must get back,' he said, 'we're fearfully late. We're pick-nicking up in the rafters. Then we've a long way to go home.'

Still silence. I so longed to speak. I wanted so much to smile at him.

He clicked his teeth at the pony and leaned and put his hand over his sister's on the reins and shook them. 'Off we go Bec. Goodbye Miss Flint.'

'Goodbye,' I said to my book.

As they moved off he called, 'Where did you say you lived?'

'The yellow house.'

'How old are you?'

'I'm over twelve.'

'What's the book?' called Rebecca.

'*Robinson Crusoe.*'

She said nothing and I looked up then and thought, 'She's not changed. She likes to be the one who knows most. He's nicer.' He must be that shadowy boy who had gone off some-where instead of playing with us.

He called as the trap started away, 'We'll leave you a footprint.'

I heard the carriage creak, the pony walk, then trot and then the hoofs drumming again, going away to the south now, and when I let myself look again, the trap had turned once more into a bouncing dot. I read

GOOD

God wonderfully sent the ship
in near enough to the shore.

I read on and on but I still seemed to hear the drumming

and the story became only words I was looking at as the sun flicked out behind the Works and the day faded and was over.

The following Wednesday it snowed and I had a headache and Charlotte's nephew came to Oversands as he did every Wednesday on his way home from school. A long walk it must have been too, all the way from the West Dyke where most of the fishermen's children went to school, if they went at all.

He was called Stanley and his Wednesday presence was as inevitable and unchanging as the rest of the timetable at the yellow house. The clocks were wound on Sunday evening, the milkman paid and given tea on Monday morning, sitting in the kitchen in the steam of the first washday of the week. Tuesdays were celebrated by the visitation of Mr Box of Boagey's, the provisions-merchants over the marsh, Mr Box taking the order for delivery in a long greenish notebook and wearing a long greenish coat which was never removed in the house. He sat at the kitchen table eating Eccles-cakes and drinking tea while Charlotte stood over him smiling her smile.

Mr Box was a ferrety man and made me uneasy because he had slippery red lips and wet eyes and because he changed—intensified—Charlotte. They always stopped talking when I came into the kitchen. Once they were not in the kitchen but there was a crash from the pantry and a scuffling and when I went running to see, Charlotte was in there with him and looking at me in a way that said: 'There's plenty for you to learn yet. If you ever do.' Mr Box said, 'Just checking on the little extras,' and sniggered.

Wednesday was a weekly festival of house-cleaning and Thursdays were for Father Pocock, the day when Aunt Frances wore a different dress and her cameo brooch and her mother's ruby dress-ring; and sometimes there was a big event, like a nun to tea.

Friday was the day of the garden-lad who was also the milk-man's-lad and Mr Box of Boagey's lad. He was a silent glum boy who was meant to tidy up the privet hedge and saw wood for the week though he never sawed quite enough. He lurked in the sheds around the yard and looked at me over the stick pile. Once he saw me unexpectedly and dropped a spade on his foot. Once—it was in spring—he came out of the chicken-house and said, 'Give us a kiss then,' turned dark red and ran away. Once he gave me some milk for a present. I was about nine. It was too deep an event to share—there were not many presents at the yellow house—and I drank the milk alone in the coal-house and washed out the jar and put flowers in it and set them on my mantelpiece. I thought deliciously of the milk-man's-lad for many weeks as I went to sleep, although I've never liked milk.

The milkman's-lad, like most of the children round about—though I saw very few of them—looked as if he needed the milk himself, for he couldn't have weighed more than three stone and his toes stuck out through his boots.

Charlotte's nephew was very different, though he was as undersized and probably as undernourished as the rest. He must have been about seven when I first noticed him but there was already an authority and vigilance about him. He was very heavy footed and his feet grew heavier and surer as he drew nearer to our back door on which he never knocked. Stamp, stamp, along he marched; click went the latch and in he came, gathering up the sixpence Charlotte always had ready for him as he passed by the draining-board. He would look across at Charlotte and nod briskly, rather like Father Pocock, profes-sional accepter of donations to a worthy cause. Then he would sit down thump in Charlotte's rocking-chair and let his hands hang down between his large red knees.

Down the side of one of his skimpy, much-darned socks he kept a ruler and in the pocket of his jacket a row of sharp pencils. 'He'll go far,' said Charlotte, 'Stanley's ambitious.' He had a purple nose and his hair fell limp like a whitewash brush all round his head from a bald spot in the middle—colourless hair and scant. His nose ran, always, at all seasons and he grunted a lot. Even if one of my aunts came into the kitchen he never stood up, and, oddly, they never asked him to and Charlotte never suggested it. He slurped up cup after cup of tea, pouring it into himself by way of the saucer, and ate everything put before him—stale cakes, old scones, cold milk-pudding from as far back as the Wednesday before. It was all kept for him. Once I remember an elderly fish-pie—or rather its remains, the old crusty bits round the dish you have to soak off for hours before you wash it up. Stanley had them hammered off with a knife-handle in five minutes. Anything freshly cooked that morning—new bread, a still-warm cake, a lush plum tart—down they all went with the rest and with no comment. If it was food, then Stanley ate it. He was more like a dog than a boy, though with little of the bounce and gratitude of dogs.

As he left, every Wednesday, Charlotte would put an apple in his pocket with his freshly darned socks and he would shoulder his satchel, settle his balloon of a cap over the miserable hair, say, 'Bye then, auntie,' and be gone. The apple would be clear of the pocket by the time he reached the chicken-house and his mouth hugely open over it by the time he reached the yard gate. I said, 'Maybe, he's got worms,' but Charlotte said, 'No. I'd not think so.'

'Is Stanley poor?' I asked Aunt Mary.

'Oh yes. They're very poor. Charlotte's sister married very badly. A very insignificant man. They live in Phyllis Alley.'

Phyllis Alley is an offshoot of Fisherman's Square and had been built and named to give the area a more sylvan tone, though looking at it, there seemed no difference. Fisherman's Square had had the cholera not many years ago, and there was still sometimes typhoid fever and typhus. Fishermen, being

used to water controlled from afar, are not good at the arrangement of drains, and the cesspits and the drinking water of the
Square and the Alley were mingled together. Mrs Woods often
spoke of the wells and the middens of that part of the marsh
and they made her eyes shine.

'What does Stanley's father do, Aunt Mary?'

'He doesn't do anything now. He was at the works, but he was
in the explosion. He lives in bed and his wife does washing and
the children gather crabs and get the scraps from the butcher. We
help as we can of course. There are four other children.'

The Wednesday visits must have been going on for years
before Stanley spoke to me, and I had quite stopped seeing
him. He was as the kitchen-table, the dock, the steel fender, the
tea-caddies, or the row of pewter meat-covers clinging like
giant oval limpets to the wall.

'Regular as the swallows,' said Aunt Frances once, 'dear
Stanley,' and she slid a penny into his hand. 'You are sure and
fair as the primrose in spring.'

I looked at her surprised and Charlotte's lips pursed up,
and two of her heavy hairpins fell into her pastry. But Aunt
Frances was not making fun. She never did that. She was smiling at Stanley and her face was looking beautiful. She put out
her hand and touched his head and Stanley stopped kicking
about at the fender and smiled up at her and a look passed
between them which said, 'We like each other.' It was a less
upsetting look than the ones between Charlotte and Mr Box
and not the sort to keep you awake at night like the smile of
the milkman's-lad: yet when Stanley's eyes found Aunt
Frances's, I felt jealous. It was the moment I learned that our
bodies are only furniture. That attractiveness has nothing to do
with looks or years.

'How old is Aunt Frances?' I asked Charlotte.

'You don't ask things like that.'

'Yes, but how old?'

'She must be forty,' said Charlotte. She slammed fiercely about with pans, 'Every day of it. Maybe fifty.'

'How old's Stanley?'

'Stanley's ten next month. The tenth.'

The first time Stanley spoke to me was the Wednesday after the angel and the blood, when I was sitting head-achey at the kitchen table doing French for Mrs Woods. Charlotte, as usual, had been baking and the room was the warmest in the house and smelled of the lines of loaves and cakes that stood about on every surface, gold and brown and cream. All the loaves stood on their upside-down baking-tins with their tops puffing out like clouds and it was comfortable because you could stretch out and pick little crazed bits off when Charlotte wasn't looking. Outside the blizzard blew and snow fell and was even settling quite deeply on the marsh, which was rare. There was an exciting light across the yard and the sea roared. I had a cold and was glad to be left to myself. I didn't intend to stir. I didn't even look up at Stanley's crumping step and the attack upon the latch or see him when he stamped his snowy feet on the mat and picked up the sixpence. Through the French I heard the usual voices—Charlotte's, less syrupy, more Yorkshire, when she was talking with her own family, and Stanley's, gruff and low; and the shake and scuffle as his coat was taken off him. I paid no more attention than when the cat had been let in.

After a time though I heard a rhythmic angry bashing which continued. And continued. I looked up and saw that Charlotte had left the room and Stanley by the fire was holding the long poker and hitting the top bar of the grate with it—bang, bang, bang, bang, bang, bang. His face was turned to me—the thin cold nose with the dew-drop, mouth open, hair still sopped. He said, 'What yer at?'

'It's my homework.'

'You go to a school, then?'

'No. They teach me here.'

'It's all homework, then?'

'Yes.'

'We don't get it. What ist?'

'It's French.'

'French?'

'Yes.'

'Can yer do it?'

'A bit.'

'Read us some.'

I read some and after a while looked at him and he was sitting with his head cocked as if he were straining to hear something else. He looked sharp. The skin over his cheek-bones was very bright.

'Gis a bit more ont.'

I read on.

'Tell us it, then.'

So I had to translate it. I liked that. French and German were easy—as easy as Welsh had been once. I went slowly for Stanley, but even so, he kept stopping me to hear it over again.

'So one's tother?' he said.

'Yes. It's called translating. D'you like it?'

'I could like it,' he said, 'I could like translating.'

'Aye, it's grand,' he said in a moment. 'Translating's grand.'

And then he threw down the poker, picked up a cinder, pulled the ruler out of his sock, put cinder to ruler and flexed it at me.

'I like it grand,' he said. 'You want to go easy—you. See?'

'What?'

He gave a huge thick sniff, narrowed his eyes and said, 'Rot you,' focussed the cinder and fired.

It hit me on the check and hurt and I shouted out, jumped up and flung the French book at his head. He ducked down and the book flew into the fire which was very hot and bright from the baking. There was a cheerful flap of flame and the book was gone.

It happened so fast, so beautifully, that we both stood still in awe. Curved-back, coffee-coloured pages with borders of sparks were poised in the red coals for a second, then collapsed and were air. Stanley said, 'Sorry, Polly Flint,' and looked at me and I saw that he had dark blue eyes and they were frightened at last.

I ran away out of the kitchen then and down the passage and up the stairs to the drawing-room where Mrs Woods was sitting alone, eating muffins from a silver dish. I said, 'My French book's burned. It's burned in the fire,' and she stared at me with a wodge of muffin in her hand. She said, 'This is a matter for your Aunt Mary. You *dropped* it in the fire?'

'No,' I said. 'Yes. I dropped it in.'

'I see,' she said, and began to eat the muffin. I ran out of the room and to my bedroom and got into bed.

Fortunately it was the beginning of influenza—or something in the nature of the week had informed the influenza it might be worth calling in. What I remember after getting into bed is very muddled. Grey people stood around. Darkness fell, sleet rattled its nails across the window as I shivered with cold and burned with sweat. Across the marsh the nuns and Father Pocock were busy with the bells and the wind howled around my headache and mysterious tears, in an eternal argument to do with French books, flames, wickedness, flames, angels, flames, crucifixions, blood, flames, and footprints in the sand.

Now and then Charlotte's voice came through. 'It's just because of the blood. It's now that the blood's come.' '*Cold* baths,' said someone. 'Cold *baths!*'

The mandarin returned and brought his friends. They nodded in conclave on tables and shelves and in mid-air. The seventy times seven Samurai. The angel kept away.

Then slowly everything was replaced by a comforting sense of defeat. A happiness. It was a happiness outside myself and after a time I realised that it was emanating from Aunt Mary. It was her happiness seeping about the room, and she was happy because she was being skilful, nursing someone, doing what she was particularly qualified to do. From the sheepskin rug she had fled. That was a dark mystery, not spoken of, stirring the many things that Father Pocock's ministry was working to discount. But sickness of the body was a matter which training and skill could overcome, and she stood beside me in a long encouraging apron, glossy with starch, a watch pinned to her chest, wiping my hot forehead with a damp cool cloth and commanding red flannel, feeding-cups, a fire in the grate, hot water, action. The fire dappled the ceiling at night and she, herself, crept in through the small hours to make it up with her own hands, her hair in fat white plaits swinging over her white tent of nightdress and shawls.

In the mornings, when I grew better, snow-light shone in at the window and the world was still.

When at last I was sitting up again, though just in the bedroom, Aunt Frances said, 'You musn't worry about the book, Polly. Accidents do happen,' and Mrs Woods arrived, or at any rate one of her arms arrived round the door, and placed something on a table. 'Breathing-lamp,' she said. 'Her breathing-lamp!' said Aunt Frances. 'She's brought you her breathing-lamp from Africa!'

'But I can breathe perfectly—'

'Say thank you—quickly, quickly. She never lends her breathing-lamp.'

'Thank you, Mrs Woods.'

'It's to ease you,' said her voice. 'We had it for Woods. Not that there was much that it could do.'

They were very slow to let me go downstairs and for a fortnight or more I sat in the bedroom wrapped in iron-grey hospital blankets brought from a lead-lined trunk in Aunt Mary's room and old enough for Scutari. I drank broth and was read *The Cuckoo Clock*. They said, 'Oh Polly dear, you have been so *ill*,' and I felt happier all the time. I forgot Stanley and his queerness that afternoon and the way he had suddenly been unable to bear me.

'What day's today?' I asked, at last back in the kitchen.

'Wednesday.'

'Stanley isn't here yet.'

'Stanley's ill. He took the influenza too, only he's very bad,' said Charlotte. 'He had it on him that day you went mad with your French. He was queer that day. Gave it you, they say.'

'Poor Stanley. Perhaps I gave it to him. I'd caught cold on the Sunday, I think. I had a cold bath,' I said, not looking at her.

'That I know. I saw the bathroom. I wasn't to mention it. You were for killing yourself likely.'

'Have you seen him?'

'I went to see him yesterday and the day before. And Sunday I spent there.'

'All day? However did we manage?'

She wasn't looking at me but out of the window.

'Here,' she said, 'he's sent something for you. We'll hope it's not tainted with infection,' and she stood on the fender and brought a dirty folded envelope down from behind the tea-caddies. In it was a torn end of paper with 'Sorry Polly Flint' written on it, and three sixpences.

Stanley died that night and Charlotte went on Friday to the funeral. She sat still for a long time when she got back, not removing her bonnet and shawl.

And with his death the even pattern of days and weeks of seven years at the yellow house ended. On the Friday evening, Charlotte still sat in the rocking chair by the kitchen fire in the funeral crêpe that Mrs Woods had lent her. There she sat.

And there she sat, and Aunt Frances brought her some brandy and talked to her and said she should have stayed longer with her family, and then left her, thinking that was what she wanted.

And the kitchen fire went out, and there Charlotte sat.

When it got nearer to supper-time, Aunt Mary came to the kitchen to say that we could look after ourselves tonight and perhaps just warm a little soup, but Charlotte did not speak.

'You've let the fire go, Charlotte. Dear, oh dear—and *such* a cold day. Now sit still. We shall see to it. I learned all about lighting fires when I was a young nurse. Polly and I will relight it easily.'

But she could find no sticks. We muffled up in coats and scarves and wraps and went through the snow to the sheds but sticks were still inside huge trunks of wood, for the milkman's-lad had been cut off by the snow. Aunt Frances found some old newspapers under the copper and I found some safety matches in a cup, and there was plenty of coal. Aunt Mary picked up the heavy axe that stood near the tree-trunks, then quickly put it down again. We needed a hot drink. The kettle hung on its chain over the fire-place, but the water in it was cold.

'Oh dear me, Charlotte,' said Aunt Frances. 'We're very helpless, I'm afraid. We can't light a fire. Could you help us, Charlotte? Isn't there some method of making the paper into twists?'

But there she sat.

'Come along now,' Aunt Mary swung round from the kettle and the grate with a sooty mark on her face but impressive—remembering herself Sister of Burns. 'Charlotte, we need you, I'm afraid. We need a fire so that we can make you a cup of tea.'

A pin fell from Charlotte's head into her lap, but there she sat.

Aunt Frances was in the pantry, peeping about under bowls

and gauze covers, looking for soup. 'You need hot soup, dear Charlotte,' she said. 'I expect you've some nice soup here somewhere . . . There's always *soup,*' she said to us, bewildered, coming back in, 'always.'

If I had been alone with Charlotte then, I suppose that things might not have gone as they did. I might have touched her. I hated touching her but I just might have done. I might even have hugged her, although she was, even in her best clothes, so very greasy.

And yet I might. I went and hung over the back of her rocking-chair instead and began to tip it gently forward and back. '*No,* Polly,' Aunt Mary said, and Mrs Woods came in.

Except for the Sunday coffee, Mrs Woods never entered the kitchen and she stood blinking now. Snow was falling again outside but today it hardly lightened the room. The stone floor looked leaden and unswept, the rag-rugs grubby and unshaken. The range was cold. No singing of the kettle or clank of the tin clock on the shelf, no kitchen noises.

'Tea is late,' announced Mrs Woods. 'What is Charlotte about?'

'Shush,' said Aunt Frances. 'Shush.'

'Certainly not. The funeral is over. Charlotte has been sitting about in her coat for two hours. Charlotte is a Christian woman. It is her duty to rejoice and continue in her path. Light the fire, Charlotte, and bring us our tea.'

'*Charlotte!*' she said, and banged her stick on the flags and Charlotte blinked behind her glasses and turned her head and got up.

'That's better. Quickly now. Polly, go with Charlotte and chop some sticks. She'll show you. Get the fire going and set a pan of water on it. Then set about the supper with her. There's yesterday's mutton-bone. It is Friday but I think we may have a dispensation from fish tonight. In the midst of death we are in life. Stanley has reached a better world.'

Then Charlotte got up and walked over to the kitchen door and got hold of the latch that Stanley had for so long manhandled. She looked at the draining-board, and then she took off Mrs Wood's crêpe and folded it and put it down where she had been used to put the sixpences. She looked at it.

Then she said to Mrs Woods, 'And who'd bed thee? Who'd ever give thee a bairn? Who'd ever want to bed thee? And what bairn'd ever want thee? What man'd look at thee—a desolate, withered, frosted crow.'

Then she went out of the back door and we never saw her again.

In the swirling and gasping and fainting about that followed I had the picture of my two aunts looking at each other quickly and hard and then looking away, printed on my retina like the black sun after you have stared the real sun in the face. There was a sort of muffled moaning and I was alone in the kitchen. The baize door silenced all beyond it and the snow silenced all outside. I sat down on the cold fender and then in time left the kitchen and walked tiptoe, tiptoe, along the clacking tiles to the hall. The house might have been empty. I sat down at Grandfather Younghusband's desk in the near dark.

Huge leather top, double glass-and-brass inkstand, papiermâché pen-tray picked out in mother-of-pearl, blotter which had supported the great manuscripts of the *Collected Sermons, The Folklore of the North Yorkshire Moors* and *Thirty Years for Christ in Danby Wiske;* the signed photograph of the last but six, Archbishop of York, another of a steel and jet woman filled with wadding—my grandmother; and the brown-pink smudge that was the cheap photograph of my mother.

I looked at this. Such a tiny woman. There am I lying on her lap, ten months old. The lap is small. I am large and fat and floppy. Look at the fragile bird-bones in my mother's head, the deep eye sockets, lovely tight-drawn-back and piled-up hair. What a romantic dress she's wearing with the lace around the shoulders, and the rose. She sits with a foreign landscape all about her—peaks and clouds and misty lakes.

But there is a crease down the middle of them. It is not a foreign place, it is a photographer's back-cloth in Liverpool. The lace, Aunt Frances has said, would have been draped around her from his property box and the rose is cloth. Outside the studio is the Liverpool lodging-house, the smelly landing and the awful plumbing: money running short and still no letter from the Captain. No work—she was a teacher, but unable to teach because of me.

Vigorous Polly. My mother is exhausted. She is the little sister who has always been made much of. Mary and Fanny's plaything. A school-teacher before she married. A wonderful teacher, they all said. But the baby is too much for her, in black Liverpool, all by herself. She can hardly hold it, laid out on her knee. She isn't even looking at it.

Her eyes appeal instead to the photographer—'Why have I got this great ungainly thing?' she says. 'I never wanted it. I am a child myself. Why does the blood have to start running down the legs?'

I heard voices at last outside the study door. Dead Emma's sisters coming downstairs after putting Mrs Woods to bed. Whispering.

Aunt Frances: 'Don't. She can't help it. It's because Polly heard.'

Aunt Mary: 'It's not that. Agnes would have found it terrible whoever had heard. Even I. Even you.'

Aunt Frances: 'Polly—would she understand?'

Aunt Mary: 'Of course not.'

Aunt Frances: 'Did Polly understand about Stanley?'

A pause. A rattling about in the umbrella-stand. Aunt Frances said, 'We should have taken him. It was wrong to take in the mother and not the son. They should have stayed together. We divided them.'

'The sister was a good woman. She made no differences. Stanley liked Charlotte. He never doubted she was his aunt. And it meant he could live in a family.'

"What a family.'

'Of his class. With a man about. Boys need a man about.'

'Drunk all day in bed.'

'Stanley and Charlotte saw each other every week of their lives. And she had *sinned,* Frances.'

'Oh—sinned.'

'Sinned.'

'I must go and find Charlotte.'

'You must not. She'll be back with her sister. There's still sickness in that house. You'll carry it back with you again. Haven't we had enough?'

Aunt Frances: 'Where will she get anything? Any work?'

Aunt Mary: 'I'll speak to someone. The nuns. I shan't of course be able to give a very good account of her. I shall have to pray about whether I am to conceal the outburst.'

Aunt Frances: 'The boy was her own. We took him from her. Where is Polly?'

Aunt Mary: 'In her bedroom. No. We put things right, if there was ever any wrong, when we took in Polly. We saved a child in Polly. I'm going to Father Pocock. Look—Father's door is open. Shut it.'

The study-door was pulled half-shut, but I could still hear them.

'Father can't hear us, Mary.'

'Thank God. Thank God.'

'For glory's—D'you think nothing of this sort happened on the Yorkshire moors? Haven't you read his folk-lore book? I've often wondered about Mother if you want to know. Emma was nothing like either of us and she came when Father was almost a fossil. And Polly's like none of us either. But Father and Mother would *never* have separated a mother and child. Never, whatever else went on.'

'Father was a saint.'

'However can we know?'

'Frances, *shut* Father's door. He is out of reach. We can expect no message from him. He was a man of God.'

The study-door was then properly shut, the vestibule-door, the front-door shut, and through the study-window I saw Aunt Mary go gliding by round the side of the house, the white bow at a frenzied angle. It was almost completely dark in the study now and Grandfather's portrait a blank. I looked to where *Robinson Crusoe* stood upon the shelf and thought of that straightforward, strong and sexless man sitting alone in the sunshine. How easy and beautiful life had been for him.

It is usually just fancy when you say that someone 'changed from that moment'. When a change starts is a matter for the angels, and even they may disagree. Historians can never be certain of anything. Dates as we know are meaningless. The Great War 'began' in 1914 and the world 'changed'. But when did the change really begin? With a student who by chance was sitting in a café when the Archduke's carriage turned down a sidestreet by mistake?

Long, long before.

And so with people. Often the intention is definable—the moment when we say, 'From now on I shall do this, do that.' But the change itself proceeds waveringly—and of course often does not proceed at all.

But changes—huge changes—do take place, and in spite of the libraries of Freudian evidence to the contrary, the deep stamp of past years and even of dreams can be eradicated, washed away, and new people can emerge: and it will be a bad day for novels when this is not so.

After the departure of Charlotte, Aunt Frances changed, and the moment was as precise as a birth and as astonishing and as complete. A plumpish woman, conciliatory, with a face that always nodded and smiled agreement or kept whispers of discord to another room, became, all at once, brisk, energetic, unflinching. Her physical appearance changed. She grew thin. Her body became more defined under its clothes. The clothes changed, seemed to be cut tighter and made from stiffer stuff. Frogging like a soldier's appeared across her day-dresses and her soft foulards for tea-parties looked almost tailored. Her dress-maker suits which had always looked rather too big and hemmy disappeared and she wore tailor-made coats of tweed. Roses vanished from her summer straws and the spectacles which she had kept semi-secretly in the floppy bag that went about with her (that went too) she kept all day upon her nose.

She began to go out a great deal, to take up church work of her own. She even 'took on a District' which meant that she and I carried large quantities of soup about a number of streets at the Works—and the streets were indeed at the Works—deep in among their furnaces: back-to-back rows of gritty, filthy houses, with women standing on their doorsteps watching us walk along, scratching the backs of their folded arms or their heavy dull hair; tired landladies of eight or ten men who slept in shifts in their tiny back bedrooms, and often drank every penny of the rent.

The new Aunt Frances strode into these houses dispensing medicine and advice as well as soup, even over the medicine she did not consult Aunt Mary. She took sweets for the children, old clothes, her own old picture-books, our left-overs of cake and biscuits and stews in jars. She never spoke of these visits at the yellow house, even to me after we were home. Often as we came back we passed Lady Vipont from The Hall in her semi-holy uniform sliding past us in her motor car, a maid beside the chauffeur with other soup-cans on her knee, but neither did Aunt Frances speak of this, nor of any other new acquaintances, and brought a face to the dining-table full of private thoughts. Fortunately for us, for Aunt Frances would probably have been the only one of us able to take on the management of the yellow house after Charlotte, we now had the Vicar's Alice to look after us.

For the day of the departure of Charlotte did not end with the revelations through the study door. When at last that night I had crept out of the study, cold and sick, I had found Aunt Frances still seated out in the hall, under the great crucifix Grandfather Younghusband had brought home from his Italian honeymoon, upon an upright chair.

'Oh Polly!'

'I heard.'

'Oh Polly. Oh my dear!'

We looked at each other and she covered her face.

'Your aunt and I are wicked women. We are Dives to Charlotte's Lazarus.'

'You couldn't be Dives, Aunt Frances—not you. You'd never leave somebody starving at gates. And you gave him a penny, often.'

'So *cruel,*' said the chrysalis Aunt Frances.

'But Aunt Mary and Mrs Woods must have thought about it and worked it all out for a long long time—prayed to do right?'

'No. They make decisions so fast. I wasn't consulted, oh, I should so have liked some children in this house.'

'Aunt Frances, do you *like* Mrs Woods?'

The chrysalis looked frightened.

'Why does she have to live here?'

'She has always been very fond of us, Polly. Could you light the lamps? She has no money, you know. She was left in penury. Now we'll see if we can boil a little pan of water on the drawing-room fire. We might make some tea or warm some milk. Aunt Mary will soon be back.'

'Could I tell you something?'

'Well anything, dear.'

'It's—Aunt, could I go away? I want to. All the time, I didn't know until now. I think it's father having being a sailor.'

'But wherever could you go at thirteen?'

'Anywhere. To sea if I could. I know I'm lucky. To be living here. I do love you, Aunt Frances, but—'

'But we are your family. You are our sister's child.'

'What was she like?'

'Your mother was very—young.'

'You can't call people ages.'

For a flicker she looked sharp. The chrysalis was beginning to thin.

'Emma's age never changed. She was always young. As a child she was genuinely young of course: very full of life.'

'But I'm young and I'm empty of life. I just am. I sit thinking about myself all the time. I can't—sort of ever forget myself and how I have to be. All the hymn-words spring up and the Collects, Creeds and Epistles. There doesn't seem anything else.'

'Oh there is, dear.'

I was surprised to see out of the window that a drunken fight was taking place, out in a narrow street—sailors, screeching women, policemen. Dirty people crowding to look down out of opposite windows. It all faded.

'I'd like to know about it. I did once I think.'

She looked puzzled and then said, 'Yes, I know. I never did.'

The milk swelled up to the top of the pan and poured insolently over the drawing room coals.

'What a fearful smell,' came Aunt Mary's voice from the hall.

'Oh please be good,' said the chrysalis, thickening up again.

'There must be more than being good.'

'How like Emma.'

'It is *dull.*'

'It is very wicked,' said Aunt Frances, sounding uncertain, 'to find life dull. It is we who are dull by bringing to life insufficient light. Father Pocock—Polly, if you would only consider being Con—'

'No.'

'Just for the Instruction. The Theology. To learn of the eternal ecstasy waiting for the redeemed—' her voice was hollow, it echoed like the bell at church; I felt that she was listening to it without confidence—'and he could give you an hour or so of Latin—'

'*No!*'

'I have here', said Aunt Mary sweeping in, 'Father Pocock's Alice. She is lent to us. What a good, good man! Oh dear there is milk on the fire-irons—even the coals in the scuttle. Alice just take away the soiled pieces of coal to the kitchen, please, with the pan and then bring a cloth to the hearth. The milk on the coal is unsightly. What is this, Polly?'

'I tell Polly that she should not find life dull.'

'Indeed no. Most certainly not. After today. But at least the day is nearly over now and we have Alice. At least temporarily. Soon there will be a nice fire in the kitchen again.'

'I will go with her,' said Aunt Frances. 'She shall start properly with proper help and she shall sleep in the spare room at first—yes—until Charlotte's room is ready for her!'

As Aunt Frances stepped into the light in her new vigour Mrs Woods receded further into shadow. Aunt Mary stayed in her twilight and I was kept so busy with my new duties that I had no time to see myself in any light at all. The music-lessons dwindled as Aunt Frances spent more and more time with the nuns at the Chaplaincy of The Rood, but the French and German were piled on hard—especially the German. For two days of the week only German conversation was allowed—German which Aunt Frances could not speak. This I soon understood was so that Mrs Woods might make a bond with me—or rather so that she could feel that she had me in bond. But Aunt Frances did not notice and my German days she simply spent away from home. And so passed two years.

Then one day a second metamorphosis took place at breakfast-time—though like the Great War we later saw the long and clanking chain that had made its way right up to the table-leg. Mrs Woods came into the room one evening quite lavender with cold from her walk home from the Celebration of the Holy Innocents and said, 'So Father Pocock is leaving us!' and Aunt Frances fainted clean away.

'Oh, I didn't know. I thought everyone must know. I had no intention of causing shocks,' said Mrs Woods. Her chest was going up and down. The lavender had turned to two flushed marks on her ivory cheek-bones and a smudge of purple round the mouth.

For it seemed that Aunt Frances—and nobody had ever dreamed of it, though (a clank from the table-leg) I did seem to remember some things Charlotte had half-said when I was a child—that Aunt Frances and Mr Pocock had been deeply concerned with one another for many years.

Looking back, I remembered the familiar silhouette of the two of them together, sometimes on the marsh, Mr Pocock accompanying her half-way home from the weekday service; and the dress and brooch for the Thursday tea; but as the Thursday tea had been the only social engagement of the week the brooch had never seemed to us unbridled. Only perhaps in one or two silences in the drawing-room when I had come in unexpectedly—I had always of course knocked; I thought that they had probably been saying some prayers—and in the way that Father Pocock always ignored Aunt Frances at the church-porch at his public greasy handshaking, had there been anything out of the common. Aunt Frances until Stanley's death had often been ignored, and if she did anything un-ignorable, Mrs Woods had at once set her straight about it. The sound of these intense, feverish settings-right upon the stairs as the two women went up their separate ways to bed had been an agony to me for years. When the voices were raised sufficiently to hear words, I had often gone down beneath the bed-clothes, not at all knowing why, and once when things became too much even for the eiderdown and three blankets to muffle I had run along the landing pretending a visit to the bathroom and passed Aunt Frances, flushed, standing up four-square to Mrs Woods, who was looking at her with what seemed hatred and banging her stick on the rug until the sea-asters and arrow-grasses trembled in their oil-green bowl.

'You know how I *love* you,' Mrs Woods was hissing.

I flew. Nobody mentioned the scene. Ever.

When the faint was done and Aunt Frances had come to herself again and been patted on the hands and put in a chair, I asked to go to bed and did so. I did not see, therefore, what happened next, but found out later that Aunt Frances had come upstairs soon afterwards, changed into her outdoor clothes and taken herself off across the marsh to The Holy Rood and had stayed there for four hours. Much later in the evening—it must have been in the middle of the night—I heard Aunt Mary and the spoons coming up to bed. She paused and came into my room.

'Polly?'

I didn't answer and she stood by the bed and said, 'Dear Polly. Oh, poor dear Emma. Oh, how difficult.'

'We must think of St Paul,' she said, turning and staring out at the wet night. "Better than to burn." Though I don't believe that Father Pocock could ever really burn. And Frances so quiet.

'I shall of course be totally on Frances's side. Totally. Even if it means she is to go to India. I believe you would agree with that wouldn't you?'

I knew that she was talking to Grandfather Younghusband, not to me, and when she had gone away, to get rid of the feeling that he was still standing about, eyes blazing above the springing beard, I lit the lamp and looked about the bedroom.

Nothing. Nothing. An empty room. The wind and rain. And Aunt Frances going to India.

Out of habit I said some prayers then, wishing there had been someone real to consult who would send me an immediate and precise answer, or some comforting gift—as when Robinson Crusoe had spoken to me and the wonderful brother and sister had appeared, so affectionate and glorious upon the beach. Some telegram from somewhere.

But none came.

In the morning my aunts sat straight and calm at the break-fast-table and although it was Saturday were drinking coffee.

'Coffee!'

'Yes dear,' said Aunt Frances, 'I thought coffee today,' she smiled.

I hadn't realised that anybody but Mrs Woods could make coffee. I had believed it was a rite only to be learned abroad. Yet this was as good as Sunday's.

'I think, Mary, we should have coffee more often, don't you?'

'Coffee? Oh it would soon run out. Agnes buys only so much—'

'There is coffee at Boagey's and at Dicky Dick's, the lino-shop. He is extending. There's no need to send for it by the railway.'

'I'm sure there's no *local* coffee Frances. And what price! It would be far from usual.'

'Nonsense. It should be usual. Coffee. Edwin has it every day. I'll make enquiries. I'd like to think of you all having plenty of good things when I'm gone.' (She had said nothing to me.)

We looked at her carefully and Mrs Woods came into the room, looking bleak. We waited for the outburst, for the smell of coffee was wonderfully strong, but all she did was to run a finger over the sideboard as she passed it and say, 'Filthy.'

And at table she examined a spoon and said, 'Naples.'

'It is perfectly clean,' said Aunt Frances.

'Since we had vicarage servants we have lived like Naples.'

'Have you ever been to Naples, Agnes?'

'I have known the filth of many foreign countries.'

'Have you been happy anywhere, Agnes? We have had the Vicar's Alice here for over two years. You haven't complained before.'

'I think she should go back where she came from. It was when she came that the rot began.'

'You'd be very silly to send her away. She's quite settled. Edwin doesn't need her. We spoke of domestic arrangements last night. Yours and ours.'

'Yours and ours?'

'Mr Pocock is leaving us, Agnes.' Aunt Mary examined her marmalade. 'You were perfectly right. He is going to India. The new priest will be making a clean start. He may even bring a wife. And Frances is also to leave us.'

'A wife? Oh, not at The Rood. Not a wife among the nuns.'

'I don't see how a wife would affect the nuns. It's usually the parsons that distract them,' said Aunt Frances.

'The Rood is too High for a wife. A married priest!' said Mrs Woods. 'And great goodness, is this my coffee? It is only Saturday!'

'We thought a little treat today. To celebrate . . .'

'To celebrate what? To celebrate *what*, Frances? What is this nonsense of Frances leaving us?'

As I left not one of them moved, nobody whispered. Nobody stirred. But when I passed the window, behind the diseased privet, I heard Aunt Frances laughing—a young laugh, light as a girl's.

Oh, I missed her so. The wedding was frightful. It seemed that Father Pocock had been vaguely preparing for the Mission Field for some years but that Aunt Frances had only known about it as his vaguest of general intentions.

As was the proposed marriage. Neither had been more than gently touched upon between them and when the results of his years or vague correspondence with old ecclesiastical cronies had at last began to solidify and necessitate publicity and the signatures of bishops, Mr Pocock had all at once become quite remote from the yellow house. Most strangely so.

'How pinched about the lips he has looked lately,' Woods had said only the week before the revelation. 'Of course he fasts a great deal.'

'Surely not at Christmas and Epiphany,' said Aunt Mary. 'It's still weeks before Lent.'

Aunt Frances said nothing.

Since Christmas, Father Pocock had scarcely been to see us. Presumably all three ladies had seen him at their weekly Saturday confession, but Aunt Frances's walks to the chaplaincy and the nuns had become brisker than ever. She had stayed for shorter and shorter times. It was some months now, I suddenly realised, since Father Pocock had even been to tea with us. There had always been reasons—but still. Aunt Frances despite her briskness had lately been looking rather white. She was not as she had been after Charlotte—in open misery, walking about with a shadow all around her, weeping for Stanley and her sin, but all, we saw now, had not been well. In the new freedom which Aunt Frances's confidence had given us, Aunt Mary at her prayers, Woods at her secret broodings and I at my books—all of us had stopped seeing her. She was just steadily, briskly, usefully there.

Now she was rosy, talkative, merry. I thought, 'Of course. That's how she used to be, long ago. When I first came. We had all forgotten,' and it was terrible to think that Aunt Frances might never have been herself again and that we might never have noticed that she was gone.

But it was terrible, too, to know that being herself again was caused by nothing one could feel happy about, and nothing in the very least romantic (I was reading Scott and Charlotte Yonge at this time) but only by her marching out on a very wet night in the most un-feminine way—and bearding Father Pocock. *Bearding* him.

It is terrible for a woman to beard.

If it were not so unthinkable one might almost imagine that she had proposed to Father Pocock herself; brought him—like someone in Wales or Fisherman's Square—up to scratch: pale flabby candlegrease Father Pocock with hands like a seal's flippers and a puffy pink sea-anemone mouth.

And there was the business Charlotte had mentioned and which Scott, Jane Austen, the Brontës and Charlotte Yonge never: 'Who'd bed thee?' Charlotte had said. Did Father Pocock understand this aspect of things? The sleeping arrangements, the lying side by side and whatever it was that happened next? And the blood? Well, presumably Aunt Frances had stopped. She was old, after all. And he must know. He had read the Bible. About the woman who had gone on non-stop for twelve years, poor wretched thing. So it might have been worse. But what would Father Pocock have made of the couch business in Wales?

What would Aunt Frances have made of it?

Did she even know? I didn't know much, but ought I perhaps to pass on to Aunt Frances what I did know?

But the whole thing seemed yet more terrible again when he came to lunch—Aunt Frances organised it for that very

Monday, giving him only the Sunday to compose himself in formal celebration of their betrothal. There he was at our dining-table, so old and pale, smiling tranquilly round and praising the steamed chicken. Mr Casaubon—so much, much worse than Mr Casaubon, for Dorothea's husband had had a massive mind, a searching scourging soul. He had breathed rare air like Moses on the mountain-top. I could understand the whole of *Middlemarch*. The passion for a scholar. It was a bit like Jo marrying Dr Bhaer in *Little Women:* you felt sick about it, but you understood.

But Father Pocock! He looked down at Aunt Frances over the cabbage, so kindly, as if by marrying her he were going to give her a very great treat that had all been his own idea. Where Mr Casaubon had breathed out Olympian sagacity, Mr Pocock gave off a bright, little self-confidence brought on, one felt, by the relief of having had his mind made up for him. 'We shan't be eating as well as this you know, ha-ha,' he said, 'in India,'—meaning 'How you must love me'—and fluffing round the sea-anemone with his napkin. 'We shall think of all this richness in our little hut.' He was as proud as if he had acquired some small stone saint and breathed it into life.

Aunt Frances said, however, in the quick new voice, 'Hardly *hut* in Delhi, Edwin. And I'm really looking forward to proper curries. They say they're quite a different thing.' And there was no doubt at all that although she—she who had read me Tennyson—had engineered this whole dread business, herself, Aunt Frances was happy. Her room became full of open seatrunks, her days of complex, delightful visits. She was endlessly at the dressmakers of the turret room, and twice, she took me with her to York, the furthest I had travelled since I was six—where she brought quantities of gigantic male cotton underwear with buttons fastened all down the front in the most outspoken positions ('You can't expect the nuns to buy them and poor Edwin has no sister').

'The main *body* of things of course,' she said, 'we shall get from the Army and Navy Stores in London. All the tropic vestments will come from Mowbray's'—for the honeymoon was to be a working one, spent mostly at the Society for the Propagation of the Gospel in Tufton Street. 'I shall see to the worldly matters while he gets on with the spiritual things,' she said.

She made great lists of most unlikely objects—she must have done considerable previous research, in the vague hopeful years, all neatly ticked off and costed out. 'It must all be very expensive,' I said once, and she said, 'Oh, Edwin's very well-to-do. We don't have to worry about that. There's more than enough and we shall be able to give away a great deal, too, I expect'—and she gave the quick happy nod she used to give Stanley when she slipped the penny into his hand. 'Oh, I shall *enjoy* being rich,' she said in a way I felt unusual in the fiancée of a missionary.

She was married in royal blue and her Leghorn straw hat with big pink peonies on it, made of silk. The wedding was quiet, and on a cold wet morning—it had to be early as they had the connections for the London train to catch. Only Aunt Mary and I and a curious-looking Pocock cousin, the maid Alice, the parson (a colleague from Mirfield) and a trickle of nuns, were in church. There was the usual devout woman at the back who always comes to a parson's wedding and cries, and leaves before the end: and Lady Vipont who slipped in just before the bride and sat apart in The Hall pew. Mr Pocock became excited at this and tried to make signs to her from the bridegroom's position: but she didn't look at him and left before the reception.

Also, I thought that just before the service began I might possibly have seen Charlotte, somewhere behind a pillar, but then I may have been mistaken.

Mrs Woods was unwell and unable to attend. And since she needed the yellow house to be quiet in, the reception was held at The Rood. Aunt Frances drove to the church in a motor driven by Boagey's First Class Wedding Services and Aunt Mary and I went with her—two cars seeming unnecessary. Aunt Mary, not a whisker in sight, sat beside the bride in a very antique and beautiful dress and a great hat of ivory silk that had been wrapped in black tissue for several people's lifetimes. She looked astoundingly beautiful and I gazed at her all the time from my tip-up bucket-seat. I could not even look at the bride.

Beside me sat an old friend of the family I had not met before, Arthur Thwaite, who had been something special in Aunt Frances's girlhood and was to give her away. He lived, I had heard, on the Yorkshire moors and I had hoped for a Heathcliff character, but he had a monocle and a drooping moustache and kept clearing his throat.

After the ceremony the motor swished through the rain to the Chaplaincy at The Rood to sherry and paste sandwiches and a piece of wedding cake. Aunt Frances bustled about, exhorting the nuns to make the most of it all—though she didn't put it so boldly—and they did, laughing I thought like children younger than me, but not quite easy with her now, and not paying quite the same reverent attention to the groom as when he had, for example, conducted their Litanies.

He, however, had not noticed. He had shone with good humour, not noticing anyone, not even Aunt Frances much, and the arc of his stomach—perhaps it was the new under-wear—moved with more than usual gravity among us and high above us all.

At the reception nobody paid much attention to Aunt Mary or to me either—I think Aunt Mary's sudden beauty had made us all shy—and I stood for most of the time with Mr Thwaite—the Heathcliff—who looked dolefully out at the rain and said at intervals, 'Fearful weather.' The Pocock cousin approached—the best man. He had a very large head which he appeared not to be quite right in. He seemed an amiable man, but when Mr Thwaite cleared his throat for the third time and said, 'Fearful weather,' yet again, he went away.

At last we all climbed back into the bridal car and the guests gathered upon the steps, a few of the less decrepit convalescents hanging over the balcony above. I sat between my aunts now, with Mr Thwaite and Mr Pocock facing us. Mr Pocock, so large above the tip-up seat that he seemed to be poised in air like God on a ceiling. He waved in various directions somberly, Aunt Frances merrily, the nuns threw a little rice and we set out for the station.

As we hissed across the marsh, the tassels of the window-blinds scarcely swinging in Boagey's Rolls Royce, the bridegroom said, 'We shall see great changes, Frances, great changes when we return. Mark my words there will be an influx soon. An *influx*. Slum clearances are on the way. The will be huge developments. I fear we may not see our marsh again, or not as it has been.'

Nobody could think of anything to say to this and proceeded in thoughtful silence. Then Mr Thwaite cleared his throat and said, 'Really frightful weather,' and I burst into tears.

At the station she said, 'Oh Polly. Don't cry. You shall come out to us. You know you shall. For a long, long stay. For ever if you want. In a year or so. When you're eighteen. You're not to fret. You're to be very brave and think and think about India. I'll write every week. I'll never miss. I love you, darling, darling Polly, I shall miss you so. You are my very own.' But she looked so triumphant as she wound down the railway carriage window to wave, with Father Pocock's great pale face above her, that I sobbed on. I tried not to. I wanted to leave a nice memory of myself. But I couldn't stop.

I couldn't stop because I knew that whatever she said she was not what she had been. She was lying. For she was not in love. Not in the very slightest. She did not love him. She had lost her true uncalculating self. She was brimful only with the importance of being a married wife.

At breakfast the next morning Mr Thwaite gave a cough and said, 'Thought of taking the girl home.'

Aunt Mary blinked at him.

'The girl,' he said, 'Polly Flint. Polly. Little break. Back to Thwaite.'

'Take *Polly?*' She sounded as if there was a host of other girls about the house. '*Polly?*'

'Little change. Little break.' He then subsided. 'Mind if I leave you? Library. Pipe.'

We looked at each other. 'Polly dear—this is very unexpected.' And Aunt Mary, her beauty muffled again in her black, looked about for her sister. It was the loss in her face at seeing the chair empty that made me say, 'Of course not. Of course, Aunt Mary, I can't leave you. With Mrs Woods ill! Of *course* not.'

I meant it, too. Mr Thwaite was a mystery and I liked the mystery: the way he commanded his interior life and was so hopeless with his exterior one. And I was beginning to like him. But when it came to it, this was no time for me possibly to leave Aunt Mary and the yellow house.

'Well, he'll stay here for a day or two,' she said. 'Let's just see what transpires,' and she rang for Alice to come and deal with the breakfast things and put coal on the fire. 'Go to the study, Polly. I'll go up and see how Mrs Woods is. Just see what he—poor Arthur—has in mind.'

The vestibule door was open and we both stood in the hall for a moment looking at the piece of tesselation in the porch where a letter might lie. 'She couldn't have written yet,' said I, 'it's only tomorrow.' I wondered if Aunt Mary was too old and good to be thinking. 'What happened? Whatever happened? How did she do? She was with him all through the dark.'

Mr Thwaite was sitting easily at the great desk in the study smoking when I went in. 'A fair collection,' he said as I slid through the doorway and sat down on a convex, cold leather chair just inside the door.

'Of books. Younghusband's books. Whose are they now?'

'Well—ours. Aunt Mary's I suppose. Like everything.'

'Very valuable indeed,' he said. 'Some very delectable editions. Do you read them?'

'Oh yes.'

'Very often?'

'Oh yes. Most days. Part of every day.'

'What—the old philosophers and saints?'

'Yes.'

'Clerics? Divines?'

'I'm not exactly—I haven't started the Divines yet.'

'And how old are you?'

'Nearly sixteen.'

'How much younger you seem.' He made a great rough noise in his throat, 'How would you really enjoy a visit to Thwaite? Plenty of books—more up to date than this—not my sort of thing, but they might amuse. Consider it.'

'Fan and Mol used to like it,' he said. 'So did your mother.'

'Fan and Mol?'

'Your aunts. And Emma.'

(Fan and Mol!) 'Did you know my mother?'

'Very well. I knew her mother, too. An old connection.'

'You must be much younger than my mother's mother,' I said.

'Yes. But much older than the three girls.'

It took a moment to understand that the three girls were Mary, Frances and Emma, one dead, two deeply aged—quite forty.

'What do you do with your life?' asked Arthur Thwaite.

'In the mornings French and German with Mrs Woods. Then piano—I do—used to do—piano—' and the great tears came and trickled down my face at the thought of the emptiness now.

'Yes, yes. Never mind,' he said. 'Play Schubert with her do—did you? So did I.'

We sat about and the Vicar's Alice clattered round outside and the rain still whispered down. Otherwise silence blanketed all.

'So now—?'

'I don't know. I'll just live.'

'The lady in charge of the languages sick and in bed. The lady in charge of the music married and gone. What point is there? You are alone? What shall you do?'

I said, fiercely, that I was not alone. I was with Aunt Mary. I was needed. He puffed and scratched about in the pipe.

'Not very good for you,' he said. 'Not very healthy. Sitting with old women. Only sixteen.'

'Gather', he said, 'your aunt wants a break, too. Said so last night. When you had gone off to bed. The other old lady not well. Not friendly.'

'She hasn't been for some time. Well, never really.'

'It's all been rather a shock for Mary. She has not had a holiday for many years you see.'

'Oh then I'll go with her. I'll come with her to Thwaite. Whenever you like. I didn't know she felt that.'

'Rather think Mary has—some sort of nunnery business in mind for herself. Oh just for a time of course . . . '

'But—Mrs Woods? And the Vicar's Alice?'

'I rather think that if you were to come with me, all might sort itself out very nicely here. Mrs Woods, I gather the doctor thinks, should be looked after for a time. Nursing home. And Alice can do the spring cleaning. Mary will go into a Retreat somewhere. She has one in mind.'

'You mean, they don't know what to do with me?'

He looked angry and I liked him more. 'Certainly not. No.

Never leave high and dry. Very fond of you. First concern. There'd be no anxiety about you though if you were to come to me and my sister Celia. For a time. Just some short time.'

'When?'

'Well, at once. Perhaps even tomorrow. Unless you want to wait for a letter from—Mrs Pocock of course.'

I said, 'Oh no thank you, Mr Thwaite. Of course not. I'll come whenever you want. If Aunt Mary wants me to. Should it be today?'

'Perhaps in the morning. Could you gather your possessions?'

'Oh yes. Yes, I could. If Aunt Mary wants—?'

'Ha.'

'For how long?'

'Shall we say a month? To be extended to three if you are happy?'

'Oh—yes. Yes. Is it very far? Of course, I'll come.'

'Not at all. Not at all far. Though everything does seem rather far from here.'

And how very comfortable I was with this old fusty man. In the train the next day, trundling across the plain of York, I was able to ask—a first class carriage and us alone in it—'Why is it, Mr Thwaite, so like after a funeral? I have never been to a funeral. But I feel I've been.'

'Oh, it was a funeral. A sorry funeral.'

The train ran gently into York, wheezed, fizzed, stopped and we changed platforms and set off again in a smaller train to Pilmoor Junction. 'These books you read,' he said. 'Which of them would you say are of greatest—use to you?'

'Which do I like best?'

'That sort of thing. Love. Love best?'

'Oh, Defoe. *Robinson Crusoe*. I read it all the time. I'm a bit peculiar about it. Especially, I think, in troubled times.'

'Have you often had troubled times?'

'It's more that I've a discontented disposition, I think. Crusoe was so sensible. And so unimaginative. He sorts you out. I love him.'

'Read Dickens ever?'

'Yes.'

'Should read Dickens,' he said. 'Get more of a *throng* with Dickens. Great mistake to keep with one feller only. This is where we get out and we hope that the trap is waiting for us. Now Dickens will make you laugh.'

A pony-carriage was waiting for us at Helperby station with a nice dog in it. A man sat dozing in the high seat at the front. A whip was stuck in a holder beside him, drooped like a plant. It was a warm sweet day and the sun shone across coloured country.

'Great change in the weather,' said Mr Thwaite.

'No, no. Pretty steady,' said the driver.

I was handed up beside the dog who laid his chin across my knee and Mr Thwaite stepped in alongside as we clopped out of the flowery station-yard between hedges full of birds. 'All well then?' asked Mr Thwaite.

'Wey, aye,' said the driver, as if how could it not be.

The lane wound round and along. The hedges stopped and seas of young green corn rippled for miles. Clumps of late primroses and fountains of cowslips stood on the verges like bridesmaids' bouquets. There were no people about but we passed quiet farms which were well painted, red roofed and large. Horses stood in the farmyards with silky hair groomed into skirts around their ankles, and shook their heads to make the polished bridles clink. Even the chickens seemed well washed. A labourer working a pink whetstone by a gate looked prosperous and rosy. On rises in the landscape we twice passed a great house standing in a park like the paintings I'd seen at The Hall. There was the sound of streams running sweetly in the grass.

We clopped over a wooden bridge with a white-painted railing and the water underneath ran fast and cheerful over polished-looking stones. All the leaves were out—even on the ash-trees—and the sun shone warm into my back. Everywhere there was Sweet Cecily in creamy lace and the new corn growing thick.

Then we came to Mr Thwaite's village—called Thwaite—after perhaps half an hour: and a pond with ducks, a cluster of red cottages and in trees, a Norman church-tower. Then we passed into a lane with a high wall along one side of it made of small dark bricks. Ivy climbed all over it and other things were spilling out from inside. White and yellow lichens exploded over the bricks like stars. We passed some iron gates all netted up with convolvulus and on them two griffins holding shields, their proud faces turned sideways in disdain. The locks to these gates were papery thin.

We turned into a stable-yard where a boy sat on a mounting-block staring at nothing and doves walked with dignity on green cobbles. Other doves paraded over roof-tops and a stable-clock struck four.

'Thwaite,' said Mr Thwaite. 'The same name as mine and the village. Thwaite House. All it means is a clearing in the forest. Exceptionally dull. There may be cinnamon. Come along.'

We left the trap and went through a door into a stone-slabbed passage with a hanging lantern in it and a smell of roses. 'Scones,' he said. 'Cinnamon scones,' and held another door and we walked over more stone slabs, passing statues and huge black furniture and crossed-swords and huge dark paintings and Chinese jars as big as men. Our feet made a very hollow noise and suddenly from far away there came an odd long note of somebody singing.

'For tea, if lucky,' said Mr Thwaite and opened a door into a room where three windows looked out over lawns and corn-land to some hills.

On a yellow silk sofa someone was lying. There was a blaze in the grate of a wood fire that never goes out, and there was also the smell of something else, very sweet. Pot-pourri—there was a heap of it in a great dish—but it wasn't that. All I could make out on the sofa was drapery and a movement of white hands and a sense of eyes watching me.

''lo Celia. Back home. Polly. Polly Flint.' Mr Thwaite did the great harumming of the throat and moved to the window. There was a valedictory atmosphere about him: I have done what I have done. I have gone through with it. He looked at the sky. 'Splendid day,' he said. 'Very poor at Oversands. Continuous rain. Very disappointing.'

'Polly *what*?'

'Flint. Emma's. Flint. Polly. Come for a little break.'

'*Flint*,' said the voice. 'Well—Arthur. On your own? Arthur ring the bell. Polly *Flint*. Come over here.'

On the sofa lay a tiny woman dressed in silk. Pampas grasses in a tall jar bowed over her like a regal awning. Her face was thickly painted—bright red mouth and cheeks. Her eyelids and brows were painted and her very black straight hair was pulled tight back across the skull like a Dutch doll, and looked painted, too. Her neck was not much thicker than a wrist and her ears glittering with round topazes were little and pretty like noisettes of lamb.

Her hands were very, very old and had veins standing on them but they were soft and unused, not as small as all that. Rather determined hands. She held one bravely out—it looked ready to drop with the weight of more topazes.

'But do come nearer.'

She examined my clothes one by one—hat to gaiters. She saw my pelisse, cut down from Aunt Frances's and very special. I had worn it at the wedding. It was draped over my childish serge coat. She seemed to count the buttons down my calves and almost ate the big plate hat. She looked lower and I remembered that there was an uncertainty about my left knicker elastic which I had meant to see to before I left.

'Thought of cinnamon scones?' said Mr Thwaite. 'About tea-time? We arrive upon our hour.'

'Polly *Flint*,' said (presumably) his sister. 'How *very* interesting. How pretty. Emma's girl. Not at all *like* Emma. Very different—except perhaps the cheek-bones. How *very* sensible or you Arthur. Has she come for a visit?'

'Seemed not unwise. Not out of the way.'

'Not at *all* unwise. But how clever. You thought of it quite alone? A long, long visit? She does know of course?'

'No time to say very much.' He looked at the polish of his button-boots.

'And did they—poor Frances—get away?'

'Yes. Yes.'

'No mishaps? No delays? No regrets?'

'No,' I said, so decidedly that the shawls stirred.

'Well. How splendid. And the bridegroom very handsome, I've no doubt?'

'Here's the—cinnamon scones. Ha,' said her brother, 'just the three of us, Celia? Nobody else en route?'

'Well, we never know. We *never* know, do we? You'll find, Polly, that people come and go here. They pass through this house with total freedom. Sometimes they are with us and sometimes they are not. You will never know for sure whom you will meet upon the stairs.'

It was difficult to reply to this.

It had been difficult to reply to anything in fact—though not many of the things they had said had been really addressed to me. I thought, perhaps it's some sort of hospital. Would Aunt Mary have known if it was a mad house? Would she have let me come? In all the years at Oversands she and Aunt Frances had never mentioned these people. They had never been to see us before. There had not even been a Christmas card. There were no photographs of them in the yellow house.

Perhaps Mr Thwaite was mad. There was certainly something funny about him. All that obsession with the weather. And the silences. And this wonderful house with the gates all locked and covered in weeds. Surely even Aunt Mary would have known if this was a private asylum.

Then I thought, oh my goodness, but she mightn't! She's got it muddled. Oh dear—she's so holy and vague. It was *Mrs Woods* who was supposed to come here and they've got it topsy turvy and sent me instead. Whatever shall I do?

But how very comfortable here. It must be a lunatic asylum for the rich. They have them in novels.

'Before long', said the sister, wiping butter carefully from her lips with a lawn handkerchief, 'we shall find you a room, Polly. I'm sure there must be a room somewhere with nobody in it?'

The huge house—I'd seen so little of it but already I felt I would never find my way out of it again—seemed so empty that if I listened I could probably have heard the crumbs dropping on to our plates.

'We are very full at present,' she said. 'Hush.'

A man came in to the room wearing red braces over a thick cotton shirt fastened with a stud, and no collar. His curly head was clipped close like a prisoner but he had not shaved. He stood staring blankly across the room. Then he snapped at the air over his shoulder like a dog after flies and went out again.

I was right.

Sister looked at brother. She said, 'A bad day . . . '

'Shall I go and have a word?' asked Mr Thwaite.

'No, no. He has to be alone. He will probably go out. It is a beautiful evening. If you pass him anywhere outside you might just say "duck".'

'Duck?'

'For dinner. He is fond of duck.'

At least one was allowed outside. And the locks on the gates had been thin.

'Excuse me,' I said, 'but could you please tell me . . . '

'Of course. What to call me. I am Celia—Lady Celia—there was a husband once—and so on. I kept the title—it was all there was. As you know, I am a poet.'

'Oh. No—I didn't.'

'Really?'

'I'm afraid I haven't read very much poetry. Modern . . . '

'Ah, that can be rectified here.'

'Novels,' said Arthur Thwaite. 'Great novel reader. Plays piano. Speaks German and so forth.'

'Ah—you are in for a great treat then. A great experience. There is to be a recital here by Grünt tomorrow. You will know Grünt?'

'I'm afraid . . . '

'My child,' she said, hauling up her hand again, 'you are going to be wonderfully awakened here.'

I realised (in the end) that I was meant to take the hand and caught it just as it collapsed. It was ice-cold, colder than the rings on it, and it lay in mine as dead.

'*How* old did you say, Arthur?'

'Har—harumph, sixteen.'

'How *wonderful*,' she said. 'How very wonderful for us all.'

Thwaite

Dear Aunt Frances,

I hope that you will read this before you go to India. I am sending it to the address you gave in London. I expect that you will be surprised at the address at the head of this letter and so, in fact, am I.

After the wedding was over Mr Thwaite asked almost

immediately if I would like to come here on a visit. He said it was near where you were born and had lived when you were all little and as I was missing you I said that if Aunt Mary could spare me, yes, I'd love to come. And so we came, he and I together, yesterday.

There is no need for me to describe it to you because I suppose that you must know every nook and corner of this house and I do wonder why you never told me about it or about Mr Thwaite. It was so strange to meet him before the wedding, walking in from the marsh in his tweeds and cape and pipe. I felt as if I had always known him. But you never said.

The wedding was very nice. I hope that you and Father Pocock enjoyed it immensely. It was a shame that Mrs Woods wasn't well. I thought that everyone, and especially the nuns, sang very clearly during the service, and the responses were very good. Mr Pocock sang well, too. I did not know that the bridegroom sang at a wedding but you could hear Mr Pocock's voice *ring out*, as at the eleven o'clock service and his shoulder-blades were going up and down like bellows. I heard one of the nuns say that it was a very *encouraging* and reverent wedding.

I did not actually sing, and I don't know about Aunt Mary. Afterwards at the reception, I felt that everything was rather quiet. The idea of your going to India is still very strange to me and sudden and I am sorry that I cried.

Perhaps in the six weeks of your journey to India it might be interesting for you to read about news of home. I thought that I would tell you a little every few days of what is happening to me here. You will be too busy with the vestment-buying and so on to read it now. Also I expect that being married is very interesting and distracting for you. But perhaps you may read this in small instalments on the high seas. I know that you have the Bible with you, like Robinson Crusoe, but I wonder if he sometimes wished for something a little lighter? And so here I am, in my bed-room, at a rosewood desk with a silver inkstand and blot-ting-paper it would be a sin to blot with. I am longing to tell you every detail.

I am sorry, Aunt Frances. I have left this letter for days.
What I have said is not quite truthful.
You see, I do not want to tell you about this place. When I begin to think how to do it, I see your face. Then I believe that I can see you in the ship, and the sun rising redder and hotter every day as you get nearer Bombay and your thoughts getting further and further from us and your old life. I see you with all your old life forgotten, dim, as was the old life of Robinson Crusoe in Hull. I see you walking about the deck with Mr Pocock, and the dolphins playing and the great seas, swinging, mounting, heaving, dropping, and Mr Pocock and Aunt Frances in the midst of them, and above you both the swirling stars. I do greatly envy you this experience Aunt Frances. And so I think—though we do not often talk of it precisely—does Mr Thwaite.

Aunt Frances, will you please forgive me if I speak to you in a way I would find difficult if I were at Oversands with Mrs Woods always just out or sight, and Alice about and Aunt Mary, who is so pure?

Aunt Frances, why did you leave me before telling me any-thing of any real use to my life? Here I am with Mr Thwaite and Lady Celia and in one sense I do feel very much at home. In another sense I am unsure. I have become even unsure about whether I should have come to live with you at Oversands—where perhaps I have become fragmented and incomplete. I don't believe that I shall ever really fit in any-where, although you and Aunt Mary have given me what Robinson Crusoe was told by his father was the greatest bless-ing. A home in 'the middle state or what might be called the

upper station of low life which he had found by long experience was the best state in the world, the most suited to human
happiness'.

The trouble, Aunt Frances, is perhaps that I am a girl. Had
I been a boy—your sister's baby boy, some solid stubborn boy
perhaps called Jack or Harry—how would you have done
then? You would have sent me away to school and please, oh
please forgive me for saying so, Aunt Frances, but the money
would have been found. It would have been a Christian sort of
school like Rossall or Repton and you would all have prayed
and prayed for me that I would become a priest. But because
I am a girl, Aunt Frances, I was to be stood in a vacuum. I was
to be left in the bell-jar of Oversands. Nothing in the world is
ever to happen to me. Since I have met these people here at
Thwaite I have begun to see what I have missed.

I love the marsh and Oversands and I know that I live in a
very compelling landscape as the Brontës did. But Aunt Frances
I am not at all sure about the Brontës. I am not sure that we were
ever meant to become knitted into a landscape. After all, I am in
no way mystical, I don't even want to be Confirmed. When
Robinson Crusoe was married to a landscape you know, he had
a hard time to keep sane. I am being dissolved into a landscape
and all hope for me is that someone will come and marry me to
make things complete and take me away.

But is marriage the only completing, necessary thing? I
keep thinking of you and hoping that you really thought it
out—whether marriage is a necessary thing. I expect by now
you will be getting used to it. It may seem quite natural by the
time you get to India. There is so much I wish we could have
talked about before you left. You have such a secret life now.
A shutter comes down when people get married.

Here at Lady Celia's, though, there are not many shutters
coming down. All is very different and nobody seems at all
sure that marriage is a necessary thing. There are many people

here, all of them artists—writers and poets and painters and musicians—and they seem to be very confused most of the time. Lady Celia looks after them. They spend a lot of time in their rooms or walking in the grounds, sometimes late into the night, up and down the lawns, forgetting dinner. They must be very serious about their work or very rich to miss such lovely dinners which Lady Celia kindly urges them towards.

There is a lady who plays a harp. She is fat and nice. When she walks she wobbles but her hands are white and small. Then there is a funny little painter who snaps at the air like a dog. The other evening I almost fell over him in the rose-garden. He was watching the sun drop down behind the hills and he said 'Into the heart of darkness or into the heart of light.' I think it was a quotation. It is all very different from Oversands— nobody goes to church at all. 'We are all free here,' said Lady Celia, yet she seems to lie on her yellow sofa holding long threads somehow, and every thread is tied to a guest.

I could not help comparing the snapping painter to Robinson Crusoe. If I had stepped out of the bushes upon Robinson Crusoe in his loneliness, he would, even after year of solitude, have behaved with greater decorum and manners than the painter, who had been talking to people only at tea-time.

Aunt Frances, there seems to be very little simple pleasure here. It does seem very queer that great artists (Lady Celia says that all her guests are famous and some of them great) should be so ugly on the whole and really rather ordinary in their con- versation. I wonder if Daniel Defoe was ordinary to meet? I said some of this to Mr Thwaite and he cleared his throat so much that I think he agreed with me. He has a great admira- tion of his sister and what she does for artists, nevertheless.

We had a piano recital the evening of the day I arrived by a pianist called Grünt. He is very famous and he is, Lady Celia says, 'the greatest living exponent of the works of Chopin'. We all gathered in the drawing-room and after a time he came in and sat down. He hung down his head so far that his nose very nearly touched the keyboard and he sat there, as praying, and we all sat in tremendous silence, except that Mr Thwaite suddenly gave a very great sneeze. First Lady Celia and then everybody else gave Mr Thwaite a look, but Herr Grünt just hung his face down closer to the keys so that the end of his nose actually brushed middle C—and then his long and bony hands reached up and he began to play.

They played quite independently of his body and even his head, which stayed quite close by middle C for a considerable time. Then his head flung itself up in the air and his face became parallel with the ceiling as the hands went on with a life of their own. His eyes were shut. It was rather warm in the room and all the poets began to sigh and groan and shift about a bit. Only Lady Celia stayed utterly still like a statue in robes.

He went on and on. It's a wonderful piano. His head is very big—far too large for his shoulders which slope away. They aren't so powerful as Mr Pocock's and I thought, well, if Herr Grünt were to get married he would not have the wonderful strength to sing at his wedding. *Down* flopped his head again, very close to his finger-tips. Then—plinkety . . . plonkety . . . plink. Very quiet. Very separate. One note. Another note. Little water drops. One, two, three . . . And a long long silence.

Then he opened his eyes and everyone stirred.

They didn't say 'bravo' or clap. They *stirred*, with a very serious, bulgy, bottomy movement and looked at one another with great meaning in their eyes, except for Mr Thwaite, who had taken out his handkerchief and was examining all the hems on it.

Then, a great murmur of awe went round the drawing-room and Herr Grünt rose and went over to Lady Celia and picked up her hand which is terribly heavy with yellow rings and he kissed it and looked at her and her lips moved and everyone began to breathe adjectives; and some people got out their handkerchieves just as Mr Thwaite was putting his away.

And I did so wish that you were there, Aunt Frances. Herr Grünt was actually, and in fact, the *most terrible pianist!*

Aunt Frances I felt so lonely.

I will write to you again. I am longing for your letters when they come from Oversands. I hope that you and Mr Pocock are enjoying your honeymoon and please forgive me if this letter is not a very controlled one, your loving Polly.

Thwaite

Dear Aunt Frances,

I am afraid that I am writing you a great many letters and it is so aggravating because I know that by now your letters to me must be collecting up at home. I shan't see them for ages unless Alice posts them on, and somehow I feel that she may not be very quick at that as she's going to be taken up so much with the spring cleaning and then to have her holiday. Mrs Woods was still in bed when I left, though I expect she will be well enough now to have gone to her nursing home.

Aunt Mary, of course as you will know, has gone into Retreat and there have to be no letters. She is so terribly good, not needing them. I must say I do—and I need to write them, too—and I keep wishing that there were more people I could send postcards to. I have sent some to the nuns.

So I am going to have to bore only you with what has happened since the Chopin recital. I don't find it boring, but perhaps it will be to you, so busy at The Society for the Propagation of the Gospel and the Army and Navy Stores. It is very wonderful here, though. Very gracious and beautiful. We live as if we are all extra-special. I'm afraid it isn't very Christian at all.

After the recital the excitement of the day was far from over. Lady Celia suggested that we all should walk on the terrace for a while and she was helped out by Herr Grünt.

He was a bit tottery because of the exhaustion of the piece and Mr Thwaite got hold of his arms and they all three stepped out together through the French doors in a row. Mr Thwaite looked very fine and knightly in his evening dress and his moustache—much more noble in every way than any of the artists and writers and I thought again that perhaps ugliness is one of the things that a creative artist has to put up with as a penance for his other advantages. Apart from Shakespeare and Byron and Shelley, most seem to have been rather plain, don't they? And they stare so much.

As I thought these things, Herr Grünt suddenly fell over which made Mr Thwaite fall over too and for a terrible minute it looked as if Lady Celia would be pulled down beneath them. And then she would have been extinguished. But the painter who barks like a dog came and slid himself cleverly underneath her.

Then there was a quartette of fallen people collapsed upon the terrace and some of them great artists. And when Mr Thwaite stood up and stood on Herr Grünt's right hand and Herr Grünt screamed, it really became quite a serious occasion.

People ran about. There was a very substantial man who is a Fellow of all Souls (I think this means a humble person studying to be a priest at a famous church somewhere in Oxford and I expect you will have heard of it) and he cried out, 'They're off! They're off! Finished—his career is finished!'

Everybody ran and helped Herr Grünt to his feet, and he was weeping, and a long lady in purple looked very deeply at a thin lady with a fringe who paints water-colours. '*What* are off?' asked the little white harpist. 'Fingers,' said the FOAS.

Even the butler was laughing—he's awfully nice—called Barker, and he and the housekeeper, Maitland, are not a bit what you'd expect. I have been invited to supper with them one night in the servants' hall.

After the multiple falling over, Barker laughed quite openly. Nobody noticed but me. He laughed in a sober sort of way but for quite a long time.

Then we all went early to bed.

This morning Lady Celia sent for me. She said, 'Child—' (I think she may just play at being Miss Havisham sometimes)—'Child, you are very *quaint*.'

I said I was sorry.

'It is not in your control,' she said. 'Quaintness is caused by circumstance. Nevertheless you ought to wear different clothes.'

I said, 'Thank you, Lady Celia, but I think Aunt Mary might not like me to have new clothes at present. I have had new clothes for the wedding.'

'Those?' she said.

'Yes,' I said.

'Oh,' she said and closed her eyes. 'Green,' she said, 'kingfisher green. Glossy. Shot.'

I said that actually kingfishers were blue. There were some in The Hall pond at home. I also said that it is virtually impossible to shoot a kingfisher. As well as being a frightful idea. Herr Grünt was sitting near, nursing his right hand which was in a bandage the size of a wasp's nest and he gave a shocked moan as if I were being remiss.

Then I heard someone laugh and it was the painter; but Lady Celia looked at him and he snapped the air.

Lady Celia's eyes gave a snap round the room, too, a fierce one. 'Quaintness may go too far,' she said. 'Help me up—no, not you—' (the big purple woman had lunged forward)—'Polly Flint.'

So I helped her up and armed her across the room feeling very clumsy and huge. I'm still growing horribly as you very well know. At the door she turned and looked at everyone, one at a time, and they mostly looked frightened (but not the painter) as if they might possibly soon be leaving.

Then we began a long journey, Lady C and I, slowly. Up the main great staircase at last, where she kept stopping and holding on to the front of her neck. You could see a vein beating in it and I was scared and said, 'Lady Celia, are you well?'

'No.'

'Then shouldn't you—stop? Shall I get Maitland?'

'Of course not. I am perfectly well. What is not well is the company in this house.'

'Oh, I'm sure they're—'

'They are not what they once were.'

'Oh, I'm sure none of them is so *very* old.'

'My family', she said, 'has entertained Tennyson.'

'Yes I see. But I expect he got old in the end.'

'His age was immaterial. Mr Dodgson has been a guest in this house. Many times.'

'Mr Dodgson—oh, did you know him?'

'Of course. He was at Croft. I was a child.'

'Oh—did he talk about *Alice*? And creatures?'

'He hadn't thought of *Alice* then. He kept asking difficult questions. Very queer mathematical things. And he was fond of marmalade.'

'Yes, I see.'

'But it was immaterial. Whatever he said or did was immaterial, for he was going to write *Alice.*'

I said, 'Oh yes. Oh *yes.*' I looked at her—all rings and paint and silly draperies and proud mouth and her old claw hands on her stick. 'Oh Lady Celia, yes.' I said it with terrific agreement rather congratulating her. She didn't like it much.

We were in her bedroom now. 'Sit me there,' she said and I settled her on a lovely watered-silk sofa with a curled end and she spread her shawls about. 'Over there,' she said and pointed at an old piece of furniture. 'Open the press.'

So many materials were stacked inside the press that it looked like a pirate's cave. A female-pirate's cave. Flimsy bits and silky bits and thick velvety bits and long, long lacy bits all crammed in and layered tight, all the colours there are, all textures, all patterns.

One of the very few mistakes in *Robinson Crusoe* is his regret about clothes—one of the jokes is his clumsy furry appearance in the nanny-goat skins. Yet there were clothes brought off the ship. He had them by him. He did not use them. Or scarcely. Perhaps he had never really cared about his appearance. I would guess this was true. One can imagine him as a boy of say fourteen, in Hull, looking not very well turned-out I think. And his parents not being enthusiastic about him at all.

Clothes on the desert island are what I should very much have missed. Different, beautiful clothes as time went by. Though I never, never seem to be wearing the right ones.

'Oh,' I said. 'Different beautiful clothes.'

'Try the greens,' she said.

'I'd love the yellows,' and I draped one after the other round myself. 'Yes,' she said, 'we could do worse than that. 'Try a red.' There was a dark red velvet a hundred miles long and I paraded about.

'Frightful,' she said. 'Try the blue. There's a blue there. Kingfisher blue.'

I dropped the red and patrolled in the blue.

'It gives you eyes,' she said. 'A start. It must be the blue. You approve of *Alice*? Many children don't.'

'I love *Alice*. I mean the book, not the girl.'

'Why not the girl?'

'She was a bit stodgy.'

'Why?'

'Oh, the bows and the frills and she did answer back so.'

'You are very decisive yourself. Especially for someone who has lived so far from the centre of things.'

'But it's the centre of things for me,' I said, 'and I'm sixteen years old. Alice was a child and everything was very everyday for her. She'd seen nothing odd. She just lived in Oxford.'

'Her dreams say otherwise.'

'She was a child,' I said.

She looked at me for ages and then said, 'Come here. Yes, I suppose you are. Older than . . .' but then she wouldn't say any more. 'You shall have the yellow,' she said, 'and the blue. I believe there is a brown velvet ready-made somewhere too—Maitland can find it—which will do for now. Wear it tomorrow. Ring the bell for Maitland.'

Then in came Maitland all pursed up and there was a great deal of talk about the lovely material and fussing about. It looks as if I am to be dressed as a princess. I sat at her dressing-table. All the silver! Great fat chunky looking-glass with fat silver cherubs flying and brushes galore, far too heavy for her and rows of glass bottles with silver stoppers.

There was a box made of pink and cream chips of something shiny—Persian people lying on benches and looking lovingly across at each other. She opened it and scrabbled about. All kinds of glittery things. The maid Maitland fastened up her mouth tighter.

'Maitland,' she said, 'shall we have Polly read us some Tennyson?'

'Yes m'lady.'

'Some Tennyson, Polly.'

An edition was produced. I read them Tennyson. *Maud.* I went on for about half an hour. Then Maitland started clanking the water-jug. Lady Celia had shut her eyes. '*The Lady of Shalott*,' she said, so I started that. I went into a sort of trance over it after a while as I always do with Aunt Mary though it upsets Aunt Mary doesn't it? She never liked it as you do, Aunt Frances. When I came to.

'She left the web, she left the loom.

She made three paces—' Lady Celia said, 'Stop!' and took a little greyish glass bottle and sniffed at it. 'The end,' she said.

So I read the end—the lovely man looking down over the bridge on the poor dead face, all of her so lovely and never even been for a walk. She must have had an awfully pasty complexion when you come to think of it. 'Wonderful!' said Lady Celia. 'Is it not?'

I said that it was wonderful.

'Do you love Tennyson?'

'Oh yes.'

She lifted a necklace out of the Persian box.

'Better than anybody?'

I watched the necklace. It swung. It was seed-pearls, with a little diamond clasp like a diamond daisy. It was small. Made for a girl.

But I had to say, 'No, not better.' And the necklace swung.

'Not best of all?'

'Well, I don't think he's quite as good as Daniel Defoe.'

'Daniel *Defoe*?' she said, as if other Daniels might have got by—the one in the lions den, or the one George Eliot wrote about, or Daniel the Upright and Discerning Judge.

'Daniel *Defoe*? You mean *Robinson Crusoe*? *Moll Flanders*?'

'Yes.'

'But my child—no trace, no *trace* of poetry. No trace of poetic truth.'

But then, Aunt Frances, I grew terribly angry and said in a fury, '*Robinson Crusoe* is full of poetic truth. And it is an attempt at a universal truth very differently expressed.'

'No form,' she cried, 'no form.'

I said, 'It is wonderfully written. It is true to his chosen form. Because of this verisimilitude it reads like reality. I have read it twenty-three times. In a novel form is not always apparent at a first or second reading. Form is determined by hard secret work—in a notebook and in the subconscious and in the head.'

'You speak of journalism.'

'Yes. Why not? With glory added. And not a lot of gush and romantic love.'

She let the necklace trickle back into the box and there was a long silence and then Maitland said, 'Oughtn't Miss Polly to be going to change?'

So I went out.

I went out rather noisily, I am afraid, because I felt very angry on behalf of Daniel Defoe. And I love you and goodnight and I'll continue probably tomorrow, Your loving Polly.

There was a thunder storm on Sunday evening this week and a tremendous sheet of rain across the plain of York. The drawing-room windows were closed and we all watched the lightning and listened to the swish and hiss of the tropical-sounding rain. Whenever the rain eased a little we opened the windows to let in the steamy summer night. When at last it had nearly stopped, the butler came and flung them wide and the sweet smell of flowers and wet grass—and lilacs—swam into the room.

The house was lamp-lit. Lady Celia and the guests sat talking in undertones very earnestly. The purple woman and the fringed water-colourist sat together in a window-seat and the Fellow of all Souls enunciated carefully to Herr Grünt who seemed to be nodding asleep. Mr Thwaite was not there, nor the painter. I wished somebody—not Herr Grünt—would play the lovely piano. I wondered if I should go up to bed, when there was a little noise beside me and I looked up and saw the butler.

It was not so much a noise he made as an easing of the feet. One, two, they went on the oriental rug. Like a cat padding. He held a tray with nothing on it for he had finished distributing Madeira round the room (the purple lady had taken two) and he was looking firmly at me.

'Message from Maitland, Miss Polly.'

'Oh, thank you, Mr Barker.'

'To speak in the sitting-room.'

'Yes I see. When?'

'Now, Miss Polly. If you have a moment. When you have said goodnight.' He looked from me to Lady Celia and back again and at once I went over to her and said goodnight, and goodnight all round, though nobody noticed much.

'Listen to the owls,' cried the purple lady. 'I distinctly hear owls.'

'Owls, owls,' mumbled Herr Grünt and went to the piano and shrill unhappy yearning noises came out of it as I followed Barker out. They cut into the stillness of the drawing-room and all its lamps and whispers as we closed the door, but the music did not catch the true awfulness of the cries of owls whose essential quality is bad temper (Robinson Crusoe was spared owls) and Herr Grünt has not the vitality for bad temper.

After a long walk, Mr Barker bowed me not into the servants' hall but into a smallish room where a fire burned bright but didn't make it stuffy in spite of the storm. Three lamps were turned up as high as they would go, one on a round table covered with thick, cream-coloured oilcloth and tacked in underneath. On the oilcloth a pack of cards was laid out. In a rocking-chair Maitland was darning and on an upright chair opposite sat Mr Thwaite, slapping down one playing-card upon another at top speed. He had removed his dinner jacket and black tie and sat in his studs and silver braces. He looked rosy and at his wrist stood a great glass of beer. 'And so and so and *so*,' he said, to the last cards, and looked round in triumph.

'And so! Out. Finish. Chess? Mr Barker. Ha—Polly. Very unsettled evening. The barometer is almost at risk.'

'Here she is,' said Mr Barker to Maitland who looked at me over her gold glasses, while her needle flew about the wooden mushroom she held to the sock-hole.

'A game of chess, Polly?' said Mr Thwaite.

'Mr Barker said that Maitland wanted me.'

'Yes—never mind her for chess, Mr Thwaite. We thought she might like a cup of tea in here with us. You two get down to the chess.'

She stooped forward and crunched the kettle down in the coals. 'We always have a cup of tea about now. And a short-bread. Sit down and make yourself comfortable. I'll have to start measuring you before long for this kingfisher festivity.'

It was funny to see the way she was in charge—not only of me the newest guest but of her husband. On the other side of the baize door Mr Barker looked and behaved like King Rameses of Egypt in Grandfather Younghusband's book of Kings. But she was also in charge of her employer—for Mr Thwaite sat there engrossed, using his head, drinking his beer, filled with the acceptance that life is very good.

'Move your arm now, Mr Thwaite,' she said. 'Let's set down these cups and saucers. Barker, take your shoes off. Put them by the fender.'

Mr Thwaite opened up the chess box as Mr Barker brought the board and they set out the men between them.

'Your move, sir,' said Mr Barker. He set down a glass for himself and a jug of beer among the tea-things. 'Yours last night.' Mr Thwaite looked piercingly at the pieces—and at length moved queen's pawn. 'They're off,' said Maitland, 'that's better. Here's your tea, Miss Polly, and we'll have a nice talk.'

'Lady Celia thinks I've gone to bed.'

'Well then, she'll be content. She's happy when everyone's safe in bed.'

'Is she? Why?'

'She likes to lie thinking of the good she's done—helping everyone, knowing that all these wonderful people are resting.'

'Why does she?'

'She believes that she was born to help geniuses and I dare say that she is right. They go away fatter than they came.'

'It's very kind of her.'

'It's *very* kind of her. Very kind. That's what tends to get forgotten in any discussion of Lady Celia. She may order them cruel but she never stops giving. Behaving filthily, a lot of them.'

'I suppose if they're geniuses—'

'There's no excuse for filthy under-drawers where there's soap and servants. Some never takes them off in a week. Mr Dodgson, of course, was very clean. Here—let's see. Turn to the door—no, there isn't enough far a long sleeve. I said there wouldn't be. You're a good round arm. You'll look well in this blue.'

'I could darn for you if you like.'

'You're here for a holiday.'

'I'd like something to do.'

'I hope you are not going to be bored with us,' Mr Barker called over his shoulder in a much more host-like way than Mr Thwaite or Lady Celia would ever have done. It would never occur to Lady Celia to enquire how anybody was enjoying himself. I was still very embarrassed about not knowing quite what I was meant to do all day and I'd been spending quite a lot of time just wandering about between meals, picking up books in the library and putting them down again. They weren't so engrossing somehow as the ones at the yellow house, being so often books people had written about other books and so many of the pages being un-cut was rather strange. You had to peer in sideways.

Wherever I walked I tended to meet the other guests walking idly, too. Not the water-colourist—she was safe because she had her easel—and not Herr Grünt. He was safe with the piano: but the rest of us, it occurred to me, might perhaps all be playing the same game. The snapping painter never painted. He stood for long periods quite still on the lawn. The purple woman poet I had met that morning, transfixed before a fat blue hyacinth which burned intensely at her feet. I said, 'Oh sorry,' coming round a bush, and then wondered why, for she had not moved a muscle. Later on I found her staring at another hyacinth right down near the great glasshouses. It was a thinner, pink hyacinth, looking rather poorly, beginning to bend a bit and go tea-coloured at the tips. I had had to say, 'Oh sorry,' again and this time she turned and seemed to come out of her trance. 'I *was* the hyacinth,' she said.

'Yes, I see.'

'I *was* it, and it was I.'

'Yes I see.'

'You see? See? If only you could. If only any of us could truly see.' We both looked down at the pink hyacinth which chose that moment to keel over. It is a rare sight to see a hyacinth collapse, being so sappy and stout, but this one tipped slowly and inevitably over like a soldier fainting and its bulb stuck out in the air with all its root threads writhing about like wire-worms. I couldn't help laughing, but she glared furiously—first at the hyacinth and then at me, and when I said, 'Oh poor thing. It's all been a bit much,' the purple woman walked off very grimly twirling her ebony cane.

Thinking about it now, darning, I started laughing again and Maitland said, 'And so what's this?' and I began to tell her, putting down the darning and taking swigs of tea. Deep breathing came from the chess players and the odd little chink from the fire but otherwise the room was quite still and utterly beautiful. I do not mean that there was anything of definite beauty—it was a cluttery dingy room—unpainted for years.

There were ugly framed family photographs, an ugly sewing machine, an ugly rag-rug. It was the atmosphere which was beautiful—Mr Barker, Mr Thwaite, Maitland and I and the blue material were beautiful. Four people happy together. Light-hearted and happy in a way that was not very usual at Oversands.

'That'll do,' said Maitland when I got to the bit about the hyacinth falling over. She was trying to make her tight mouth deny itself.

'And what of the hair-cutting?' called Mr Thwaite from behind his hovering knight. Maitland said, 'And that'll do from you, Mr Thwaite.'

I said, 'Oh no—please, what about the hair-cutting?'

So he told us the story about when a very famous writer indeed was staying at the house and there was a poet staying, too, who had been here so long that his hair was getting in his soup and he wanted it cut. Lady Celia liked it, however, and said there was no barber nearer than York and so secretly the poet asked the very famous writer just to trim his hair a little on the quiet. While Lady Celia was resting, they spread a bed-sheet on the poet's bedroom floor and the writer came to borrow Maitland's scissors but they were not adequate. He needed very long sharp scissors he said, and Maitland had been rather worried, but had sent for horse-clippers and shears.

'Needlessly,' said Mr Barker, 'needlessly worried. That was not one we ever had trouble with. Melancholy at times, yes. Suicidal and dangerous, no.'

I wondered whether to tell them that when I arrived I'd thought it was a lunatic asylum but then thought they might be hurt. 'I shouldn't think geniuses would be very good barbers,' I said. 'It is quite difficult for an ordinary man to cut hair. Even a practical, very very sensible man like Robinson Crusoe couldn't cut hair. It was a great drawback to him. I always wondered about that though. I'm sure a woman would have found a way. Like gnawing.'

'He made a very fair try,' said Barker, 'A very even finish, the novelist,' and both he and Maitland looked across at Mr Thwaite, and I saw that servants do not laugh before their employer at the guests of that employer. Mr Thwaite said, 'No bad hand at it at all. Trouble was he had a bit of a go at his own afterwards and a lot of hair got scattered off the bed-sheet around the room and they tried to get it up with the hearth-brush and left some soot-marks on the carpet. Then they burned it.'

'What, the carpet?'

'No, the hair. They lit some paper in the fireplace and burned the hair on it and then they gathered up the bed-sheet hair into the grate too and the bed-sheet caught fire.'

'Yes, I see.'

'Then they crammed the whole bed-sheet into the fireplace to try to choke out the fire but there was quite a—well, a very fair blaze. Not many actual flames but rather a great deal of smoke which went billowing out and they flapped it about the room with pillows and things to try and do something about the smell of burned hair and then the pillows caught fire. Somebody sitting on the lawn—we were all waiting for tea—heard them and saw the smoke and cried: "Fire", and Mr Barker and the stablemen had to go running with buckets and a boy was sent to Pilmoor brigade, but they didn't get here for two hours.'

'Whatever did Lady Celia do?'

'Oh, she was quite wonderful. She never said one word except at dinner. She asked the great writer why one side of his hair was six inches shorter than the other. He hadn't been able to finish you see.'

'What about the poet?'

'He disappeared.'

'Check,' said Mr Barker.

'Serves me right,' said Mr Thwaite. 'Not concentrating.'

'You do have fun here,' I said.

'We have our little moments,' said Maitland. 'Not much for anyone your age though, Miss Polly. No young life. You're the first child I ever remember.'

'I'm not a child. I'm sixteen.'

'You are and you're not. You're younger than many a twelve and you talk older than many a one we've had here of forty.'

'She makes these utterances,' said Mr Barker. 'My wife is a very wise woman.'

'I didn't know you were married to each other.'

'Does it seem so strange?'

'No. It seems perfect.'

Mr Thwaite cleared his throat and said, 'Excellent. A very excellent arrangement.'

'I think everything here is absolutely excellent and perfect,' I said. 'I've never been so happy.'

'You should go to bed now though,' said Maitland, 'child or no child. There's something for you to look forward tomorrow. Did you know? A new one.'

'No. What—a new guest?'

'Yes. Something special. A poet. The most hopeful thing since Shakespeare, we understand, and he must be. He's to have the green room.'

'I hope he doesn't snap the air.'

'He's scarcely more than a boy,' said Mr Thwaite. 'Celia is very fond of boys.'

'I think she's asked him for Miss Polly.'

'Oh, I shouldn't count on that.'

'For *Miss Polly*,' said Maitland very firmly. 'And there's a new blue linen and a good hat for you you'll find in your wardrobe as well as the new brown velvet. I had a roust about. And I took the liberty of discarding the pelisse.'

*

The motor went off for the poet the next morning—not the trap. This guest was important.

I heard it leave and I can't say that I waited about for its return but as I sat reading on the lawn until luncheon I found that every now and then I stopped to listen and often looked up.

But at luncheon nothing was new. The dining-room was dark—the pale blinds drawn against the sun and Lady Celia playing with curls of toast and examining her sole. There were not many of us. The poets all seemed to be resting and the water-colourist had not returned from her morning session by the wheat-field. The snapping painter had completely disappeared and only Herr Grünt sat dismally at the far end of the table, his long blue under-lip extended as a ledge for his spoon.

Afterwards, I wandered about, wishing for Mr Thwaite. He was said to have gone for a walk somewhere after breakfast and I wished he had asked me to go with him. He had gone across the fields, Maitland said, towards Brafferton and if I took the hedgerow paths and then the river path I might just meet him coming back. He had probably gone by Thoralby and Roundstone.

'Thoralby?'

'The Jewish people are near Thoralby.'

'Jewish people?'

'Yes. They live near Thoralby.'

'You mean a sort of—tribe?'

I couldn't understand her or why she laughed. I had never met any Jews as I had never met anybody black or a Roman Catholic. Jews were in the Old Testament. 'A great family,' she said, 'rich as princes. They are industrialists.'

'But it's all farms,' I said.

'They have bought a manor house here. They have houses all over the place. They've branched out from Tyneside somewhere—they're foreigners. Originally from Germany or some place like that. Thwaite doesn't mix with them. Not socially.'

'But you said Mr Thwaite might have gone there?'

'Oh, Mr Thwaite mixes everywhere. Mr Thwaite, we don't question.'

'Doesn't Lady Celia know the Jews?'

'No. She wanted to. She thought they might be musical. When she found out they were just industrial she was very disappointed.'

'Yes I see. I'd love to meet some Jews,' I said. 'Do they worship idols?'

'They worship the same good God as you and me and Jesus Christ,' she said. 'Hist?'

There was a crackly noise of the motor arriving and after a moment Mr Barker came in—we were in the kitchen—to say 'Three trains have been met and no guest alighting.' He and Maitland exchanged a long look.

So I set off across the gardens to a gate in the wall and along the hedgerow paths and down to the river and along the meadows hoping to meet Mr Thwaite on his way back, perhaps accompanied by some of the industrial Jews. I imagined them walking together in a little group like on the road to Emmaus, but it was difficult. I felt like poor Robinson Crusoe when he first saw the cannibal boats, staring and staring as hard as he could but making out nothing because he'd come out without his expanding-glass.

It was lovely after the storm—the grasses by the river in shiny clumps and feathery with seeds, all the dandelions and meadowsweet polished and clean and the water running fast in the streams. The meadow smells were not like the marsh smells—the rushes and blites and spurreys and scurvy grasses.

I was wearing Maitland's 'blue' which turned out to be a lovely floppy skirt and top and a sailor-blouse with white on it with a big bow and a straw hat with ribbons. I had undone my hair, all loose and long. Maitland said this was acceptable since I was in the country—until I was seventeen. At seventeen, up it must go. I kept imagining Mr Thwaite appearing round the next corner with a cluster of disciples—strong fishermen-type people with hook noses? Very brown, and sandals? Country people—except of course, St Luke, who was a doctor. I wondered how doctors dressed in Galilee about 30 AD and if they carried a bag of any sort and I sat down and took a reed and pulled the brown tufty sprout off it and began to suck the worm of white sorbet inside. I licked it and tapped it with my tongue.

It was a very hot afternoon. I took off my hat. I lay down and looked up at the sky. Then I sat up. There was not a sound anywhere. There could be no people for miles. The path I'd been following was hardly a path at all. I took off the top of my sailor suit. It felt stuffy and hard. Then I took off my liberty-bodice and then I took off my vest and I lay down with no clothes on the top half of myself in the long grass and listened to the river running by. I thought of the disciples walking talkatively along with Mr Thwaite. And then I fell asleep.

When I woke up there seemed to be a disciple looking at me—very serious and reflective. He had a twitchy sort of nose and bright black eyes and I felt he was some old friend. But when I sat up he was not there and I knew that he had been part of a dream.

The sun had gone. It looked like rain again. I knew it was much later. I looked astonished at my bare arms and then more astonished at the bare huge rest of me. I must have been mad. Lying half naked in broad daylight in the middle of the plain of York! I scrabbled back into the blouse, pushed the vest and bodice into the skirt pockets, tried to get myself straightened out round the waist. Then I thought I heard voices calling somewhere along the path and I was filled with wonderfully exciting shame. I found the hat, crammed it on my head and ran frantically back along the way I had come.

I ran for nearly a mile until I came to the door in Thwaite wall and slid through it and leaned against it, then walked quickly along inside the wall, past the bonfire place, the glasshouses, the pink hyacinth still displaying its unseeable underparts to all who passed by like the man who fell among thieves. I sidled into the house and up to my room and saw in the glass a ruby-red face on a rough girl like a well fed gypsy with torn stockings, wild hair and her vest hanging out of her pocket.

Outside on the lawn the guests were beginning to gather for tea from their creative activities for the next part of the comforting time-table Lady Celia had provided for them against the assaults of their calling.

Seeing them pacing so soberly, acquiescently forward, I found that I was crying and the reason for this seemed to be that I had now to go down and join them. I, so nondescript and friendless, and wearing all my clothes. And somewhere, Charlotte peeped from a corner of the room with some triumph and there were some queer shadows behind her from Wales.

Below me, Mr Barker was walking like Rameses over the lawn following two parlour-maids in black and white. He carried a cake-stand and they the heavy trays of silver and the tea-cups. Mr Thwaite had arrived—no sign of the disciples—and his sweet smile brightened at the sight of the cakes and made me calmer. 'I shall have to join in,' I thought. 'I shall have to go down.'

'Beggars can't choose,' said Charlotte from inside the wardrobe as I changed my dress. 'It's not as if there's anything else for you. You've no excuse to be different. You can't write poetry or paint or play very well and you'll never write a book.

You've never been to school or felt you were a hyacinth. All you can do is speak German and talk about *Robinson Crusoe*. There's no genius in you.'

So I walked sadly on to the landing and there was somebody there. He said, 'Oh thank goodness—I know absolutely no one. May I go down with you?'

Thwaite

Aunt Frances, most dear and best beloved, I have fallen in love. Paul, he is called, Paul Treece, a friend of Lady Celia and the most beautiful of human beings. Oh let me tell you what has happened.

He was standing on the stairs yesterday as I came out of my room to go down in the garden for tea, and he is twenty years old, which is old, I know, but from the first moment it did not matter. He has quite a godlike air but he has not at all a godlike certainty because he said, 'Could I go down with you? I don't know a single soul.'

It seemed amazing. It was exactly what I would have said to him, the very words. I felt that we had changed souls. I said, 'Oh yes,' in a very stiff way and we walked downstairs side by side but very far apart. He walks all bobby up and down and bouncy—and all the time he talks—very fast and excited. He is a poet and in his second year at Cambridge. He is very eager all the time. Out of the sides of my eyes I kept getting a look at him and his profile is—oh Aunt Frances—most utterly perfect. His nose could be a nose in a textbook of fine noses.

On the lawn there were two other new people just arrived—very important new ones making their way to Wooller in Scotland: writers of some very significant sort—a melancholy brooding man and a very thin woman in old expensive clothes with the hem coming down, who was beautiful. Even her raggedness looked queenly. She was rather wild about the eyes which were in very deep caves in her face, and the corners of her mouth turned down in a desperately forlorn and anxious, yet sweet way. Her hands were long and bony and she clutched her tea-cup tight. When Lady Celia introduced us all, this woman looked for a long time and then turned her head away, but I think she was thinking of other things. The man smiled gently and nicely at us.

I perhaps noticed them so particularly because since meeting Paul Treece I have noticed everything with very precise and crystalline pertinence, Aunt Frances, as if a skin had been peeled from everything, a gauze or a glass. Even when Paul Treece turned brick-red with awe at the two writers and sat by the bony woman on a stool at her feet and turned on her a very passionate gaze as he put scone after scone in his mouth (which is a bit red. It's a pity) without looking where it was going, and I went over to sit by Mr Thwaite—even then I thought, 'Nothing, *nothing* will ever spoil this day. We arrived on the lawn together. They will think we belong to each other.'

Mr Thwaite said that it was hot for the time of the year and I asked if he had enjoyed his walk. I told him how Mr Barker had been worried by the chauffeur meeting so many trains, because he loves talking about train-times, and we discussed trains generally for a while. He then said, 'Know who they are, these new cough-drops?'

Mr Thwaite never asks questions—well, so very seldom. You know. He spoke quite loud and it fell very clearly and flatly into the tea-party because nobody was talking much. That is an interesting thing that I have noticed: great artists do not actually say very much in the ordinary way, but go in for great silences. The more famous they are the less they utter at tea-parties, which makes me think that Paul Treece cannot be a genius as he is the most tremendous talker and was only silent at that moment with awe and scones.

Several heads turned to Mr Thwaite and everyone looked at him with long intellectual stares and I felt so sorry for him until I noticed that he did not seem to care at all. He simply opened his mouth over a beautiful piece of black fruit-cake and munched. Lady Celia said melodiously then, 'When the evenings grow longer, later in the year, we come out here after dinner and listen to the doves.'

Again nobody said anything and the sentence—she has a light slow fluty voice a little like Aunt Mary—hung about among the tea-things for a time and then floated away. In ones and twos then people began to say things blankly—unconnected things, unhurried, and it turned into a discussion soon between a number of people, quite fast like a chorus. Then between only one or two people, and more dropped out until it was just two—the dark new man and the snapping painter who talks Cockney with a bit of a foreign accent (the lady looked up into the trees. She is called Mrs Wolf which is inappropriate for she is more horse or unicorn-like) and it got very difficult for me to follow.

At least the dark man—Mr Wolf, though he is more dog-like—said something that sounded like the ultimate word of truth, and everybody murmured and stirred about like at the end of a concert. Paul Treece was left stranded by the unicorn lady, who had now closed her eyes, so he came over to Mr Thwaite and me—talking—and said, 'Mr Thwaite—what a perfectly beautiful garden. What a house! May I ask if you were born in it?' Mr Thwaite looked quite surprised. Lady Celia's friends don't talk to him much. He said, 'Harrumph grunt grunt ha—yes. Ha. Good old place. Romantic old place. As it happens, yes.'

'I expect that you must be lord of the manor?'

Lady Celia was listening, though she did not turn her head. Mr Thwaite looked across for guidance from her.

'Well—my sister, Celia, has taken on all that—' he said, leaving things trailing. 'Though I am, in fact.'

'Might I—might we—walk about a little? I'd love to see.'

'All means. Delighted. At once,' said Mr Thwaite, pleased as a cat and got up and went striding off with us after him.

We walked everywhere, Aunt Frances—miles of gardens and shrubberies I hadn't seen, down to the spinneys and along the near bank of the river, Paul Treece talking all the time and bouncing and springing on his feet (which are very big and may become flattish in later life, but never mind. He is very tall) and making little runs here and there. Once he said, 'Oh quickly—don't let us miss this glade, Miss Flint,' (Miss Flint!) and ran to a gate and rested his elbow on it, his chin in his hand. He sighed and said some Latin. 'Horace,' he said.

'Odes One,' said Mr Thwaite. 'Rabbits everywhere. The very deuce. Gun?'

'I beg your pardon?'

'If you've a gun—care for a gun?'

'Oh not at—No thank you.'

'See about one, tomorrow?'

Paul Treece and I found that we were looking at each other at that moment, very steadily, and reading each other's thoughts. I knew then everything about him and I felt sure again he knew all about me. 'Never', he said, 'a gun. I could never handle a gun.'

'May have to,' said Mr Thwaite, 'before long.'

'I am a poet, sir.'

'Ah well. Some of them did. Horace.'

'Horace fled the battlefield leaving his shield.'

'But thought it a disgrace. There'll be other Horaces. Before long. War coming.'

He went off then by himself, saying he must see the farm people and leaving me and Paul Treece together.

With love from Polly—I won't write again for a while, as I think I'd like to see the letters that will be waiting from you at home.

The next morning I woke up and went to my window and saw Paul Treece standing with his back to me on the terrace, looking out over the meadows and watching the sun rise. It was a rose-pink sky on the horizon with navy-blue above it and the dew on the nearer grass where the mist had not yet touched it was like rime. Paul Treece's bony figure looked gawky in the dawn and his clothes which seemed to be the same as yesterday's—he had not even changed for dinner—looked crumpled as if perhaps he had slept in them or just dropped them on the floor. They were noticeably now too big for him. Also, as I saw him for the first time not in profile, I noticed that he had oval ears, standing out like shells at right-angles to his head and the rays of the sun as I watched shone through them and made them glow.

It may have been the ears that gave me the confidence to dress in two minutes and go down through the early morning house and out to the terrace to join him; though when he turned and saw me all my awe of yesterday came back. I stopped still and said (very silly), 'It's early.'

'It's not six. Look, here's the sun.'

We stood side by side and as the sun burst up, listened to the tremendous palaver of the birds. The red farms on the plain were standing now up to their knees in mist and the river-bed was a gentle snake of cotton-wool crawling away to join the Ouse at Ouseburn to the south. He said, 'It's like *The Mill on the Floss*, isn't it? All the prosperous farms,' and my shyness went away. I said, 'Oh no. It's much prettier. They were great dark ominous places. Solitary. Great barns and things, all heavy and obvious—more like where I live.'

'Oh—is that near Northamptonshire?'

'No. I don't think so.'

'But you know Northamptonshire?'

'I don't know anywhere. This is the only piace I've ever been to stay in except for home. And Wales when I was a baby, but I don't remember much of that.'

'But the Midlands?'

I hadn't realised *The Mill on the Floss* was in the Midlands—or anywhere except in a book. I hadn't realised you could use a landscape in a book. I'd thought you had to make new ones. I knew the landscape of books—the weird sea-coast of *Sallee*, the primaeval wastes of *Wuthering Heights*, the rich isles of the Caribs, all the fancy places of French romance; the expanding-glass places of Gulliver. I knew every inch of Looking Glass Land and the underground places that open out from rabbit holes. It was the landscape of maps I found unreal—that's to say useless to fiction. I hardly ever looked at Grandfather Younghusband's globes now, in the study. I feared them rather. I said, 'I'm not even very sure where The Midlands are.'

He said, 'Where is "home"?'

'To the North.'

'I'm from the North-West. But I met Lady Celia in Cambridge.'

'Have you known her for a long time?'

'About three weeks. I met her at a concert. I sat next to her—she was visiting somebody grand. I'm in my second year there. She asked me to stay here.'

'Yes I see.'

'I'm a writer.'

'I expect she had heard of you.'

'Nobody's heard of me. I haven't published anything yet. She is good to poor writers. I was lucky to sit next to her. She invites anybody she thinks is promising. She is quite noted for it.'

'Are all the others here promising?'

'Oh goodness, yes. Some of them are Olympians. Are you considered promising in some way? I expect you're still at school.'

'I'm a sort of relation. I've never been to school. I don't think I'm at all promising.'

'Well, you've read *The Mill on the Floss*. It's a start. Do you read many novels?'

'I've read two hundred and eighty-three.'

'Good heavens. I didn't know there were—Were they mostly romantic?'

'No, I don't think so. I just read them in sets—they're all in the study. Scott, Dickens, Hardy, Richardson, Fielding, Sterne, Disraeli and so on. Most of them I think were my grandmother's though the study was my grandfather's really. He was very stuffy. He read mostly holy things and about stones and so on. The Swift is his though. Swift is very good. I've read all the French ones too, but I don't think he read those. He must have kept them out of sentiment when his wife died.'

'Did you meet Lady Celia in a cultural way?'

'No. I said—I'm a sort of relation. There was something between one of my aunts and Mr Thwaite. She's just got married, so it's rather a tense time.'

'I am coming to *adore* Mr Thwaite.'

I thought, what a very strange thing to say.

We walked across the lawn and out of the door in the wall and headed for the water-meadows. Our feet were soaking. Paul Treece's trousers were black with dew half way to the knee and clinging round his legs, not very engagingly. I said, 'You'll catch cold. You'll have to change when you get in.'

'Oh, I shall be all right.'

I felt troubled as we walked on and wondered why. We

passed a man out hoeing turnips early and a string of cows, red as the farm-building they were leaving. The cows looked hesitantly, one by one, out of the byre and then stepped from it with a dainty step. They swung very slowly across the yard and into the lane watching us, edging by us with anxious eyes. They smelled milky and warm and blew damp mist from their noses. Cocks were crowing about the land and sun blazed up, round and brilliant above the stack-yards. How could I be troubled?

We came to a footbridge—a wooden plank on old stone pillars with a hand-rail polished smooth. The water ran quietly, wrinkling round the stones, and Paul Treece stopped on the bridge and stood smiling at the water, his hands on the rail. He was jumpy with pleasure. I had thought that poets were ruminative and sage—like Wordsworth and Tennyson—but Paul Treece was all arms and legs and jitter.

His trousers were drying and I looked down at my own wet shoes and stockings and realised why I wasn't totally happy. When I'd been concerned for his wetness he hadn't given a thought to mine. Also—another thing—one bit of grit can set another scratching—'I adore Mr Thwaite.'

How could he *adore* Mr Thwaite? He'd hardly met him. It was not manly. Could one imagine Robinson Crusoe saying that he adored Mr Thwaite? Imagine Swift or Thomas Hardy! No, they would not. It did not do.

And how self-sufficient he was, springing about by the bridge. Now he was on the other bank picking things up and throwing them in the air. He was a bit dotty—as dotty as those Olympian Wolves at tea yesterday though at least he wasn't so miserable. Dotty as the snapping painter.

He wasn't the least bit interested in me either. Whatever was I doing walking along the fields with him, hungry and wet before breakfast? He just liked being watched. That was it. He liked a girl looking at him and feeling, 'I am walking in the meadows with a poet.'

He was nothing.

Just then though as I crossed the bridge he took my hand.

He didn't stop talking—he talked all the time and about everything he saw—'Look—the wheat. Look at the lines of it. Look at the hedges. D'you see how the May is dark red? D'you see how red the hedges are—a different red? Bright. There's so much red in a hedge—right from the start. The new shoots in January—well it's January in Cambridge—later here no doubt—what about your part of the world? Are there hedges? The sap is never green you know, rising. It's red. Like blood. That's a fact. And a poetic concept—' That's how he went on and in the middle of it, had taken my hand.

The talk was sure enough but the hand-holding wasn't very expert and I knew he hadn't done a lot of it before. His fingers were very nice and his hands thin but somehow it was all very disappointing. I had expected that holding a man's hand would be rather better.

'I'd like to go back now, please. We could go back along the path and get home this way, I think.'

We had come to a field end.

'Yes, all right.'

He turned obediently. He was endlessly amiable.

'You seem a very happy person,' I said.

'Happy? Well, yes. Very happy. I don't, as a matter of fact, think—I don't think I've ever been so happy—Cambridge and Lady Celia and—I'm very lucky. Oh dear—'

'What?'

'Is this the right way? The right way home?'

'Yes, I think so.'

'You can't see Thwaite from here can you? We seem to be in a valley bottom. Do you read Meredith?'

'No. I haven't heard of Meredith. Look I think—'

'Or Yeats. Do you read Yeats?'

He did a sort of dance. 'To think of it!' he said. 'To think of it. You are so innocent and yet aware. You have everything to come. Yeats and Meredith!'

I thought, he's so beautiful and joyful and I am alone with him in the early morning. I'm talking to him about all the things I most care about, like poets and wonderful books. Why can I only think of breakfast and that Lady Celia must be right—I am not in any way promising?

'Shall we try this way?'

After a time to my great relief we saw a man coming along through the fields in working clothes—black trousers tied at the knee with whitish, hairy string and a shirt without a collar, just a brass stud. Paul Treece was going on very loud, quoting from the writer Yeats but I said, 'Could we just ask do you think?'

'Ask?'

'Where we are. That man. How to get back.'

'Get *back*? Do you want to get back? Do you want this to be over?' All the time he had still held my hand and his big brilliant eyes looked at me very excitedly. I had a sudden comprehension of Fanny Brawne. I wanted to kick him.

'*Please* will you ask this man?'

'Good morning,' said Paul Treece. 'We're slightly lost. Early morning walk. We're trying to find Thwaite again.'

The man put down on the grass a bucket of milk he was carrying. It slopped about, pink at the edges. 'Thwaite?'

'The Hall.'

'What Hall?'

'Thwaite. Thwaite Hall. Lady Celia—'

'You're nearer Roundstone Hall. It's next village. Past Thoralby.'

'But we are staying at Thwaite.'

'Then you're away off your course. You're five miles off. Now Roundstone Hall—'

'That would be no good, I'm afraid. We have to be at Thwaite for breakfast.'

'Then it's a fair step. It's way beyond the river. The bridge is two mile back or two mile forward. Good day to you.'

'Five miles,' I said. 'Five miles! It can't be. We can't have walked five miles. We're absolutely lost.'

Something in me wanted him to say that how could we be lost and together, that I needn't worry, that we were so happy.

'Roundstone,' he said, 'Roundstone Hall. Well good heavens, did he say Roundstone Hall?'

'Yes, I think so.'

'Well I know it! I know Roundstone Hall. I know the people.'

'Oh yes?'

'I'm at Cambridge with a chap from Roundstone Hall. He said it was in Yorkshire somewhere. Theo Zeit. Come on, young child. We'll find a breakfast.'

The boy and girl of the pony and trap stood on the stairs, the girl not much taller than she had been then—rather short-legged, but the same glorious hair. Theo stood on the step above and so seemed very tall indeed. He looked quietly at us as his sister covered her mouth with a shriek at the sight of Paul Treece.

'Oh good heavens!' Out shot her arms. 'The *Poultice*, The Poultice! It is—how can it be—The Poultice?'

There was the most tremendous smell of polish and newness everywhere. Every surface was soaked in it. Fine mahogany chests and cabinets and chairs like thrones swam with it. A rosewood pedestal glowed with it and the sabre-leafed plant that stood on it seemed polished, too. In the dining-room sideboards like streets, a vast table and twenty chairs were rich with the hours people had spent rubbing at them with wax and soft cloths. The table-legs had flown from some Indian temple and there was a good deal of brass and copper about. At the end of the table a woman sat very upright and amused by us. She had papers beside her and a pen in her hand.

'Well, good morning.'

'Mother. This is extraordinary! Paul Treece from Queen's. And—Miss Polly Flint. Walking before breakfast and lost. They're staying at Thwaite.'

'Lost—oh dear. How do you do? And before breakfast.'

'They set off very early. About dawn. They've walked in circles.'

'The Poultice is a poet, Mamma.'

'Poultice? Ah, yes. A poet—they have a good many of them at Thwaite I hear. Good morning Miss Flint. You must be a poet, too?'

'No, I'm just—'

'You are just. Well done. Come at once and sit down. No—go with Rebecca and wash. You must be longing to wash. Then come back again—at once—for food.'

'Thank you. I'm just slightly—'

'Worried? There is no need. We shall telephone.'

'They aren't on the telephone. It's not what Lady Celia—'

'Then I shall send a message. Wash. Return and eat. Theo will see to Mr Poultice.'

She was quite little but with a large head, black hair in ropes in a nest on top and a face most dreadfully plain with a floppy undefined sort of mouth that strayed over it. But she had a smiling look about her and gave the general impression that everything in her world was remarkably pleasant. Her hands were very certain of themselves as she tidied the papers and letters beside her. When we came back from a wonderful bathroom white tiled to the ceiling with taps like something in the Works—she was gone.

Paul Treece sat at the table instead in front of a plate mountains high with kidneys, bacon, sausages, eggs. He was talking hard, waving his fork, and his eyes quite wild with excitement.

The delicious but not robust food at Thwaite was meant to pass unnoticed, incidental to the spirit, and it came in very small quantities.

Rebecca sat near him watching the mountain diminish and Theo stood by the window, his red head against a velvet curtain which had bobbles all the way down it like thistle heads. He had the same look of general happiness being the order of things as his mother and smiled and said, 'Come and have kippers.'

'Oh—no thank you.'

My heart thumped too desperately for eating.

'Coffee? Tea?'

'Oh, coffee please.'

'It's a bit of a wash, the coffee today. Difficult to get round here.'

'We get ours from London.'

'*Do* you indeed! On that marsh? Do you still live on that marsh of yester-year? Does the coffee come in on the tide?'

'No it comes from Mrs Woods. She has connections with Africa.' Rebecca spluttered. She said, 'Oh God—I'm sorry. Africa!' Theo gave an elderly smile (but not unkind). 'That marsh and Africa,' she said.

So I knew I must defend it.

I looked round at the money—the plush, the carpet, all turkish red and blue, gold-framed pictures on brass chains on brass railings supported by fat gold brackets in the shape of fat gold flowers. A gold-tubed clock set between marble supports under a glass bell, on the chimney piece struck nine. 'Oh the marsh is a *really* rich place,' I said.

They were quiet.

'We're going to have our house ready soon,' said Theo. 'It's on the way to being finished now. It's for us all to get lots of healthy sea-breezes in the summer.'

'Yes, I know. It doesn't seem to be getting on very fast.'

'It's been Mamma's plaything for years. She keeps changing all the plans. She thinks Father ought to have somewhere healthy to go to not so far from the Works as Germany—which is where he is now, and very often. At the Spa. The Works are only across the estuary.'

'The Works are getting nearer all the time,' I said, 'and the smoke's nearer too.'

'We shall be neighbours,' he said. 'Next year the plan is that we shall be there for ages—all the summer.'

'It's all astonishing,' said Paul Treece, stretching for fresh toast. He took a great many small bites at it, examining the shape of each and then took a great many quick little sips of coffee. 'I know nothing about any of all this. Nothing.'

The brother and sister collapsed again.

'The dear old Poultice,' said Theo. 'You know he's a genius, Polly Flint? Writes the most amazing stuff. So I'm told. Publishes it in the greenery-yallery magazines. He's supposed to be like whatsisname, the famous one.'

'*What* famous one?' Rebecca was wiping her eyes. She seemed very close to her brother, catching his thoughts. 'Oh, we're being beastly, Theo. Sorry Poult. I'm terribly sorry Polly Flint. You see The Poult knows and puts up with us. You don't. We're utterly hopeless you see, Theo and I. All the Zeits are. At arty things. Even though we're Jewish and German— we can't sing a note or play a thing and we never read a book. And behold the pictures! Dying stags. Mamma bought them from a baronial mansion in Scotland because of the frames. We're *terrible* philistines. Aren't we, Paul?'

'They're *fairly* hopeless,' he said, dolloping on the butter.

'I thought—philistines are a particular Jewish sect?'

'We are philistines and we are atheists.'

'I've never agreed about that,' said Paul Treece. 'You love mankind. You're not atheists. Your family gives away goodness knows what. Millions.'

'Well, we are atheists, aren't we, Theo?'

'You are,' said Theo, 'and Mamma, and so, I *suppose*, is father, but he will never discuss it. He thinks things out by himself. In Baden-Baden. In the mud. And he'd give you his last pair of trousers.'

'Whyever should Polly Flint want father's last pair of trousers?'

'I mean he is the *best*, not just the good Samaritan. And he is probably very sad that he can't believe in God. How about you, Miss Flint? I shouldn't think God comes into things down on the marsh very much.'

I felt cold and the furniture glowed in vain.

'More coffee? Is something wrong?' Theo came and sat beside me and looked at me. Rebecca had been looking at me too, noticing that I was looking awful—elderly, quaint and not pretty. And not a pretty shape. Theo looked as if he was concerned for me, though.

'She's probably not met many atheists,' said Rebecca.

'I never—I don't really ask—'

'I don't suppose there are many people *to* ask on that marsh.'

'Ask in the Iron-Works slums and you'll find atheists,' said Rebecca.

'Some aren't,' I said. 'Well they say "God bless you" some of them when we go round with soup. Some don't speak for hate of us, but I don't think they're all atheists. Actually at Oversands we—my aunts—are very religious. My Aunt Frances has just married a priest. They've gone to be missionaries in India. They sail—tomorrow.'

Rebecca groaned and put her hands through her great fizz of wild hair. 'I can't bear it.'

'What?'

'I'm sorry. I can't do with all that.'

'All what?'

'Tosh and missionaries. I'm sorry. I have to speak out. I'm not like Theo. He's nice. I'm very bold and crude. Nobody likes me much at Cambridge. I can't keep my mouth shut.'

'You mean', I said, 'you honestly don't believe in God?'

'No. Not a bit. I can't. It just all sounds like fairy stories. There seems absolutely no sense in it. Old men in the sky looking down and watching over us. I haven't the beginnings of an idea how an intelligent human being can believe that. It's why I didn't read Philosophy. History is mystifying enough.'

I saw the queer procession of my aunts, Mrs Woods and me, pacing towards the bell every Sunday, rain or shine to worship an old man in the sky.

'Shut up, Bec. Live and let live,' said Theo. 'I go to church at Cambridge every Sunday, don't I, Poult? My God, He lives in King's College Chapel.'

'He lives in toast,' said Paul Treece, 'peach jam, in Polly Flint and Zeits.'

Theo said, 'Polly—we have upset you.'

'It's all right,' I said, 'I'm not Confirmed.'

'Oh *I* am. I was done *en bloc* at Eton.'

I felt sick and shy again and said, 'Paul, I think we ought to go now. It's so late. We never said we were going out.'

'All is perfectly dealt with,' said Mrs Zeit sailing back among us. 'I'm just sending someone over to Thwaite with a note. I've said you'll be staying here for the day. It's a perfect day for the garden and we've tennis and croquet and some more interesting people from Sunderland coming to luncheon.'

'More interesting than what—or who?'

'—m' said Rebecca.

'I'm afraid', I got up, 'I really should like to go. Don't you think so, Paul?'

'Oh well—'

'If you want to stay, do stay. I want to go.'

'But you *can't*,' said Rebecca. 'It's nice here. Come on. They're all old *things* at Thwaite. Creepy crawlies. Pianists.'

'They'll mind,' I said, 'I'm sorry, Mrs Zeit,' and surprised myself by folding my napkin, getting up and walking over to her. 'It's been so kind of you.'

She was wearing yellow silk with ruching and diamond brooches. In the morning. Her eyes were very displeased. Then, instead or taking my hand she held out both hers and took both mine and her eyes smiled again. She held tight. 'My *dear* little girl,' she said, 'have some *fun* here with us.'

But I said, 'No. I must go home.'

When I reached the drive, Paul Treece followed me and walked beside me and near the gate a great quiet car crept up behind us with a chauffeur in it. It passed and stopped and the chauffeur got out and held the door for us.

'To Thwaite, sir?'

'Oh—well, yes.'

'I'd like to walk,' I said, but felt that this was overdoing things and got in, Paul Treece beside me. He was silent and only said once, 'Look Polly, look at the corn.'

I looked but did not really see the miles of silvery stalks and the blobs of poppies and the sky above them. 'See them wriggle,' he said, 'in the breeze. What a lovely summer. There can't have been a more lovely summer since the beginning of the world.'

At length the crumbly walls of Thwaite appeared and we got out.

I knew perfectly well that nobody had noticed that we had been away.

The chauffeur, as he opened the motor-car door for us, handed me a letter addressed to Lady Celia and said that he had been told to wait for an answer. I said, 'Oh no—that's all been changed. That letter was to tell Lady Celia we were not coming home—'

He said, 'No miss, that was the *first* note. This one's been written since. It's why you had to set off without me and I had to catch you up. Mrs Z is a right fast writer. There's new plans afoot now.'

The Poultice was standing waiting at Thwaite's door so I took the envelope. 'It might be a while to wait for the answer,' I said. 'Shall I tell Maitland you're here? You can go round to the kitchen and have tea.'

He said, '*No* thank you, miss,' and gave me a look.

In the hall Mr Barker was putting out the post, keeping aside on a salver a pile of very personal-looking letters, some faintly coloured with ripply edges to the flaps. 'Put that one on the top of these,' he said. 'They're all for Lady Celia. They're just going up to her.'

'Oh!' I pounced and knocked his Pharoic arm. I had seen Aunt Frances's writing on a letter laid out on the chest.

'Hold hard,' said Mr Barker. 'That there's not for you, it's for Mr Thwaite. Here's yours.'

I grabbed—but it was not from Aunt Frances. How could it be when I came to think about it. She didn't even know I was here. Her letters to me would be waiting at the yellow house. And this letter was in a cheap envelope, very thin, the hand-writing round and wobbly like a child's and it spelled my name wrong.

'Dear Miss Polly,' it said. 'Sorry to trouble you on your holidays but would appreciate advice about matters here which are not good she is worse even in my opinion not right at all and Miss Mary gone. Have called the doctor and think you should come back yours truly Alice Bates.'

'Lady Celia wants you to go up,' said Mr Barker. He had come down again from the bedroom and stood with his head bowed a little towards me as a butler should, but he said,

'Something wrong, Miss Polly? You're gone to a statue. Mr Treece is away for some coffee. Shall I—?'

'No thanks. Oh—'

'You're to go up there, she says. If you don't want coffee, go now and get it over.'

'I must see Maitland. Lady Celia will be answering the letter the chauffeur brought. He's waiting. I've time.'

'No—get sorted up yonder, miss. Roundstone waits. We don't faff with Roundstone.'

'Yes, I see.'

Lady Celia's exhausted head was propped on a hummock of pastel-coloured pillows and above them drooped a spray of peacock-feathers and gauzy curtains like in Tennyson. Her breakfast-tray, a still life, was untouched upon the bed and she was looking out of the window and her hand holding Mrs Zeit's letter seemed hardly attached to her. It was a dark bedroom. I stood at the foot of the bed.

She said at last, 'You have called then? At Roundstone?'

'No. Yes.'

'No-yes? What is this no-yes?'

'We got lost.'

'Lost?'

'We went walking. Paul Treece and I. We went much farther than we meant to and then we were told we were near Roundstone and Paul Treece was absolutely thrilled because he knows the people there.'

'Ah.'

'I said it was rude just to go in.'

'You were right.'

'But they are his very *close* friends.'

'Paul Treece has very many "very *close* friends".'

'They're all at Cambridge together. It's all very under—'

'Paul Treece', she said, 'is a go-getter. An enchanting boy, but a go-getter. You should be warned—though I don't see

him in great pursuit of you. The Zeit girl and her millions perhaps. He can write poetry—to a certain extent. This is why I
invited him. He is very poor.'

'Yes I see.'

'And also he is in love with me. As much as that sort of man
ever can be.'

I said nothing. She must have been fifty.

'It is not unusual in this house. It is something I have to put
up with very often. It killed my husband—my intense attractiveness to men of all ages.'

'Yes I see.'

'Will you please stop saying, "yes I see". And please understand that we at Thwaite do *not* know those at Roundstone.'
There was a sort of electricity in the pillows as she turned her
head and glared at me; a patchiness about the face which was
not rouge. 'They are people we are not able to know socially,'
she said. 'Do you understand?'

How could you know people unsocially?

'Yes. But—' I was about to say 'But Mr Thwaite goes to
Roundstone often,' when I remembered his nice lanky old
figure in its breeches going off like a shadow towards the
meadows.

She didn't know.

'They all seemed so very—interesting there.'

'They are not. They are not interesting in the very least. Not
at all.'

'You mean because they are Jews and foreigners?'

'Certainly not. Thwaite is full of Jews and foreigners. It is
because they have no conception of anything we stand for.
They laugh at aestheticism. And they deny their God. They
find us *amusing!*'

'I hated it about God,' I said. 'It seems so much worse
somehow when they are Jews. But some writers don't exactly
believe in God. Isn't that what they were all talking about on

the lawn yesterday? All that about a primal force? And the Zeits do give millions of pounds to the poor.'

'And told you so?'

'Oh, not—Well, in a round-about way. Somebody said—'

'Exactly. For us such people are without reality.'

'But they all seemed so very real,' I said. 'They all seemed a bit too real. Very—solid.'

'Ha! Solid—solid is exactly it. Up to now we have avoided Roundstone. I have never called. Yet this shameless letter has invited you and Treece to spend the day with them tomorrow. Picnics—no doubt with silver canapé-dishes and everyone dressed up in diamonds and high-heeled shoes. Motor cars. Businessmen from Tyneside in gloves. Please go down and ask Barker to send the chauffeur away.'

'What shall he say?'

'That a reply will be posted. They are *philistines!*'

'Is he to say that they are philistines?'

A flash from the pillow. 'Of course not, you fool of a child.'

I said, 'Actually they know that they are philistines. They told me so. They say they can't help it. I don't think they're at all—subversive.'

'You seem—and come back: throw this letter in the waste-paper-basket by my dressing table—you seem to have got a very long way at Roundstone in a very short time.'

I dropped the letter, and in the looking-glass saw the peacock-feathers and the gauzes and the drapes of birds and flowers, an easel with a portrait on it of someone very rich but of spiritual expression, in a cravat—the husband killed through his wife's magnetism for men. I wondered whether I liked aestheticism very much.

'Oh we did get a long way,' I said. 'You see, I'd met them before, long ago when I was young, the two Zeit children. We got a long way then, too. It was on the beach. I loved them at once, and very much. And I couldn't have gone with them tomorrow anyway, Lady Celia, because I have to go home.'

I did not see Paul Treece again before I left, for Lady Celia took him aside with her that afternoon and they were in close conversation all the evening. He smiled in my direction over dinner and after dinner I made off to the servants' quarters where I felt they were sorry that I was leaving, and this was balm.

But I didn't say much. Just sat, held Maitland's knitting wool, listened to the cinders drop, the kettle sing. Nobody asked any questions about my being called home and I wished they would, for it might have strengthened me to say in words why I must go—for I had not explored the reasons why I was so sure. Yet in another way I liked being left alone. It was adult.

Maitland did say when I said goodbye at bedtime—for I was to leave early in the morning—that she hoped all would be well for me. I said that it couldn't be well, exactly, with both my aunts gone.

'Then who's to greet you?'

'I shan't be *greeted*. There's just Alice the maid, and Mrs. Woods. Mrs Woods is ill. That's why I have to go.'

'Who is Mrs Woods?'

'She's someone who lives with us.'

'A servant?'

'No, just someone my aunts have been kind to.'

'Ah—a paid companion?'

'Oh no. Not *paid*. She's very important. I don't really know much about her. But I think she's always been important. For years.'

'Well it seems to me it's not very nice of you. You with your own life beginning. We'll all miss you—won't we Barker? We've taken a great fancy to you. Do you realise that?

Mr Thwaite—we'll miss Miss Polly.' Mr Thwaite didn't look as though he were going to miss me much. He was examining a bishop.

'It's good to have some straightforward young life here,' she went on. 'Now you're to write to us. Will you write to us?'

'Yes, of course. I think I'll write very often. I think I might need lots of advice. If I'm to be in charge, with just Alice.'

'In charge of this important old companion who is sick—advice you'll need. What's this Alice?'

'Oh, she's—she keeps apart. She's very quiet and hard-working. She came from the vicar, she's my age about. She's the maid. But we think she may have to go, now that Aunt Frances and the vicar have gone.'

Maitland raised a long arm in the air and held her wool aloft for an extended moment. She said, 'You're to write, if *ever* you're in trouble. No one manages alone.'

Mr Thwaite surprised me at the station—he had driven us himself in the trap, I and the snapping painter who was returning to London—by saying the same thing in his own way.

'Letter not come amiss,' he said. 'No joke alone for a girl.'

'I'll write to Lady Celia tonight.'

'Apart from bread and butter. Collinses. Personal to me. No S.O.S. ignored, directed to Arthur Thwaite.'

I wanted to thank him, to love him—standing there looking high above our heads, his Don Quixote shoulders in the old Norfolk jacket, blue eyes peering about at the station traceries, examining the baskets of geraniums, the little swinging sign, checking the station-clock with his gold watch, thin as a biscuit. 'Thank you very much for been the most marvellous—'

"Here she comes. Right on time.'

Along the dead-straight track, puffs of smoke preceded the round face of the engine. 'Here we are now.'

The painter and I got in.

'Perhaps, let me know?' said Mr Thwaite. 'What you hear from India?'

'Of course.'

'Deplorable business.' He touched his temple with the whip of the pony-trap and swung away, and I saw how blank his face had become.

The painter's train to London did not leave for some time and so, on Darlington station, we sat together on my platform and waited for my train to the marsh.

He looked as mad as ever. He wasn't snapping so much but he twitched his fingers and pulled at his hair and kept getting up and sitting down again. The day was grey and cold—the wonderful weather of Thwaite seemed already to belong to some sealed-off conservatory somewhere, some hot and distant island. Rain began to patter on the high glass roof of the station and a wind blew down the platform from the direction I was going to take. I shut my eyes.

I didn't bother to speak to the painter and he didn't bother to speak to me and I sat with my eyes shut until I heard my train clank in and then I climbed up and put my bags on the rack and let down the window to lean out and shake hands.

But instead of taking my hand he put a piece of paper into it. It was a picture of me sitting on the platform asleep, and it was the most beautiful drawing I had ever seen.

'A young woman on the threshold of life,' he said, and snapped the air and twisted his face about; and I laughed, because although the drawing was so lovely the face was also the most miserable face in the world.

'The doomed traveller,' said he.

And looking at him I saw what a miserable, smug, self-righteous lump I was. What a heavy weight I must have been. And yet, for all that, he had missed none of the few good things. Seeing all, he had forgiven all, and had shown that, though I was young and stupid, there was some sort of hope.

'Oh,' I said, 'oh it's wonderful. It really is *very* good,' and he looked at me sharp and sideways—a 'thank you kindly, Miss No one'. The whistle went, the flag flapped on the slamming doors. 'You'll be someone I'll think of,' I shouted, 'I think you're going to be very famous. It's just *like* me. Oh I wish I didn't understand things only when they were over. I'm not really a misery. Not by nature. Thank you, so very much. I'm a sort of Robinson Crusoe. I'm all washed up at present.'

Doors slammed.

'Robinson Crusoe wasn't so bad,' he said. 'A bit too bloody sane, but not so bad. Goodbye.' He reached up a hard, warm hand then to the back of my neck and pulled my head down to him and kissed me. He stopped kissing me and then kissed me again harder, opening my mouth, pressing my mouth until it hurt, pulling his tongue inside so that I gasped out. The moving train jerked him away and was nearly off the end of the platform before I could breathe.

I could tell from his figure walking in the other direction that I was already forgotten.

Hearing people talk now, or reading about it, one imagines the four years of the Great War passing in England in benign and golden sunlight, occasional gunfire on the channel-breeze as we tended roses, rolled bandages and drank cups of tea, or handed white feathers about the pleasant streets. We are also told, endlessly, that the war burst and shattered us like a thunderbolt from a summer sky, like Crusoe's demon pouncing upon him in sleep.

Neither is quite true. Even on the marsh we had heard uneasy things for some time—for about four years. For months before August 4th, 1914, Mr Box of Boagey's, the doctor, the vicar had all spoken of a coming war and I remember Aunt Frances telling me years before her wedding when I was still a child, 'Father always said that there will be war with Germany in the end.' I had heard Mr Box tell Charlotte, 'There'll be war again, you'll see. With Germany. I can't stand Germans, but if I had to choose between them and the French as friends I know which it would be. Never the French.' Charlotte said, 'One foreigner's as bad as another. I can't abide Germans neither'—though wherever could she have met one? Or Mr Box a Frenchman? There was still, on the marsh, a faint shadow of pride going about that we had beaten Napoleon, and a curious Nelson-Worship—something to do with H.M.S. Victory—always called 'Nelson's Flagship Victory' on the marsh, presumably because so many people remembered local men being pressed aboard her long years after Trafalgar.

Through the spring and early summer of 1914, when the possibility of war was mentioned, I remember no patriotism, only sombreness. Perhaps, of course, on our queer island on the marsh we were different and dour. Certainly we were on August 4th, 1914, which was by all accounts throughout the rest of the country a most glorious golden morning.

With us it was raining. Round the yellow house there hung a cold, early-morning sea-fret and Alice and I looked out at whiteness as we dealt with Mrs Woods's slops and dirty sheets and made ready for the day. Out of her window we could hardly see the little privet hedge. The sea might not have been there, but for its insistent whisper—the long wave from the Gare to the breakwater turning and collapsing, turning and collapsing just out of sight. Not a bird uttered and we could hardly hear the bells.

What Mrs Woods could hear, of course, or see or understand about war or anything else, goodness knows, for she had had a stroke and for more than a year now had lain looking at the ceiling, not speaking, but groaning a great deal when Alice and I lifted her twice a day.

For I must now say what happened when I came walking home in 1913 over the marsh from Thwaite towards the yellow house—a changing marsh, for I had been a month away.

I noticed how it was shrinking. It wasn't just that I was two feet taller than when I first knew it, so that the flowers and grasses were so much further off. The marsh itself had diminished. The chimneys had crept up on us, and so had the workmen's houses on the mud-flats with all their plumes of smoke bending together away from the sea. And the streets up around the church were closer too and there were more of them. There was a large and prosperous blossoming of lodging houses.

And I noticed what must have been there for a while, a broad tarmacadammed road running along and out towards us before the sea, stopping well short of the yellow house certainly, and cracking here and there with sprouts of persistent grass—brave ugly grass, which might win yet. But it was a road.

The yellow house stood high with its big windows flashing and the sea behind it tossing and the big ships sliding along the horizon waiting for the tide into the estuary. Oh, beautiful house.

I climbed the steps and the door was flung wide to an empty hall and the vicar's Alice turning her head away from me with embarrassed relief.

'Tooken bad five days,' she said. 'I got the doctor.'

'Is Miss Younghusband here yet?'

'She's not come. I wrote. Like to you. The nuns up at The Rood say a Retreat's when you're closed off from things.'

'Yes, but not in a *crisis*. Mrs Woods might have died.'

'Well, Miss Mary's not here. There's been me alone.'

She was very frightened. Wisps of hair and a dirty apron.

'I'll go up. Is the doctor coming every day? You've done wonders, Alice. I came as soon as I could,' which was true. But how in the last few hours I had yearned to be back. I dumped down my bag and went up and held Mrs Woods's bedroom door-knob.

In all the years of my childhood I had never been inside

her bedroom but I knew that when I opened the door there would be a smell—the sour, dreadful smell of her. I knew that she would be looking towards the door as it opened, looking at me with the resentful bitter face I'd scarcely ever seen soften or smile. I prayed, 'Help me' and thought 'Praying— how ridiculous.' The people at Thwaite would not need to pray—the Olympian writers who had come to tea, mercurial Paul Treece, the snapping painter. Or the Zeits at Roundstone. Strong effective brilliant people who knew how to enjoy their lives in long summer visits, and endless pleasures—never with morbid thoughts of God. None of them believed in God. They had the wonderful freedom of not believing in God, the freedom denied even to Robinson Crusoe, otherwise the steadiest man in the world though very likely not Confirmed.

Look where praying had got my aunts. To India with Mr Pocock, to a cell where they wouldn't let you out to look after your friends. Look where it had got Mrs Woods—a husk on a bed with no one to love.

I wondered then about Mr Thwaite, if he prayed, and at once I knew that he did; and it was seeing his mediaeval face in my mind rather than a message from anything higher that gave me the courage to turn the door-knob and go in.

I saw a clean room, very bare, a thin carpet with a broad surround of blank floor-board, a white cotton bed-cover, no curtains, and over the fireplace a cross. The window was wide open and the swish of the sea came in, comforting and steady. The room smelled salty. She was not looking at me but straight upwards, the side of her face drawn slightly down and dribble was coming out of her mouth. She was wearing a thick white very clean night-dress, her arms out of sight under the quilt. She seemed exceedingly small. By not a blink or a flicker did she show that she was glad to see me, or could see me at all. The expression of ferocity in her eyes had gone. They held none. Her hair on the pillow I noticed for the first time was thin and there was a pink blob on the top of her head where it had worn out.

The horrible thinness of the hair had to be looked away from. I said, 'Mrs Woods. Hello. I'm so sorry. Whatever have you been doing—frightening us all? Well, I don't know! You can't be left alone for a minute.'

What was all this? Kindness? I was awkward with kindness. I had never learned it. You have to learn kindness very young indeed. Kindness had been sketchy in Wales.

'We must brush your poor hair,' I said (We!). 'Dear me, we must set things to right.' I hated her still.

And a tear formed then in Mrs Woods's good eye, welled up over its red under-lid and spilled crookedly down her awful cheek.

Aunt Mary did come back to the yellow house but not then. Not for some time and her return was almost a worse surprise than Mrs Woods, for like the marsh she seemed to be shrunk and poor, unrecognisable as the tall beauty in the oyster-silk at the wedding scarcely more than a month ago.

Stepping out of the taxi she seemed pinched up, strange, and old, in the familiar crazy black veiling. She scarcely noticed me as she came into the house, glanced at the pile of letters in the hall and passed them by, looked at Alice as if she were uncertain who she was and examined the barometer for a long time. Then very slowly she took off her gloves.

At last she said, 'Polly?'

I tried to hug her but she pushed me vaguely away. 'No, dear, let me just think.' She went across the hall and looked round the study door and stood there for ages. Then she crossed over and looked in at the dining-room. 'Oh how nice!' she said. 'I hope the spoons are safe?'

I said, 'Mrs Woods—'

'Yes. Never mind. Another time,' and we went up to the drawing-room and Alice brought tea.

'Are you all right, Aunt Mary? Was the Retreat—nice?'

'Very nice, thank you.' She sat upright holding the flowery tea-cup.

'I had a—marvellous time. I met all sorts of famous people. It's a wonderful place, Aunt. Thwaite. You never told me. It's a vast house. There are suits of armour and things. Lady Celia—'

'Lady Celia,' said Aunt Mary. 'Hah!'

'Oh—don't you like her?'

'Celia Thwaite, we do not talk about. She is a destroyer. She has ruined lives.'

'Goodness—Yes, she might.'

'She did. She has. Arthur Thwaite was born to marry a good woman. At the wedding—'

'Oh—oh yes. I see.'

'Celia is a wicked woman given over to sin.' The ring of the old Aunt Mary made me feel better. 'If you don't mind, Polly, we shall not speak of her again.'

'No, of course not. But', I said, 'I can't see why he—Mr Thwaite—listened to her? About getting married?'

'He is weak. All men are weak. Pocock—your father. Not of course your Grandfather Younghusband, but he was one apart. Women are the strong ones, Polly, but we are not allowed to show it. We have to await men's pleasure. We can never ask *them*. If we do there is a fiasco. Like Frances—'

'Oh, have you heard from her? There are letters from her in the hall—all to you. None to me.'

'I heard before I left the Retreat. Something or other to do with the armed forces. Shopping in London.'

'Oh please, can I bring the rest of the letters in?'

'Not just yet.' She sat looking queerly at the brown and gold pansies on her tea-cup. 'I've been so happy while I've been away,' she said.

After that she took to wandering about. For the next few days she drifted round the house looking out of all the windows. Then she spent hours sitting still. She ate almost nothing. Once she went to see Mrs Woods, but soon wandered out again and when the doctor called, though she seemed to be listening to him intently, her eyes were on other things. 'Mrs Woods may well live for many years,' he said. 'She is improving all the time. We're getting her up—Polly and young Alice—now. She will soon be getting downstairs again. I don't think, since she's not—er—, that there should be much extra washing. So that we need not think of moving her. I shan't recommend hospital at present, or nursing home.'

'There is no money for either,' said Aunt Mary. 'It would have to be the nuns. Or the workhouse. She is penniless.'

The doctor tipped his sherry-glass about. 'The nuns only take the convalescents of the working poor.'

'We are the idle poor,' said Aunt Mary. 'I am nearly penniless too. Frances and I had very little and Frances has taken her share to India. I have only the house and no one would buy that. We are as poor as Our Lord.'

One night I woke up and found Aunt Mary standing in my bedroom looking out of the window again. It was moonlight and she stood still, watching the sea. After a minute she went out. She looked even thinner, madder, with her great white nightdress floating all about her, one hand holding a candle and the other the case of spoons.

I lay awake then until the sun began to rise, thinking about her and about everything that had happened to me since I was born, and how perhaps a dog, a couple of cats, a handful of goats and a parrot might be quite jolly companions.

A week or so later she came into the study and said, 'Polly, if I went back to the Retreat, could you manage? It is very cheap and I don't mean it to be for very long. I do so miss it there. Just until I feel better? I don't seem able to underst—to organise anything here any more.'

I said, 'Yes, I see. Of course. I'm sure with Alice—She's very good.'

'I don't want to do *wrong*,' she said. 'You're not seventeen. Could you ring for Alice?' Her eyes glared and stared.

'I'd miss you very much,' I said.

'Alice, come in. Could you and Miss Polly manage alone for a little longer? If I were to go back to the Retreat?'

Alice looked at me as if she were about to have her throat cut. 'Yes Miss Younghusband. Yes, I'd think—'

'I cannot be as near to God here as I should like. Miss Polly understands, although she is—sadly—un-Confirmed. Now I shall go and write the letter.'

When she had gone out Alice said, 'Oh Miss Polly!' and I said, 'Is she ill, Alice? What shall we do? She's not *here* any more.'

'We must bide with her,' said Alice.

'Alice, I'm frightened.'

'I'm frightened, too, miss, but I'd think it might be her age.'

'What does that mean?'

'Well, her age. Her time of life. We go funny, women.'

'*Funny?*'

'My Mam did. But she'll come through it. Bear up.'

'Yes, I suppose so.' (Would I ever know anything? What was this 'funny'? There was nothing about women going funny in novels. Perhaps if Robinson Crusoe had been a woman— Did men go funny, too, and who was there to tell me?)

'We'll fettle grand,' said Alice uncertainly, but she was watching me. I saw kindness in her face and something better— something that meant she could be strong if need be. She had only to get used to an idea. 'Oh, we'll fettle grand,' she said. 'We got me Mam through right as ninepence. She took a great fancy to bloaters and we humoured her. She takes in washing again now—strong as a lion, and so'll Miss Younghusband be.'

But she was wrong for Aunt Mary died a month later from a tumour on the brain and was buried in the churchyard near poor little Mr Woods, which would not have pleased her.

To tell Aunt Frances was the first concern. I wrote at once, of course, but knew that it would be weeks before the letter arrived in Delhi—long before she did, for the Pococks were travelling very slowly. Rome and Naples had been visited and at present they must be steaming across the Indian Ocean. I thought that at the funeral I might be able to ask Mr Thwaite about the telegraph to cable to ships, but Mr Thwaite had bronchitis and could not attend the funeral. After worrying about it—and being advised about it by the Church and The Hall and Mr Boagey and Mr Box and several of Aunt Mary's nuns—even going to the post-office to enquire of Dicky Dick who had expanded the lino-shop to become the first postmaster to the new esplanade terrace (he had no first-hand information about cabling facilities but gave me tea) I decided that there was no need for haste after all.

Aunt Frances could not come back. Even if she could have done, what sense in it would there be? I was only wanting sympathy.

So I wrote a note to the Society of the Propagation of the Gospel in case they had someone else going to Delhi who might be a comfort to her in her sad loss, and tried to keep my head.

I took to going to church regularly after Aunt Mary's death, sitting in her pew, using her white prayer-book, thinking about her a good deal. The church-people were kind. They turned round from the pews in front with wide smiles and sympathetic nods and at the church-porch the new young priest thrust out at me his Cardinal Newman jaw and his hand gripped mine like a vice.

He came to the yellow house to see me, too, often stayed after bringing Mrs Woods her Holy Communion and threw back several glasses of sherry, sprawled out in the button-back chair.

After Evensong once—I even started going to Evensong, though I suppose I did let my mind wander rather—watching the new priest tearing about the chancel, scrabbling in his vestments for his handkerchief, singing cheerfully like a Methodist—after Evensong once, a large important woman asked if I would like to do a vase, but as I didn't know what she meant I said no, and there was rather a cooling off after that.

Then one day I went to the church and met a great blanket of gloom as I stepped through the door. I was handed a prayerbook by Mr Boagey bent in to a hoop, and the ladies here and there had handkerchieves about them as openly as the vicar and nothing to do with hay-fever from the marsh. The vaselady turned from the pew in front and covered my hand with hers and when Lady Vipont slid into The Hall pew, it was like the arrival of the cloud that worried Noah. 'Thank God', said the lady of the vase, 'that it was painless and swift.'

It appeared that Mr Pocock had died at sea. The vicarage had heard only that morning.

'My child—you didn't *know*! We were sure—! We heard just before the service—a telephone message to The Hall and The Hall to the Vicar. We would have come to you at once—' After the service clusters of ladies stood talking in whispers in the churchyard and only the nuns, being professionals, looked composed. And only the nuns said 'Your poor dear aunt. Oh Polly, your poor dear aunt. And still a bride.'

Alice said—we had a brandy together in the kitchen— 'Look at it this way, Miss Polly. She'll not want. He was a rich man. That's not nothing. Miss Frances was liked by all when she was poor and now she'll be the belle of the ball. And she's so young-looking, too!'

'But she'll be coming home, Alice,' I said, just realising it. 'She'll be home again. Oh Alice!'

And then the most astonishing thing happened.

Superstition, habit, respect, what you will, I could not write a letter on a Sunday with the sepia eye of Grandfather Younghusband on me from the wall and the holy eye of Aunt Mary from the clouds and so it was Monday morning before I had the letter of condolence to Aunt Frances ready for the post.

Alice and I did Mrs Woods that morning as usual. I wrote the letter and decided not to wait for the postman to call, but walked across the marsh to Dicky Dick's myself. It had not been an easy letter to write and I brooded all the way on whether or not I had hit the right note—Aunt Frances had always known very well that Mr Pocock and I had not been the best of friends. He had no idea what I looked like for a start as he had always been intent on something far above my head; and he had hardly addressed a word to me since the business of the refusal of Evensong. I said what I could—the terrible shock, the short time together, and so forth, and described the dreadfully sad atmosphere in church yesterday and the long prayers we'd had for both of them, alive and dead. The last bit was the real bit. Oh when, when, when will you get home? Darling Aunt Frances, when?

At Dicky Dick's I got another cup of tea and a long discussion on burials at sea and foreign germs. Then we moved to the new vicar and how the nuns were threatening a strike on laundering his albs. 'As to his cottas,' said Mrs Dick, 'they say they're shameless. They don't know what he does with them—and his surplices ripped and filthy round the hem like a Roman. It's the way he rives about in the pulpit. And that sneezing. Mr Pocock, God rest him, always behaved so stately.'

'Here's post for you, Miss Polly,' said Mr. Dick. 'from foreign. Just arrived.'

I seized and ran—and on the marsh peeled the large envelope from the front of my coat where I had slapped it against me—and gazed. It was. A letter from Aunt Frances. To me. Addressed to me. At last. I ripped it open.

It was heavy and stiff, not like the letters on the hall-table to Aunt Mary, which, still unread by me, had accompanied her to the Retreat. In fact it was not a letter at all, but a photograph taken on board ship and it showed Aunt Frances dressed as a pierrot in a stiff white ruff and a pointed hat with black pom-poms, a satin skirt and bodice cut tight. Surrounding her were other pierrots, male and female, some of them smoking ciga-rettes in long holders and holding wineglasses at angles. Everyone had a very shiny face. A large man in the middle who was wearing a monocle which accorded strangely with the pom-poms had the shiniest face of all. He was holding a bottle and had his arm round Aunt Frances's waist and on the back of the photograph in Aunt Frances's hand-writing were the words, 'High Jinks on Deck.'

It was after tea before I told Alice. She said as she came to take my tray, 'She's managed three scones and honey and she's walked to the window. My feelings are she could do them stairs now even by herself, if she had a mind. You're quiet?'

'Yes. I've had some news. I forgot to say.'

'*Forgot*? Now what's this then? Letters?' (I thought, Alice is changing.)

'Well, it wasn't a letter. From Miss Frances. It was a photo-graph. Taken on board the ship.'

'Oh Miss Polly,' she said, reverting to status. 'Oh, how lovely. Oh, she'll be glad she had that taken in time. Just the two of them together. Especially after no photos at the wed-ding. Even our Min had wedding photos. You'll have to take it round to all of them at Church.'

'I don't know that I will, actually. Mr Pocock's not in it.'

'Oh dear, I expect he was sickening. Oh!'

She looked at the photograph closely. For a long time, then turned it over and then back.

'Which one is Jinks do you think, Miss Polly?'

'I don't know. It's rather puzzling isn't it?'

'Miss Frances looks rather—over-done. I don't think I should show it to Mrs Woods.'

'No. Maybe I could show it to the new vicar?'

'Well, we could,' she said. 'They say he's a man of the world.'

'"We",' I thought. 'Yes, Alice is changing. They'd all have had a fit about "we".' And then I thought, 'Whatever should I do without her?'

'I had this from Aunt Frances,' I told the vicar the day of the post-Communion sherry and he choked violently in the button-back chair and went wheezing and hacking round the room beating his chest and ended up with his head against the marble chimney-piece. 'God in Heaven!' he cried and remembered himself before looking at the photograph again with a grave mouth, his eyes streaming.

'D'you think it's some sort of mistake, Father? I hardly recognise her.'

'She does seem rather—over-excited,' he said, getting out the handkerchief.

'Alice has a brother who was stoker on a liner. He told her that people do get rather excited on board ship. It's vibrations of the engines, though I don't see quite why.'

'Harra—yes,' he said. 'Did you see the postmark?'

'It was posted ages ago,' I said, and left it at that. He kept looking at me however, and at last I had to say, 'Aden.'

'Aden?'

'Yes.'

We looked away from each other then, because we both knew that last Sunday we had prayed for the repose of Father Pocock committed to the deep, and that the deep referred to had been the Mediterranean. An ocean which the Aunt Frances in the photograph had left far behind her.

To the best of my knowledge, that vicar who stayed such a

short time with us and whom I missed very much (there was a hay-fever and incense revolt) never told anyone about the photograph. I put it deep in a drawer where it stayed for many years, taking it out only once, a month later, when we heard that Aunt Frances had died of amoebic dysentery on the way to Chandrapore. I looked at it for a long time then and felt mystification as before, but a sort of elation, too, at the dizzy joy in her face.

The war began for us, then, with a rainy morning and mist wrapped about a stunned house of death and disease and metamorphosis; and also with the front doorbell giving a loud and tremendous jangling cry.

'Law, I can't answer it, look at me,' said Alice at the dirty fireplace and held out black hands. I said, 'I'll go, it's all right.'

'That you'll not. Whatever would they have said?' She tried to push bits of hair back under her cap and left a black mark on her forehead.

'I'm going,' said I. 'You go off and wash before you go up to the bedroom. I'll come and help soon. You're a show, Alice,' and I opened the door to Paul Treece.

He looked eager, rose-pink and dripping.

It was more than a year. The sight of him meant Thwaite and Roundstone, and there was a great surge of excitement in me. Simultaneously there was the surge of disappointment at the girlish slope of his shoulders, the ears, the overbrightness.

'Polly—Miss Flint! I came over at once. I had no idea you were so near. I'm at The New House. With the Zeits. I was staying for a visit. None of that now, of course. I'm joining my regiment this afternoon.'

'You're frightfully wet. Come in. I didn't know you were in the army. It drenches you, the mist. You're flooding the tiles.'

'I didn't stop for a coat. I thought I'd get right over to you at once.'

(Goodness! Goodness, goodness, Paul Treece!)

I said, 'I heard the Zeits were coming at last. But it's been so long. I don't go out much.'

'No. I heard. You're alone looking after a crowd of sick aunts. They're very sorry—the Zeits. I was to say so. Look, I've a letter here. You're to go over. I'll be gone though.'

'I can't go over, Paul. Come through to the kitchen and I'll get you a towel to dry your hair.'

He rubbed at his hair like a small child, going round and round his head in circles.

'I didn't know you were a soldier.'

'I jumped the gun. Made enquiries. I got my papers this very morning.'

'You said you couldn't bear guns.'

'That was long ago.'

'I saw this coming. Well, it has to be done.'

'Saw what coming?'

He took his face out of the towel—his ears vermilion, the hands in the towel bony and big—'But you know? You've heard?'

'No.'

'We're at war. It was all up yesterday—well, it was all up in June. The declaration was this morning.'

'I heard nothing. Did the bells ring?'

'No. There was nothing. It's just seeping around. They have a telephone at the Zeits.'

'We're—rather cut off out here.'

'Well, it's the war. There's no doubt about it. No choice if we're to keep with France. May as well get it over—it won't last long.'

'A *war*.' Trying the word over, it sounded mad. Such a random thing. A boy with a gun in Bohemia, one afternoon. The lunatic world.

'It comes from so far away. Such a foreign, hysterical sort of thing. It happens all the time in historical novels, the shooting of dukes, but the world doesn't join in.'

'It's not nothing to Austria. It's as if our Prince of Wales had been assassinated in Ireland.'

'Well, yes I see. That would be frightful. But it makes me think we should be on their side.'

'What a desert isle you live on.'

'Come through,' I said. 'We'll take the tea to the study. D'you think—d'you suppose we'll actually notice it? Up here?'

'All the men will disappear,' he said. 'They say a hundred thousand are going to France. Theo Zeit says there is a plan to make a new army—overnight. Everybody—the butcher, the baker. It will be mediaeval. Magnificent. Otherwise I dare say it won't change your life here very much—unless there's a bombardment from the sea. But that couldn't happen in the North-East I'd think. You'd be a huge target here of course—in this house—you're almost in the water.'

'Yes, almost.'

'You must mind these books,' he said. He was moving fussily around the room, touching the shelves. 'Take care of them. Maybe you should let the Zeits look after them at Roundstone.'

'What's happening to the Zeits?'

'Nothing yet. Theo isn't in any hurry for the army. He's very quiet. You know how he is. Rebecca's all agog. Talking of nursing already. But there's a snag or two. For all of them. Not very pleasant.'

'Oh?'

'Well—foreign blood and so on you know. They're Germans, after all. German Jews. Schieswig-Holstein or somewhere extraordinary—there are a good many in the North-East. They've been here for a generation. Everyone calls them German though. And since Theo's father died—'

'Oh did he? I didn't know. I never saw him. Mr Thwaite liked him so much. I'm sorry.'

'Grand old country gentleman. Typical English country gentleman, if you didn't know. He collected butterflies. She was the power house always. The genius Ironmaster was Theo's grandfather and Mrs Zeit took up the reins. Theo'll take over in time of course and be magnificent. He's a marvelous chap—you can feel it, can't you? He keeps his own counsel. You can never get very near him. But everyone likes him. He'll have a hard time. The Iron-Works are in poor shape aren't they?'

'There have always been people thrown out of work there, I think. It stays like that. We don' t really know much about the Works on the marsh.' (And all the time I was saying: Paul Treece, Paul Treece is here and Theo not two miles away.)

'Theo will change things. He may stay here now. There may just be some trouble about him getting into the army you know. He may be more useful here at home.'

(Theo upon my doorstep. Theo near me all the time!)

'Could I?' He took down a book and looked at it with love. He stroked it and smelled it. 'When I come back from the war,' he said, 'I shall sit still all my life in a room full of books.'

I liked him again. He was standing in profile too.

'I see you here,' he said, 'a hundred years behind your times, reading Jane Austen—what an edition!—through endless afternoons. Sitting up straight, as you do!'

'I don't like her much.' (He's noticed how I sit.)

'Good heavens, don't you? Of course, I'd forgotten. Defoe's the one isn't he? Is he still? People usually move off from *Robinson Crusoe* after childhood.'

'I shall never move off.'

'Perhaps you will always be a—' But he caught my look, I dare say. I'd noticed this before in people. I hoped it wasn't something I'd learned from Mrs Woods.

'Now why on earth is that, I wonder?' he said instead.

'"The granite rock of English fiction" and so forth, but not *high* in the imaginative stakes. Not *exactly* given to flights of poetry.'

'Neither's Jane Austen. And imagination—you're mad. Have you ever tried to imagine it? Twenty-eight years of life, minute by minute, solitary, out of touch, nothing but the Bible and some animals? Not a soul to open your mouth to with hope of a proper reply for nearly thirty years? And all those years in holy dread? And the creation of a whole landscape? Out of nothing? He wasn't much of a traveller, Defoe, you know. D'you think he'd really seen bears and the Indies and cannibals and the sea-coast of Sallee?'

'Goodness me. There are *qualities* of imagination you know. Jane Austen's was water-colour. Subtle. She had the poetry of the intricate mind.'

'Oh get on,' I said—and looked round to see if it was someone else speaking. For a moment I thought I'd said one of the words from Wales. 'Water-colour. *Etching,* more like. And I'm a bit lost with intricate minds to tell you the truth. I like large obvious minds. I suppose it's because I'm large and rather obvious but—I love people who are very rational. Who *do* things. I admire it. Not that *I* am rational—I have to work very hard at it. I'd much rather go soaring off somewhere in the imagination, but you can't face things that way. It's not brave. Robinson Crusoe was very brave. And strong and oh, so clever.'

'How long since you read it, Mistress Flint?'

'I read it most years. I read Defoe all the time, but *Crusoe* separate from the rest. He's a separate, real person Defoe, struck upon by accident. A sort of divine accident. I think that this is how most characters who are going to survive get born.'

'But he wasn't brave,' said Paul Treece. 'You said there was terror on the island. There was terror all the time. He was afraid of everything. Sleeping up trees, building fortresses with secret back-doors—and after years—years—when he'd not been troubled by any living creature, he gets the shakes over a dying goat. After he spotted the foot-print he had the shakes for two whole years. And he only started praying out of fright. He prays non-stop for twenty-eight years—*out of fright.* He never sits still. He's a bundle of nerves. He lives in fear, refined and pure. He's magnificent when the shooting starts, I agree. Smell of cordite, whites of eyes and so forth. But for a quarter of a century, waiting for the fun to start he's a dithering, boring coward.'

'Perhaps he did have some imagination then.'

'Oh well—I don't know. Instinctive cowardice I'd call it. How would you have liked to spend the years with him?'

'Very much.'

'You could hardly have loved him? You'd have been his good woman. He'd have been worse than the dreadful father of *La Famille Suisse,* which is saying something. Nobody really loved anybody—have you read Part II?'

'Yes.'

'Crusoe and women? He never needed a—gave a thought to a woman all those years. As for Friday—what about the way he treated Friday? Called himself a Christian and didn't even ask his name. Gave him a new one he'd thought up himself.'

'That's not un-Christian. Christians are always changing their name.'

'"Friday"—how ridiculous. "Good Friday" I suppose. Someone will be calling it all religious allegory soon I expect. Maybe it was—though I'd doubt it, in a journalist. The Crusoe-fixion. Ha!'

'Of course it's not. And Defoe wasn't just a journalist. I don't think Crusoe was very religious as a matter of fact. He was possessed by guilt and discontent and this tremendous inborn lust for travel. He was the last man on earth to endure imprisonment on an island, but he came to terms with it. He didn't go mad. He was *brave.* He was wonderful. He was like women have to be almost always, on an island. Stuck. Imprisoned. The only way to survive it is to say it's God's will.'

(I had had no idea that I thought all this!)

'I agree with you about the praying,' I hurtled on. 'It wasn't love of God, like we're meant to have. It was awe and fear and at last just habit. That's why I won't get Confirmed—it would be just habit. That's why I think marriage is so dull—after you're married it becomes just habit. But they're both a sort of crutch to help you along. You get in a mess without them. Habits.'

'Habit and journalistic device,' said Paul Treece. 'The Godly element in Crusoe was only put in to hang a few sermons on. People would read anything then if it had a sermon in it. Times change. I tell you—Defoe was a journalist. You've glorified this book into a gospel.'

I wasn't really listening. I was hot in the face and felt that I had to talk on and on or burst.

'Actually, with my aunts the habit didn't work.' I said, 'It wasn't strong enough. They missed out on marriage or they muddled it and the praying got—oh, too important. They both went mad a bit I think. It's more difficult you see. Women's bodies are so difficult and disgusting, though they're supposed to be so fragrant and beautiful and delicate. We have to try so much harder than men.'

'I've lost you, I'm afraid,' he said, looking dreadfully embarrassed suddenly. Before I'd mentioned women's bodies he'd been looking handsome and excited and happy—and as delighted to be talking about Defoe as I was. Now by talking about my body I'd stopped the only real conversation I'd ever had in my life.

'The painter at Thwaite understood,' I said.

He recovered and his ears dimmed.

'D'you know what Dickens said?' He put the *Sense and Sensibility* back on its shelf. 'Dickens said that *Robinson Crusoe* has never made anybody laugh or cry.'

'Why does everybody read it then? I go on reading it. I have done since I was eight. Everybody loves it. Crusoe's everybody's hero. I laugh and I cry. I expect Dickens was jealous. Most people don't remember when they first heard of Crusoe—that's the test. He just always was. He's very human and at the same time almost a god. He's my *utter* hero.'

'Oh, you get these books,' he said, 'books to possess you. You ought to rid yourself of him or he'll stick fast. He'll retard you. It's like love. Often the book that gets you is the first you've really read for yourself—or maybe you pick it up at an important moment in your life—at the time of some passionate event. Like ducks. Little ducks, you know—the first thing they see when they step out of the egg, they think is their mother. Even if it's a cow, they'll follow it about. I live on a farm, I've seen it. It is an imprint. "Love" is only an imprint, most of the time.'

'I'd love to live on a farm,' I said.

'That's part of the Crusoe complex. The good hearth. Distrust it.'

'How do you know so much about books?'

'I was born that sort.'

'Yes. So was I. I was lucky to come here.'

'I've had to suck up to people to get any books,' he said. 'I'm fairly shameless. A parasite and a go-getter. Otherwise no books. We're pretty poor at home.'

I thought, 'He is an honest man.' I was beginning to love him again.

'But I'm not a duck.' I said. 'I don't think *Robinson Crusoe* is my mother.'

'That's something.' He came up near to me and touched my hair and ran a finger round the edge of my face. He patted it in a motherly sort of way.

'But it's true about love,' he said. 'It's the girl who happens to be there at some important moment who becomes the obsession.'

'That's a bit unflattering.' I moved a step back.

'Like that morning,' he said, giving a little jerky jump forward. 'That extraordinary dawn. And the cows. And the rolls of mist on the river and the pink milk. They cast a spell.'

'Yes. There was something then.' But I thought of years berore, when the pony and trap came up out of nowhere on the sands as I had sat freezing on the seaweed.

He said, 'I'd better be off, I suppose,' and stepped back again. In the new talkativeness and sureness, I said, 'You're very cautious for such an emotional man. And a poet.'

The quiet book-room had grown quieter, the big windows blanker and whiter. The mist was beginning to shine and the sun would be through now soon. 'I always seem to be with you in mists,' I said.

'Yes. Well. I had better be off. I wondered if perhaps I might write?'

'Write? But don't you?'

'Write to you. You might write back if you have time. I dare say we'll need some letters wherever we're going. Of course, I don't want to compromise you in any way—'

'No. I suppose not.'

'I have asked a number of girls to write. I wouldn't want to—embarrass you. You're very young. I mean—it's early days.'

'Yes, I see.'

'Here's Mrs Zeit's letter.' He handed it over, looking above my head. 'I say, that's a lovely drawing of you.'

'It was done at Lady Celia's. Well—on the way home.'

'A surprise. I didn't know you were so pretty. What's the matter? Have I said something wrong?'

'About six things,' I said, 'but never mind. You'd better go.'

'I'm sorry. I'm not good at it. Talking with a girl alone. I do talk too much I know. They say I'm rather naïve. I write better.'

'Yes I see.'

'It's odd—you shut away out here. You're not at all naïve.'

'I thought I must be, quite.'

'No. I'm very direct,' he said. 'You like the direct. Defoe.'

He stood about. I thought, 'Oh Lord, go away. You're hopeless. Go. You're hopeless after all.'

He turned at the foot of the steps as if he'd never move again and stood still, examining his wet boots. Water was being almost visibly sucked up from the marsh to join the soaking air. I said, 'Wait,' and ran back to the passage where there was a cape hanging from when Grandfather Younghusband strode the landscape in it, and I gave it to The Poultice. His body became invisible inside it, a soft, poor tortoise in a noble shell. 'Oh *jolly* swish!' he said. 'I'll tell them to let you have it back. Don't like getting wet particularly. I'm not sure that I'm going to be all that keen on the outdoor aspect of this next business. Still—I expect I'll be all right when the shooting starts. Like himself.'

'Goodbye Paul. I will write.'

I watched the triangle of the immense cape vanish into the lifting mist, bobbing here, bobbing there through the long pools and the salt-hills. It moved in cheerful jumps and splashes. I could hear him after he had disappeared.

His letters were slow in coming, but when they eventually began to appear, continued thick and fast, first from O.T.C. camp, then from the local battalion he had joined as a private in order to get more quickly into action, and finally from France where he found himself a second lieutenant within the space of three months. The letters were very perfect—the handwriting neat and confident, sentences beautifully constructed, adjectives consciously correct. There were no endearments, only carefully-judged phrases of appreciation which had been looked over for a long time and sometimes, I felt, changed to give better cadences. Whole letters may have been re-drafted to achieve this—there was never a crossing out.

They were exercises. But little did I care, for I read them quickly, only interested because they were letters I had received from a man. I liked the look of them waiting on the hall-table. I often didn't open them for hours.

For during the next months, as the soldiers fell in thousands, off Belgium, I was at The New House every day, being welcomed with flamboyance by the Zeits. I turned pink and merry overnight and got Alice to put up my hair, which had become shiny and curly and taken on a life of its own. Rebecca approved me and Theo was there.

Theo was there all day. Every day. At every meal. He was quiet while the sister and mother talked and talked—so cleverly, so fast—but he seemed always to be looking at me and when I caught him looking at me he never looked away, but smiled. We walked in the gardens together and we sat together indoors and he saw me home across the marsh at night. In October he and Rebecca went up to Cambridge but I still went to the house to help Mrs Zeit with her war-work—she held something called 'The Depot' in her morning room, and rather-awed, respectable local ladies from the terraces rolled bandages there. Flowers came from Theo once to the yellow house, thanking me for helping his mother. He returned home before his term had ended and was closeted with her for hours.

Walking back to the yellow house with him one evening, looking at the belching Works he said, 'I don't want them. I don't see them as mine. Well, the war will decide things I suppose.'

'Shall you—do you think you'll enlist?'

'It's all confused at present. I'm not sure I shall be allowed to. We have a German name. We didn't change it like most people. They are embarrassed for us—and suspicious of us. It would look like fighting our own side we're told—though I don't feel it. We're waiting.'

'Yes. I see you can't feel very passionately patriotic.'

'No. Have you heard from the redoubtable Poultice?'

'Oh yes,' I said. 'Often.'

'Are you—d'you mind my asking—engaged to him?'

'Oh heavens, no!'

'I thought you might be. I'm sorry. You looked so very much together the day you came walking in to breakfast in the country.'

'Oh that was just accident. It's like that at Lady Celia's. The others there were all famous and old so we were rather thrown together.'

'Arty-crafty place isn't it? It'd suit the poor old Poultice.'

'I think he loved it.'

'Did it suit you?'

'Well some of it.'

'Bit of a delicate flower, isn't he, actually? If we're really honest. Something of a joke.'

I said nothing. He said, 'I've put my foot in it. Dear God, I'm sorry. And you must be so worried about him. He'll be back soon, you know. He'll get some leave.'

'He wanted me to go up to London for his embarkation leave but of course I couldn't.'

'Really? I'd think it would have been fun for you. Well, "it'll be over by Christmas", so we are told. Endlessly.'

We walked on the beach and went out in the trap and visited The Hall—but nobody was there. The shutters were up. There was a chain across the mausoleum door. The sun shone every day as if it were a festival year—a deep, beautiful autumn. Rebecca left Cambridge and briefly visited us, then departed with set jaw to London on political matters, she said. 'She's anti-suffragette,' said Theo, 'like so many bossy women.'

He taught me to play tennis on the new court and laughed at me for being so stately, not making it seem foolish. I spoke German with him and with Mrs Zeit—they said they would forget it all soon and could only speak it when the servants were not about. 'How beautifully you speak,' she said; 'a perfect accent,' and I said, 'That's Mrs Woods.'

But I had forgotten Mrs Woods. I had forgotten home altogether—the household, the housekeeping, Alice. I went home only to sleep and pray for the next day to come fast.

I woke up very early one day and wondered why. It was sunny and still. I felt that something had just stopped and went to my window and saw outside the yellow house Theo sitting in the pony-trap in the early light. He was not attempting to get out but simply sitting, staring ahead. He had a queer, patient, staid look about him and seemed to be staring at, but not seeing, the old convalescent home where soldiers were now marching on a newly-made parade-ground, up and down, up and down. The tinny bark and echo of the sergeant-major bounced towards the house occasionally. Surrounding Mr Pocock's old Chaplaincy by the nunnery, a city of tents had gone up, spreading out onto the marsh itself. The broken-ended esplanade had been extended.

Theo was sitting so remarkably still, even for him, that I dressed and rushed out to him without doing up my hair and he turned and looked down at me.

'Are you warm enough?'

'Yes. It's a lovely day.'

'Could you—jump in?'

'Yes, of course.'

The front door stood open behind me for the sand to fly freely in, and I had not looked even to see if Mrs Woods was all right, and I had not seen Alice, and I was not wearing a hat. He leaned down and helped me up beside him and we moved off inland, turning away from the lane-end that led to the Zeits, away from the sea. We meandered inland towards the church, but veered away from it again, and on past a farm and haystacks, then northward towards the Works. We sat watching them across the stubble—fields which were growing new flowers among the straw, for the summer would not cease. It was quiet except that I thought that I had never heard so many birds. He said, 'Polly, we've just heard from Rebecca that Paul Treece is dead. He was killed a week ago.'

The birds went on and on and the smoke from the chimneys stood in the blue sky. The horse shook its head vigorously and clattered a shoe. It moved to the hedge and began to pull up and crunch the grass beside it. After a time Theo put an arm round me and I put my head on his shoulder. He smelled of soap and man. I had not smelled man before. I began to cry, not because The Poultice was dead but because of my wickedness in being so excited by the smell of Theo Zeit.

He turned the trap with one hand and we drove back very slowly to The New House with my hair against his face. I believe that people passed us and saw, but I didn't move and nor did he. When we reached The New House drive I still did not move, but there was a flash of light from somewhere above us and I jumped and sat up; but he still held on to me.

'It's all right. It's the telescope. It's being dismantled. Government orders. They think we're German spies.'

'I once thought I saw an angel up there.'

'I saw you once from there. You were trying to fly like a bird.'

'I was twelve. It was years ago.'

'I thought you were lovely.'

I disentangled myself and sat up straight and tried to sort out my hair.

'Could you take me home?'

'Not yet. You're to come to us. Mother ordered it,' and she was standing on the steps in her funny over-decorated dress, all brooches and necklaces, her face lifted up like Hecuba with tears on it, her short, plump arms held out. I thought, 'She looks as if she's going to sing,' and nearly laughed.

'My dear, dear child!' Such hugs and kisses as I had never known, and had no notion what to do with. But I felt them less than I felt Theo standing near and watching me; and I cried again at my wickedness at having been made happy by a death.

I hadn't even thought about the death yet. I would get to that when I went home.

'Would you very much mind if I went home?'

'My child, very much, very much.'

I sat down to coffee and then breakfast with cheese and small sweet cakes, but I didn't like to eat them. Maids padded about outside the door, people spoke in whispers. Down the creamy cheeks of Mrs Zeit the tears flowed and she was unashamed. I thought, how foreign she is.

But Theo sat beside me.

'I must go and get tidy,' I said and Mrs Zeit took me to her bedroom and I sat at her dressing-table before a forest of photographs: powerful short men with short beards, women with chins and frilled crinolines and mountains of crinkly hair and firm, gigantic bosoms. Rebecca, a sparkling child, and Theo—no one but Theo—a baby with watchful loving black eyes. He wore a satin suit and sat firmly on a satin chaise-longue.

'You are to stay here with us for a little while, Polly, my dear. A day or two.'

'No, I must go back. There's Mrs Woods.'

'Polly, soon we are to talk about Mrs Woods, you and I together. It is time that something was decided about Mrs Woods.'

'She's got no one.'

'Which is no reason that you should sacrifice your young life.'

'Please, I don't want to talk now.'

'Of course not. Of course not. But we shall be talking soon. I have decided. We are to talk about your future. About the university. Yes. I have decided. It is to be Oxford I think. Please do not look at me so. It is to be Oxford for you.'

I said that I wanted to walk home and Theo came with me

as far as the terrace. I felt his gentle eyes watching my back all the way down to the faraway gate. I tried not to think of this—to think only of Paul Treece—dead Paul Treece, the ears, the sloping shoulders, the hands that had touched the books, had touched my hair, all rotten, limp, bundled into a hole in France. I managed for a minute or so.

At the gate I turned back to wave to Theo but found that I had been wrong, for he was not there.

I helped Alice when I got home. We changed Mrs Woods, talked about meals, domestic things. 'D'you want a rest?' said Alice. 'You look right lowered.'

'There's somebody killed,' I said. 'It was the young man who called the day of the Declaration of War.'

'I remember him,' she said. 'He was artless-looking. Well. He'll not be alone out there. Mr Box of Boagey's has gone and many another more. There'll be many and many a hundred yet. It said in the papers "The Greatest European War in History". It's hard to believe, isn't it—being a part of History?'

I went each day to the Zeits' for four weeks then and for four days after that, and the late autumn was still golden and hot and berries shone on the trees and hedges. The house was busy with comings and goings. We were allocated the billeting of Belgian refugees, though I never saw any. Great consultations went on usually behind closed doors and I sat at Mrs Zeit's desk, writing the letters, checking endless rather obscure lists while she went about the rooms, talkative and busy—often talking apparently to herself. She set up another desk for herself near a giant telephone and Theo, amused, delighted with her, often caught my eye including me in his affection. She was in total command. Sometimes, however, the discussions behind the locked doors left uneasiness in the air when the doors were opened.

'We still don't know what they're going to do with us,' he said.

'What could they do with you?'

'Stick us in prison. Intern us.'

'Oh Theo, how ridiculous. You're English. You're as English as I am.'

'Yes. I'm sure it won't come to it. It's all very haphazard. Shall we go down and look at the sea—as near as we can get? We're rich, you see. There's jealousy. In Newcastle they're interning all Germans who aren't naturalised, whoever they are. Newcastle's where we started from in England—the family. When we left Europe. It's hard to believe we don't belong.'

We walked by the sea and we walked in the fields and as late as early November we sat out after dinner on the terrace. When it grew colder they found me an old fur coat. It was silky. 'They're sables,' he said; 'you are a princess.' He kissed me sometimes. I found that I was very good at kissing after a time, as good—rather better—than he.

A letter came from Paul Treece with a poem in it called "At the Gate of the Past." It arrived a week after he was dead, posted the day before he died. The poem floated along on the top of my mind and I did not allow it to go deeper. I carried it everywhere with me, and although I was never so indecent as to let it be seen, I knew that my motive for having it always in my pocket was not a pure one, and in the end, I did casually mention it to Theo. 'You were in love with him,' he said, so solemnly that my heart lifted.

'No,' I said, 'no I wasn't, not in love.' But I said it with an inflection on the 'I'.

'You and he were very close though. Books and so on. Weren't you? I felt it. I suppose you'd known him a very long time.'

'Oh—a year or so.' (Not, 'I had met him twice.')

'You've known me longer. You've known me for five years and I've known about you for longer than that—since the day you were being a bird, behind all the old birds.'

'Not *known*,' I said.

'I'm afraid I don't read much. Only the Sciences. Well—just the books everyone has to.'

'You'd read *Robinson Crusoe*. You said so on the beach.'

'Well everyone knows about the footprint. That's not a novel though, is it, *Robinson Crusoe*—isn't it biography? He was real, wasn't he?'

I was sleeping at the Zeits now, only going home occasionally. There was to be a Christmas party at The New House—just a few close friends of the children, Mrs Zeit said—and I had written to Maitland—we wrote every month or so. She wrote funny formal dry little letters back and always said that I was to say if ever I needed anything. For the party she had sent me a dress—with Lady Celia's blessing, so that I was supposedly forgiven for the defection at breakfast last year. The dress was of pure silk muslin, golden-brown, with needlework bands and a high neck stitched with blue silk thread. I was thinner than when she had measured me at Thwaite and Alice had been altering it. I went home for this dress only and Alice was as pleased as I was with it. So we arranged for Boagey's to bring a car for me on the night of the party and at The New House we worked at preparing the party all the day before until we were tired. In the evening Theo said, 'Come out. Put on the sables, Mistress Flint, and we'll look at the stars.'

It was as a frosty night at last, but I was warm, and we walked about the marsh and on the sand-hills. We lay down in the sand-hills and under the sables he undid my dress. I said, 'We'll be seen. There are soldiers. I don't think we should be here anyway. Even if we are just walking.' But we did not go. We stayed there for hours.

'We'll go home,' he said. 'You're staying tonight. We have the whole night ahead of us.'

And so I went to bed at the Zeits and waited for him. I wore my silk nightdress, Maitland's last Christmas present, and I brushed my hair two hundred times as Aunt Frances had taught me. The big clocks downstairs struck eleven and then twelve and at last, oh at last, some time after that, the handle of my bedroom-door began to turn.

Mrs Zeit came in to the room and sat on the end of my bed.

'How we shall miss you, Polly. Oh we shall miss you so. As a daughter and as a sister. The whole family will miss you. We'll be gone in three days you know—only three days left before London. Now, we want you to know. We *all* want to help you. We're not going to let you waste your life here.' She picked up the sables which were lying across a chair and put them comfortably over her arm.

I said, thank you.

'Somehow or other we are going to get you to Oxford. Now what do you think about that? Go to sleep. Go home in the morning and don't think of coming in again. You've worked so hard for the children's little party. Just have a good rest at home until it's over. And if we just *don't* see you again before we leave, you must not think we have forgotten you. We shall never lose touch, dear Polly. Good night my child.'

She left the room, stroking the furs, and I lay awake until the pale, cold morning came and, still dark, the maids began to stir about the house.

Theo was very affectionate when we said goodbye, and kissed my cheek and Mrs Zeit kissed me, too, as the chauffeur held open the Daimler door. Mother and son stood side by side upon the steps, she with the kindest of faces, he to attention, looking over our heads, not exactly smiling but not quite achieving the blankness he was aiming at. But perfectly in control.

'We can't have you walking home,' said Mrs Zeit, 'after all you've done. *Such* hard work. And the car can go on afterwards to the station and pick up the guests.'

At first, in the car, I allowed only the most immediate things room. How to tell Alice about the dress. Whether I should tell her that I'd made a frightful mistake. That it had never been intended that I should be at the party. But I saw the disappointment and hurt for me in her red, rough face, and then the fury rising up and knew I couldn't bear it.

As the car slid past the church and the ghosts of my saints, I prayed, I think for Alice first: 'Dear God, set this to rights. Oh, amidst the chaos of nations and the deaths in France and the great disasters in the turning world, and although I am still un-Confirmed into the Church of England I pray through Jesus Christ our Lord that this miserable hurt in my worthless grain of a life may somehow or other be resolved and used at last.'

'Why, the poor old sowl!' said Mrs Treece, 'And after years. Just gone in a minute! Well, it happens. Gone in her sleep. But just as you stepped in from visiting? You'd feel badly, not being with her at the end.'

'Well, yes I did. You see she was the last of the people I've known since I was a child. I felt so guilty. You see, she and I had never been friends. She'd resented me when my aunts took me in. She'd always adored one of my aunts you see, and when I came, that aunt began to adore me instead, and—'

'Nose out of joint,' said old Mrs Treece. 'Well, she's to be prayed for. Strokes is terrible things. I remember my father lying.'

She was so small that her feet scarcely touched the floor and the rocking chair she sat in stayed upright and steady. She wore black of course, for Paul—black ankle-strap shoes like a child's, over woollen stockings, and even the upright, soldierly collar round her child-size neck was trimmed with black lace as was the long apron over her woollen dress. Out of it all her face shone clear and rosy and her hair shone silverish. She was peeling big potatoes over a newspaper and washing them in a bowl beside her before dropping them into the pan on the fire.

Outside the farm kitchen it was snowing fast and the snow had gathered in the same corner of each of the nine little panes of the window over the stone slab sink where we washed the dishes. The fire was bright with precious small-coal for the cooking and I sat on the fender in my friendly brown-velvet dress, my back warm against the copper where the water heated in a deep dark font. A chicken was roasting in the fire-side oven, for it was Christmas Day. My invitation to stay at the Treeces' farm had been waiting for me at home the morning of my banishment, when I had walked in upon Mrs Woods's death.

'And her funeral a sad tale, likely?'

'Oh yes, it was. There were so few there. Some nuns—she was very keen on nuns, though she never really got to know any of them separately. She hadn't the touch for friends at all, poor Mrs Woods. She was awfully clever. She spoke three languages and she'd been all over the world. But she'd got into the habit of being grim.'

All my life I have felt that I would find it very easy to talk to people if I could just once get started and here, at last, on a farm in the North-West fells, with Paul Treece's mother I was achieving it—though only, perhaps, I thought, because she keeps to her own unselfconscious track. And maybe it was her grief that had made her so totally uncritical, so accepting. It might well not last.

At present however I felt that I had lived with her for years.

'The poor old *sowl!*' she said again. 'No friend to mourn her? Paul has his mourners, and in high places.'

'Yes he has.'

'Paul knew some of the greatest in the land, even before he went to college. His room's full of letters from people very well born. Writing, clever people.'

'Yes, I'm sure.'

'Which is how I found you out, Polly, among all the letters

from universities and lords and ladies. I went and sat up there and I read everything that there was in that room, on and on. On that first day his father and Laurie left me. They fettled for themselves. Maybe three days, all by themselves. There was bread and ham and a bit of cheese and some potatoes. What I did, when the telegram came, I took cloths to cover the pictures and the mirrors and I opened the windows all over the house. Bitter weather, bitter. I went up and sat in his room. It's always been the coldest in this old place, Paul's room, but he never ailed a thing, never. Mind he wasn't here these last years, scarcely, and I did think he was looking terrible thin just before he went to France.

'I liked it being cold up there in that room as I read. The room was full of him. Electric. You know how he was? Electric. Oh—so tidy! I never seen a pencil not set straight. His books all graded along the bed-shelf and on the ledge and on his floor on newspapers and little slips of paper for dividers and on his table all his exercise books right back from school and through college. Oh he was a wonderful scholar, his writing that neat and clever-looking. Well, we never could think where he could have come from, Paul. No more could his teachers. Latin was nothing to him. French he could write as fast as English, all the little marks this way and that way, neat as print. I'se seen him up there writing Latin as young as twelve, freezing with his ears turned rainbow. I knitted him a cap once, but I don't recollect him wearing it. I would take him up his supper when his father wasn't by. His father'd say, If he can't come to table he does without. He wouldn't let him have a lamp, neither, with the price of lamp-oil. I've known him have a lamp under the clothes up there when he was still at school—for his homework. It's a wonder he wasn't cinders. Yet he was always lucky, Paul, till now. He seemed charmed. Lately his father was proud of him and he could do what he liked. Didn't even expect him to help with the farm work—

well he weren't much advantage when he did, dreaming about. Paul was a mystery to his father, and to many another, but he's properly mourned—not like your poor person.'

I had walked from the Zeits' Daimler, praying and thinking of dresses, and up to Mrs Woods's bedroom, to find Alice turning from the bed.

'When, when?'

'Now. It must have been just now. I was up with her at breakfast. She had some breakfast. She's dead.'

'She *can't* be—' I wouldn't look. I had never seen anyone dead. 'How do you know?'

'Look.'

'I can't.'

'You can and should. Stay here. I'll go for the doctor. Take her prayer-book. Read some prayers will you?'

'I can't.'

'Very well then, go downstairs. Get yourself a hot drink. I'll be back when I can.' She was out of the room.

I paced about the house then and Mrs Woods was everywhere. She stood on the stairs, she sat in the chair by the ferns, she peered round the study door with her knitting, her walking-stick tapped across the coloured tiles; she gave commands at the kitchen door. When I looked out of the windows there she was, huddled over her hot-water-bottle, scurrying over the marsh to church. In the dining-room she sat glaring at a child with her nose level with the forks. Outside my bedroom she whispered on the landing and out in the yard she was looking down from between the net curtains of the staircase window, holding one of them back on a finger. In the end my feet took me to the one place she was not, her bedroom, where a nothing lay under the cotton counterpane—a nothing with a young face, quite gentle and pretty, and the room calm.

'Now just go through to the dairy,' said Paul Treece's mother, 'and on the stone you'll see pork sausages. We'll fry them for the chicken on the fire. The bread sauce is at the bottom of the oven and there'll be room. The plum pudding's well away. There's room for another pan. It's a fine pow-sowdy. I'se not my usual self this year. Most-times I'se brisker. Maybe it's soon to be bothering with Christmas, but Paul wouldn't have wanted us overcome.'

'Why did you choose to write to me out of all the other people? Didn't you tell the other people?'

'No. Some seems to have known. There've been some messages. None of his letters—they sent them back to me from France with his things—even his fountain and his photographs and his brushes—none of his letters from other folks was so homely as yours. Being from famous people I suppose they couldn't be. Very dignified they mostly was, as if to someone lower, but time would have changed that. When I comes to your letters, thinks I, here's a quaint-spoken, old-fashioned girl and fond of Paul.'

'Yes, I was.'

'And like to have married him.'

'Well,—'

'I thought, "I dare say out of all the grand ones she'd have been the lucky one. All she had to do, this one, thinks I, was play her cards right and she could have had him." He'd tell't me of you.'

'Oh—did he?'

'He'd tell't me of others—ladies and sirs and Bells and Wolves, this and that. Says I, "Paul, they're all foreigners to me. However you keep up with them I'll never know. Moneywise alone it can't be easy, with only the scholarship." I didn't ever like the way he was stopping with first one and then another, not giving back a penny. That's another thing I couldn't think where it came from. It's not like our family. I kept it from his

father. I went by myself to his college for the graduation, long
since. His father might have drawn attention to hisself—not liking south-country folk, them not ever doing any work.'

'Did you meet his friends at Cambridge, Mrs Treece?'

'Not so many. They were stand-offish I dare say. I looked
for thee, Polly Flint, or one like thee. One that loved Paul.'

'Oh, I didn't—'

'Say no more. I can tell. When I read the letters I said,
"She's the one I want about me now."'

She had forgotten the potatoes and let her hand holding the
little worn triangle of knife drop to her lap among the peelings.
She looked at the fire. I said, 'Let me finish,' and took the
things from her. 'Sit still. I'll see to it'—I, who was hopeless
and hadn't cooked a potato in my life.

Then the door opened and Paul's father and brother came
in from feeding calves, carrying buckets, and stamped snow off
themselves, clattered and called about, paying us no attention.
They kicked the dogs into a corner and Paul's father stuck his
wet cap up between a sagging black beam and the ceiling to
dry. Paul's brother slapped the dirty bucket under the sink
ready for us to wash up after our dinner. Their boots left pools
about the patches of linoleum which were so sparse on the cold
slabs that the floor seemed to be occasionally painted with dim
flowers and leaves and squirls and bare in patches, like the
traces of an antique pavement.

We sat to dinner quietly. There was a rough black settle covered in a pattern of red birds. There was not much of a cloth
on the table, shreddy linen, but very clean. We drank from
mugs not glasses. The knives and forks were poor and crooked
but shining. The pudding was served with a queer plain sauce
like starch. 'It's a good pudding,' said Paul's brother, shovelling
it in. 'It's a grand pudding.' 'It's carrot and potato,' said his
mother. 'There's plenty currants in it,' said the brother, looking
defensive, watching me for disgust.

After dinner the farmer took off his boots and heaved himself on to a high wooden meal-chest at the back of the kitchen and fell asleep. His feet, pointing at the ceiling, were in socks as thick as chain-mail. Mrs Treece and I washed the dishes and then the animal-buckets at the sink and the brother Laurie sat at the fire, grinding branches into it from the stick-corner until the sparks flew. At length he leaned back and slept too.

What had Paul done on Christmas afternoons? I thought of him reading Yeats in the cold bedroom, writing careful letters to the famous, poetry of his own.

'Do you go to church ever at Christmas, Mrs Treece?'

'No. We never bother. Only harvest festivals.'

'We're very religious where I live.'

'Well, some it suits. The parson's been over about Paul. Not that he knew what to say for all the practice he's had. Eleven in Paul's carriage from this parish sets off for France, and nine of them dead in a week. What could he say, if ever? What it's for's beyond me. I make no pretence of understanding. I'll go up now to change my dress.'

I sat opposite the sleeping brother. He was short and thick-set with huge hands, hanging loose between his open thighs, his head flung back and sideways, his hair soft and young. His coarse trousers were rolled up and his stockings like his father's had big darns in them which were beautiful. He lay heavy and still, uncaring and unaware of me or any stranger. A year younger than Paul, this boy and he must have been babies together playing on this rag-rug, learning to speak with the same country accent, before Paul unlearned it again, going together to the same village school. Paul had never mentioned Laurie.

Laurie's eyelashes were like Paul's. His ears were usual. He had a nicer mouth—a sleepy, hungry mouth with the lower lip fuller than the top one. Looking at the mouth I began to think about Laurie.

'What ist?' he said, waking up. 'It's goin' on dark. It's bare three o'clock. Canst thou mek tea?'

'Yes. I'll make tea. Shouldn't we wait for your mother?'

'She'll bide. She'll be sleeping maybe. She's slept little. It's in yon caddy.'

He pointed up to a red tin with the King and Queen looking out from it in patchy gold on the chimney-piece. It was so high that I had to stretch even standing on the fender, and he watched me and did not help. I found the teapot and warmed it and threw the slops out of the kitchen door as I'd seen his mother do and some of them blew in at me again. Then I poured the water from the huge kettle on the chain over the fire—it needed two hands—and then set the teapot on top of the copper-lid to stand. Laurie said, 'That's a good lass. Thas't not a bad lass.'

'Thank you.'

'You and Paul was sweet-hearting, then?'

'Well—'

'He'd never had one. Tell truth, I never thowt he would. He was missing in that direction.'

'Did you—were you quite close?'

'Aye, under the year.'

'I meant close. Close friends?'

'I could never make him out. Aye, we was friends. Did you have a ring from him?'

'Oh no. Nothing like that.'

'You knew he was from farming people?'

'Oh yes. I told him I'd love to live on a farm.'

'You did, did you? What made you think that?'

'I don't know. I'm telling the truth though.'

'Have you changed your tune now?'

'No.'

'D'you know we works twelve hours a day all week and never a holiday? My mam walks eight miles to a shop to save a penny on the bus—and she's scrubbed this floor for twenty years, not being money for a hired girl—and her a boarding-school girl herself when she was young. Well born. She's an old woman now at forty-nine. We never get an egg—they go to be sold. Most of last year it was potatoes, potatoes. You're rich, aren't you?'

'No. I haven't any money except a little bit I was left and a house.'

'A house is rich—and that dress is rich. This house in't our own. We's tenants. We could be thrown out tomorrow. Paul would have come rich, mind, you could see.'

'Why did he go to the army so soon, Laurie? He didn't have to.'

'Christ knows.'

'You won't?'

'Not required and won't be. I'll be reserved occupation. Catch me, anyway.'

'I suppose Paul went for his country.'

'My country needs me in it.'

He leaned forward soon and took my hand and watched me, and his hand began to tighten. Then the old man stirred on the kist-top and Mrs Treece came in without her apron, pleased to see the pot of tea.

'Could you not stay longer?' she said at the New Year. 'We's got used to you. You've brought comfort.'

'Aye, you've done that,' said the farmer, surprising everyone, 'you've brought some comfort.' The simple words seemed to surprise the speaker too. For the first time in the brave house I felt near tears.

'Why not stop on?' Laurie was watching me carry down my bag and the big parcels of Paul's papers and books which his parents had quite fiercely said were mine. He watched me wrap myself up in gloves and scarves and lift up my things into the cart behind him. 'I can't. There's too much to do at home. Alice is all alone.'

'You'll come again mind?'

'Thank you very much.' (I knew I never could.)

'I'll drive you then.'

We squatted side by side in the front of the cart drawn by the brown cart-horse. I kept Paul's box of papers between us, and watched over the bundles of books tied together with hairy twine. The floor of the cart was caked with old dried mud and between the cracks in it I watched the rough road go by between the long hedges up the hill. The high wheels went wobbling round—they had once been painted red and yellow and must have looked like a carnival, when Paul was a baby. A daily fairground. I saw the baby watching the coloured wheels turn and the red shoots of the hedges all about them.

Laurie let me get down from the car alone and then passed me all the things and some butter and eggs wrapped in oily paper. He watched me go with the old station-master helping me up the station yard and I waved goodbye and stood in the waiting room stamping my feet and looking out at the miles of snowy fell.

The sun shone. The station stove made a clinking and dropping of coals and there was a louder clinking and xylophonic dropping of water outside, for all along the pretty carved edges of the station buildings the icicles were melting. Then I could hear the train coming.

As I gathered my things together again, Laurie suddenly appeared and took my bag from me with a funny sideways, sly-look, not speaking and I thought, Good gracious, after all he's shy.

I opened the carriage window and he looked up at me and said 'If you was to sell that house you could come here and live. Think on. Think on now. I'll say nothing further.'

'Thank you very much.'

'I'd not have thowt to fetch up with a woman of Paul's, mind. Seems we wasn't so different after all.'

'Thank you very much.'

'What say then? Think on?'

I said nothing and he began to hop and run by the train. He had anxious, over-bright eyes. I saw Paul in him now so clearly for a moment that my own eyes filled properly with tears and this time the tears fell. For I knew that Laurie and the Treeces were not for me.

'It's grand here in spring and summer,' he called. 'You'd like that. The lambs and that. And harvest time. It's a grand country. I'd not leave it.'

He'd think later I was a strange girl, crying, never answering him, though he'd not think of me for very long.

The most famous heart-stopping incident in *Robinson Crusoe* is, of course, the foot-print, yet it was never to me the most terrifying. A glorious idea, with no known parallel in fiction, as simple and splendid as the idea of the book itself, at once an astounding and completely credible sight.

Yet I was always slightly disappointed by it—that it was just a print, not Friday's print as everybody has come to think. Just the print of some quite anonymous foot, probably crunched up on a later occasion around the cannibal fires.

Secondly it had always seemed disappointing that years had to pass by before any living foot followed the promise of the print of one—even though the casual lapse of time is consistent with Defoe's unhurried pace, his grandly confident unrolling of the years.

But much more frightening seems to me to be another occasion: when Crusoe, after his first foray in his home-made canoe, gets shipwrecked again on an unknown part of his island and hears his own voice calling out his name.

'Robin, Robin, Robin Crusoe, poor Robin Crusoe! Where are you, Robin Crusoe? Where are you? Where have you been?'

(His parrot.)

'However, even though I knew it was my parrot, and that indeed it could be nobody else, it was a good while before I could compose myself. First I imagined how the creature had got thither, and then how he should just keep about the place, and nowhere else. But . . . I got it over and . . . he . . . continued talking to me, "Poor Robin Crusoe! and how did I come here? and where had I been?" just as if he had been overjoyed to see me again: and so I carried him along with me.'

Would Alice have kept about the place, I wondered, coming home from my own foray to the farm, away from my island? There was really no reason for it. Whyever should she stay now in the great yellow house out on the marsh, all alone with me? There was other work to be got with the war. Soon she would be able to make twice—four times—the money. And she was only about my own age. There was no purpose in her staying to wait on me there, as there was no purpose in my own life there, either, come to that. Or anywhere.

What I was to do with my life now I hadn't the least idea.

And if my life at the yellow house was odd—and dull and lonely except for my books—how much worse it must be for Alice. She had never given much sign of liking any of us particularly and I knew that I had never been a real friend to her, not seeming to know quite how to begin. Yet she had toiled and slaved and nursed and cooked for us and seen to my clothes and cared about my new mysterious life at the Zeits. My last week there had made her eyes sparkle when I told her of all the glamours. I had still of course not told her that these glamours were done and I shamefully rejected, treated as a dismissed servant, as we would never, never, have treated her.

I had begun to be a little afraid of Alice, I realised, as I walked home over the marsh with as many of my belongings as I could carry from Paul Treece's farm. I wasn't sure exactly how I should feel if I found a dead house and a letter of farewell from her lying on the hall-table.

Perhaps a freedom?

But the chimneys of the yellow house smoked, and as I walked in with my butter and eggs and bundles of poems, there she stood, saying, 'Well, you're back. Praise be. I wondered if you'd stop. I'd half a fancy they'd seduce you away— and then where'd we be?

'There's been a great bombardment here,' she said. 'Hartlepool—and dozens dead.'

She was wearing a most unlikely hat, like a long felt blue-bell stuck with a painted fish-bone pin, and she had a hand on her hip and was smoking a cigarette. 'Butter and eggs,' I said, looking away. 'Such nice people, Alice. Did you have a happy Christmas? It's good to be back,' and I knew as I spoke just why I was frightened of her.

'Yes I see. *That's* a good thing then,' she said, examining the parcel.

It was my own voice using my own words.

She was in charge—and had probably been in charge, though I had not known it, for ages. Gone long ago were the wisps, the grubby sharp face and the big skivvy aprons. How long since I'd seen them? Alice was her own woman and had been so at least since the day of Mrs Woods's death when she had turned from the bed and ordered me what to do.

But when I got used to the change I liked it.

And I clung now quite desperately to my island. I went nicely about, day after day, industrious in the yellow house, behaving like the soul of serenity. The house needed a lot of looking after. Even in the midst of war, at that time it was not so strange for a woman to give her life to a house.

Also, I invented work. I had kept the schoolroom habit of sitting at a desk surrounded by books each day for years and now, with Paul Treece's things about me too and his manu-scripts, I began to write myself, starting, of course, with *Robinson Crusoe*, which I decided to translate into German.

It was a totally pointless exercise but demanding in its way and I took pleasure in the pile of glossy exercise books I bought and in my clear handwriting covering the pages. I wrote page-numbers in red ink and underlined in green. Then as time passed I discovered the satisfaction of footnotes. These I also wrote in red with an inked black line between text and note. There was a vast amount of double underlining.

I translated for four hours each morning, the translation was fast, but its transference to the page I tried to make so beautiful that it was very slow, and soon I was as abstracted as a monk at a Book of Hours or a child with his first crayons.

After lunch I often worked at The Poultice MSS which I copied out and arranged in order. Nearly all was poetry—pastoral, direct. There was some love-poetry—alarmingly passionate. Strawberries and nipples. It made me thoughtful. Rather shocked. There was a series of poems about some simple but very confident girl who lived inside her head and drove men mad. It seems that she was very desirable but as far as I could make out, half asleep. He had said that he knew a lot of girls.

Some of the poems were strong and witty and there was a lovely fortitude in them which reminded me of *Robinson Crusoe* and I began to see that under the mud of France there was dust that might have become of great account.

Then, in the evenings, I read. There had been some critical works in Paul Treece's library and they interested me, being the first modern ones I had seen. While it seemed to be an extremely arrogant way of getting into print I think that they may have been the start in me of a greater organisation of my ideas. This was a sort of physic.

I made notes about everything. Whenever my mind and

heart began to stir I made notes more feverishly, meticulously still and uselessly for the demon at my back was not Paul. It was of course still Theo.

But no letter had come from him. No message had come from any Zeit. No card, no word, no whisper, no local gossip. His face, at first I blotted out with hurt and shock, helped by seeing another kind of suffering—the raw suffering—at the farm. Now however it kept returning, surprising me at aimless moments—on closing a book, or looking up quickly at the tap of the acorn on a blind-cord in the wind. Often I heard the Zeit pony and trap at the door and looked out at an empty road.

Since the winter night, lying there with him, I had not been able to walk on the sand-hills and would take a huge half circle round them to the town, and the soldiers guarding the camp, and the sick in the old convalescent home watched me. I heard one soldier say once, 'Is she a bit peculiar that woman in that house?' and in Boagey's Son and Nephew a loud lady said to old Mr Box, 'Whatever happened to that young Miss Flint? She was wanting a bit, wasn't she? Slow?'

But I was still there. No recluse. Not seeking solitude to weep in. It was only the sand-hills I couldn't face.

Sometimes I tried to talk to the people I met on the marsh. The convalescents were no longer the Warrenby poor our soup had failed to cure, but the wounded shipped from France and the North-East ports and distributed about. They lay out in the convalescent home, such as could, under grit-brown blankets in crowded rows. Some sat in the sandy blowy grounds staring. Others wandered the marsh, wooden and apart. It was they who turned from me when I came near.

The New House stood empty. Because I had never been quite alone there with Theo it was possible still for me to bear to walk in its gardens. Through the long windows of the drawing-room spindly gold chairs were stacked in heaps, abandoned presumably after the Christmas party. I could see the magnificent piano (which no Zeit had ever played) covered with a thick dust-sheet tied in at the feet and the chandeliers of 'the best rooms' as Mrs Zeit had called them, hanging in huge bags heavy as swarms of bees.

There was a lackadaisical care-taker. He had been the church's sexton, ancient and sly, and I had never liked him. He used to dig the graves with an awful relish and slowly deck their walls with leaves of privet and sea-lavender held in with big black hair-pins. He would watch you at ankle level as you passed. Alice once said with rare venom, 'I'd like to kick the face in of yon.' 'Bitter,' he used to say even on pleasant days. 'Bitter weather again, Miss Flint. I hear Mrs Woods is failing?'

At this time I seemed unable ever to get quite free of images of mortality and met the sexton everywhere, at last coming face to face with him in The New House drive where the imported orange gravel was now all hazed with green weeds.

He said, watching me, 'They're putting them sand-hills out of bounds. There's young girls out there shameless with the soldiers. Going at it like tortoises. I've thrown water over cats for less.'

I didn't go back to The New House after that, but often wondered about tortoises and exactly how they went at it. When my own memory of the sand-hills came to me there was no longer the lurch of pure joy as he unfastened my dress. Only tortoises.

'Are tortoises funny?' I asked Alice. "You know—unnatural?'

'I don't know as I've seen many outside Boagey's Pet and Corn shop.'

'You know—sexually peculiar?'

She gave me a queer look.

In the spring of 1916 when the slaughter of the Somme was such that each army sometimes ran out to retrieve the other's dead, Alice and I were busy with the sexuality of tortoises. We cleaned the library, getting down the books from every shelf for the first time in memory—possibly ever—and behind a row of works of the Reverend Thomas Fuller, up against the ceiling, we found a small copy of a novel by Cleland and I took it to the window and examined it. I stayed there for a very long time.

'Aren't you coming to your tea, Miss Polly?'

'Just a minute.'

'Your supper's ready. Whatever've you found?'

'Read it,' I said, 'take it to your bed.'

The next morning we did not look at one another in the eye. Washing away at the shelves from the top of the steps, she said, 'That *Fanny Hill*! Life's full of surprises. I'll say that.'

'Did you—know all that, Alice?'

'Aye—some of it.' She was still servant enough not to ask whether I did.

'I didn't,' I said. 'I didn't know any of it. Well I knew some things. It sounds a lot better than I'd thought. D'you think people really go on like that?'

'I'd think so. Mind, it was in History. They seemed to have enjoyed themselves more then. All the long skirts and that. Romantic. Well, exciting-like!'

'They didn't seem exactly to get in the way.'

We began to giggle and laugh. 'Where's the book now?' I said. 'I want to read it again.'

'I'm ashamed of you, Miss Polly.' Alice had turned a brick-ish colour. 'You can't have it till I've read it again.' So we sat together in the kitchen that evening, reading bits silently then staring at each other, then dissolving with joy.

'However did it get up there? D'you think it was the Archdeacon?'

'Archdeacon nothing,' said Alice. 'Didn't you see? It says Gertrude Younghusband, large as life on the fly-leaf. Shameless!'

'Maybe she wrote her name in it before she'd read it?'

'Well, she didn't burn it up or throw it away.'

'*Alice!* Gertrude Younghusband was my *grandmother*—the Archdeacon's wife!' We both went and looked long and hard at the matron in whalebone with the imperial nose on the Archdeacon's writing-desk.

Alice began to have a great many more evenings off after this. I, less extreme, only started to teach myself to cook. *Fanny Hill* had cheered us and though it should have made us restless in some way in fact it made us rather calmer, and more assured, so that for the next two years until almost the end of the war we seemed to swim in rather more hopeful waters.

For the next two years.

'For the next two years', like Crusoe, 'I cannot say that any extraordinary things happened to me; but I lived on in the same course, in the same posture and places, just as before.'

Then one day in 1918, Alice ran into the kitchen where I was beating something in a bowl and bread was rising rubbery white in ten tins.

'There's someone here.'

'Who?'

'I don't know who.' But she looked very wild. 'It could be Mr Zeit.'

'*Could* be?'

'I don't say is. Here—give us that skillet.'

I walked through to the front of the house with my sleeves still rolled up and my apron on and my hands floury. In the hall was nobody, nor in the dining room, nor in the library, nor upstairs in the drawing room. I stood in the hall before the glass again and rolled my sleeves down, wiped my hands upon the apron and took it off. Outside on the scrag end of marsh that was all that remained stood an army-green motor with driver. A man sat in the back, very old and empty-looking about the eyes, but they were still Theo's.

'Can you drive with me somewhere?'

It was cold. I went in for a coat. Then I sat by him in the car and saw how his hands shook like the hands of the men at the convalescent home and that he clasped them together and still they shook. When he spoke it was with long pauses between words and sometimes the words got stuck and he spluttered and gulped. I asked, 'How long were you in France?'

'Since you saw me.'

'Is your leave long?'

'It's been long. I'm about ready to go back.'

'Are you?'

'Well there's a Board next week.'

'Aren't we going to The New House? We've gone by.'

'No. It's full of soldiers now. It was commandeered.'

'Yes. I heard. Where are you all? Where are we going then, Theo?'

'Mother's up in Newcastle. She was interned you know. For nearly two years. But she's running the North again now.'

'Yes, I see. I hadn't heard.'

'Rebecca's in France, nursing. So is Delphi Vipont from The Hall—and fairly hopeless at it I gather. I thought we'd go to The Hall now. Bec wants me to collect some things for Delphi.'

The Hall was so much of a ruin that even the army had not wanted it. Parts of its roof had gone in, its shutters hung crooked or were gone, its drive was so choked that Theo ordered the driver to go and leave us at the gates which were overgrown, immovable, and we climbed through between one of the stone posts and the great broken hinges. We walked through the courtyard and in through the front door, stuck open under its swaying fanlight. The long stretch of rooms, one opening out of another, stood empty. Rats had eaten holes in their floors, a volcano of soot sat in each beautiful grate, the milky marble above dulled and daubed with bird-droppings. 'It's all to be pulled down soon,' said Theo. 'There'll be nothing here. She's too late for her keepsakes.'

We walked about. Old newspapers were stuck to the black and white of the eighteenth-century saloon, the staircase was splintered. He tried to help me up the stairs but I had to help him too, he seemed so uncertain.

His hands were so cold. In the bedroom we opened a shutter and found a four-poster bed all by itself on the bare floor still with a dark old counterpane and hung with crimson silk, each fold of the silk with a velvet edge of dust. A prie-dieu stood beside it and it all had a daunting ecclesiastical look.

'It must have been Lady Vipont's. She was very holy.'

Theo said, 'Delphi must have started in that bed.'

His hands were shaking again and he sat on the window-seat. Across the window wistaria hung so thick and gnarled that the window had to be pushed hard against it to open at all. Rain fell on the green leaves, pattering, though the sun still shone through them. Large glassy drops hung on the long grey flowers. 'I've thought of you every day,' said Theo, 'but it was thinking of someone else's woman in another century.'

'You sent no message. It's been nearly four years.'

'No.'

'Have you written no letters? Not to anyone?'

'Only to the parents of my men. When they die. Saying that they died bravely. I only write lies.'

'I've heard nothing. Nothing. Not from any of you. You all vanished. You might all have been dead. You threw me away.'

He said, 'I am dead. We are all dead, Polly. This country died.'

We lay down on Lady Vipont's bed in each other's arms until it grew dark and we said almost nothing. In the great cold house I became warm and I felt my warmth warm Theo and he held me fast. We did not make love, yet we lay as one person for hours. We lay till dark.

Before we left he said at the top of the stairs, 'I'll just look for something, in case—' and went off, feeling and looking about in a room or two. 'There's a bit of old junk in the back of a cupboard. She wanted something from the mausoleum really.' We passed the mausoleum all boarded up and tied round with barbed wire. 'D'you remember in there?' he said, 'All pearl and pink. D'you remember that day? The hymn-books? Beccy running? You like a round flower?'

At home he said, 'Go in quickly. Go. I'll write this time. I promise, when I can write letters again the first will be to you. I'll see you next leave. The war can't be long now.'

Then he said, 'I do love you, you know.' But the words seemed to be very difficult to understand. We both stood considering them as if we were hearing an old primitive language.

When the car had gone I stood outside the yellow house until Alice came out and said 'Miss? *Was* that Mr Zeit? I can't think it was Mr Zeit,' and I didn't know what to reply.

He did write and at first quite often. The letters began to arrive three weeks later and continued for about a year. I answered every one and sent two or three extra in between.

In my letters I told him everything in the whole world so far as I understood it: about Wales, about the marsh and about the sad years when everybody prayed or died or vanished. I told him about my wish that I might be a good Christian but my certainty that I was not ready to Confirmed, about my sinful disgust at Mrs Woods and God's answer to my prayer with her death; about my fear and awe of Alice—how I knew that she had hated looking at and touching Mrs Woods and feeding her with a cup and putting little bits or food in her awful mouth as much as I did. The lifting her. The washing of her. Yet never once had she flinched or mentioned it.

I told how I still missed Aunt Frances and of the mystery of her silence to me after she had gone away; and how I had felt at home so seldom—only in the old sexy memories of

Wales, the housekeeper's kitchen at Thwaite and walking on that one morning with Paul Treece. I told him how sick I felt and worried because I had not liked Paul Treece's looks, had not wanted to touch him. I told him about Virginia Woolf and the poets and famous people at Thwaite, and the memory of my father; dancing and singing the sea song; of Mr Pocock, and the table-top swimming with polish in the dining-room, so that I had looked out over a shadowed lake, with the brooding presences around its edges, like in Wordsworth's *Prelude.*

I told him how my life was now divided before my lying with him on Lady Vipont's bed, and afterwards; and I wrote how much I loved him in such a tremendous and passionate way that I often stood looking at the post-box after the letter went flop inside it, thinking, 'Could I have written that? Could any woman ever have written so much to any man before?' I saw his face which never told a thing, reading it and I thought, if he is killed, will all the letters go back to Mrs Zeit? Yet, I continued to tell everything, everything, as I am doing in this book, and as women are not supposed to do.

Then, thinking of what women are not supposed to do, I would go quickly away and write another letter saying yet more. About wanting him and needing to sleep with him, though I did not say sleep. Wanting, wanting, I said—and in just what ways, day and night, indoors and out, wherever he sent for me. I drew deeply on my knowledge of the novel which my grandmother had prized. I wrote unlike a granddaughter of a Victorian Archdeacon, unlike even the women in D. H. Lawrence whom Alice had taken to lately. (Well, Lawrence's women hardly say anything.)

Had Moll Flanders, Cleopatra, Emily Brontë loved Theo Zeit they could not have told him so with more passion and with less restraint. And they were I dare say the wiser women.

Theo's dry, short letters grew more and more difficult to

read—the writing smaller and smaller, almost tormentedly careful. Then they stopped.

They stopped not after any especially naked one of mine. I thought, 'He is killed.' Then after two months, 'Had he been killed I would have heard by now.' I re-read his last letter slowly, slowly. There was no clue. I re-read all the letters then and I found that they had been nothing. I was left with nothing and I had then a great terror that I had been mad. The bed in The Hall had been fantasy. '*Was* that Mr Zeit?' Alice had said, 'Surely it can't have been?' I had dreamed it. I did not fully remember what happened. I did not remember how he got home. I had dreamed.

A hole in the air.

I read and re-read the letters, on and on. At the end of each one he had always said 'love'. I clung to this wonderful fact: that he had always said love.

And I began to feel sorry for him—that he had been burdened with letters like mine. All the things I had said were the things that he so prudently would have felt were best unsaid. I had based my great trust that we felt and thought and saw alike on the fact that when I was twelve years old he had said that he would leave me a footprint, and that when he went away the last time he had said that he loved me.

Such a correct and truthful man. Such a nice man. Everyone said so. Would he tell lies? Oh, of course he would not.

So I thought on my island.

There was one night—I had been translating Crusoe for hours, colouring in the chapter-headings, underlining with very exquisite care, letting the fire die, the lamp go down, my feet grow cold. All sound in the house and outside it had ceased. Only the clocks.

I said, 'It is time. It is time, Polly Flint. It's time this stopped. He is nothing. You are sick. No woman need suffer like this. It is wicked and mad. Forget him.' And telling myself this with great authority, some of the burden did fall away, as did Robinson Crusoe's on awaking from his fever to a spell of God's peace.

The next morning, since I had gone to bed at almost dawn, Alice brought me up my post and there was a letter from Rebecca Zeit to say that she was coming to The New House to arrange for the sale of it, or of what the soldiers had left of it, and might she come and see me.

Her writing was huge and black and spluttery and she arrived a day or two later, exactly as she wrote. I heard her voice right up in the drawing-room calling out to the taxi out-side to come back in an hour. 'In *one hour,'* the voice called like a bell, 'now *exactly,* Mr Boagey, not more, not less. Yes.' The door-bell jangled loudly and I heard her laughter as the wind took all the mats in the hall and wafted them about. Alice showed her up and she swooped forward in a great flurry, still talking, though whether to Alice or me or to herself wasn't clear.

She had turned into a still rather alarming but rather merry woman in tight-fitting clothes, with fur at the neck and cuffs, very fashionable: an ugly, long-draped jacket, short skirt, and her hair short as a man's but still curly crammed under a beau-tiful helmet hat. She talked and she talked, seeming unable to keep still. Bright green eyes searching about.

'You're *exactly* the same! Exactly. Oh, Polly, I don't believe it! You've been here all this time. *Nothing* has changed!'

'I couldn't leave.'

'The old woman—the aunt-person. Did she die?'

'In the end.'

'But couldn't someone—? Wasn't there anybody? She wasn't even a *relation.'*

'No. But—'

'Yes, of course. I remember—you were terribly Christian at the yellow house. But you're not all alone here, Polly?'

'Well, we've had some officers billetted—'

'You must have *noticed* the war?'

'They bombarded Hartlepool. At the very beginning. But I was staying away on a farm.'

We had tea.

'And no romances? With the officers?'

'I hardly saw them. Alice looked after them. I'm not very romantic.'

'Yes, I remember. Factual downright Pol. *Robinson Crusoe.* You were always the plain woman.' She realised what she'd said and tried to set it right, 'I mean the straight woman—salt of the earth. Dependable. You'd have been wonderful in France you know. But perhaps you're lucky.'

'It is over without me. It is over and we've won.'

'It's over,' said Beccy, 'that's all.'

'What will you do, Beccy?'

'I'm stuck nursing in a private nursing home—but I'll stop now. Get back to Cambridge and finish.'

'Yes, I see. Is Mrs Zeit—?'

'Oh, Mamma has survived. But it won't be long now—'

'She's ill?'

'No, no—Mamma's never *ill*. No, the war. We've made a decision. We're going back to Germany—all of us. It's mother's idea. We all agree though. It won't be easy here—everything of ours in England's sold up—it was mismanaged, neglected. Mamma was interned you know. Theo in the Army. She's suddenly feeling very continental—very German-Jewish. She wants to work for post-war Germany.'

'But can you? Live there after it all? After all you've seen of Germans?'

'Yes. What makes you think they're so different? Somebody must start somewhere showing that all countries are the same. Just people. If we bleed Germany dry now there'll be another war in a generation. You'll see.'

'Do you tell people this?'

'No, no. I must say we don't. It would not be the moment.'

'Why d'you tell me, Beccy?'

'Well, you're not just anybody are you? It's funny, I've always felt you were a sort of part of our family. Yet when it comes down to dates and times I suppose it's almost nothing. That day on the sands—you know—I felt we'd known you always.'

'Yes I know. It was the same for me.'

'And I think you were even closer to Theo. You and Theo—I think you knew him better than I did.'

'Knew?' I was standing and held on to the back of the chair. 'How is Theo?'

'Oh Theo's perfectly all right. He was wounded pretty early on you know. Bit of shellshock, but he never quite broke up. Had a good long sick-leave. Very brave, our old Theo—could have got right out of it if he'd tried. Of course, you never quite know what Theo wants. He's survived—playing it fairly carefully. D'you remember that queer Treece person? He lasted no time at all. It wasn't just that Theo was careful, though. He's lucky. He's the sort who'll never get cancer or TB or be run-over or have accidents. D'you know, Mamma and I never really worried for him. Isn't that weird? He's amazingly his old sweet silent self as a matter of fact—oh, look here, ducky. Here's the taxi, I must go. It's been lovely to see you, Polly. Mamma often talks of you. I think she feels the least bit guilty you know. She had such schemes for you—to push you into a university. D'you remember? She still makes these wild decisions.'

She was firmly pulling on gloves.

'There wouldn't have been the money for it, Beccy.'

'Oh, she'd have seen to that. And she'd have seen that you had the right qualifications—she'd have got you coached. She had a pull with Somerville. Modern Languages—that's what it was to be, wasn't it?'

'I've no idea. And I couldn't have gone. As things were.'

'Mamma would have seen to the old woman. It was the war. It swamped her. All of us. She had a worse time than me in the internment camp you see—ostracism and so on. Two years. And it was so *ridiculous*. She can't bear to be ridiculous. But I do know she feels guilty about you—just a teeny bit mis'.'

'There's no need. I would not have been helped.'

'Oh, Theo's getting married. Maybe you knew? Delphi Vipont of course. Never been quite my sort—or Mamma's and we've told him for years she's not his. Besotted with her. As ever. Well—it's been a life-long thing. D'you know she never wrote to him *once* when he was in France. She was pretty wild. The Viponts lost everything in the war, you know—so he's a haven for her now.'

We were at the taxi. She looked me quickly up and down and gave me the sharp, assessing bird-look I remembered. She said, 'It's been lovely. Look—we'll see each other again, Polly, won't we?'

It is considered usual that anyone in great solitude of mind for many years will run mad. Alexander Selkirk, after only four years upon his island ran mad as a hare, as did most of the other historical characters who may or may not have been Daniel Defoe's inspiration for *Robinson Crusoe*. Indeed, it is a sign of a human being's sanity, perhaps, that he should run mad in such circumstances, and perhaps Crusoe himself was insane when he arrived on the island, for his twenty-eight years in residence show only the growth of a most extraordinary and unnatural steadiness.

This growing, rather frightening sanity proceeded from a very affectionate analysis of himself, his ability to stand apart, to watch and to muse upon his shaggy and unlovely figure walking the great beaches, perched upon the ferocious cliff-tops, treading the forest and saying: 'Well, I don't know. Look at me. I have God and myself to talk to. How much better to have God and oneself to hand than almost any other of one's acquaintance. "That man can never want conversation who is company for himself, and he that cannot converse profitably with himself is not fit for any conversation at all."'

Oh, the stability of this great Yorkshireman! After the two years—*two years*—of digging the trench for the sea to introduce itself to his great beached boat he finds that the sea will never reach it. He stands sagely and calmly by and says: 'How great is the human condition. A man may learn from his mistakes.'

Occasionally the passions flower. Occasionally they even threaten to take charge. Yet they never do take charge—not wholly. For as they manifest themselves they are monitored, dissected, pondered—and dispersed.

There are some secret, moving springs in the affections which, when they are set going by some object in view, or even not in view . . . that motion carries out the soul in such violent, eager embracings of the object that the absence of it is insupportable.

When that happens, the hands of Robinson Crusoe clench, and Robinson Crusoe watched them clench, so hard into the palm that anything in them (he reflects) would be crushed.

Crusoe feels Crusoe's teeth involuntarily clamp together so that he can hardly part them again. 'Doubtless,' says Crusoe, 'these are the effects of ardent wishes and of strong ideas formed in the mind.'

'How very interesting,' says Robin Crusoe, and tick-tock, in time, Crusoe's body, Crusoe observes, begins to behave itself again.

Monumental, godlike Crusoe. Monumentally and deisti-cally taking control of his emotions. And I, Polly Flint, after the knowledge of my loss, set out to be the same. Theo's face and being and presence at her shoulder, Polly Flint blots out, and lets the noble and unfailing face and being and presence of Crusoe become her devotion and her joy.

Crusoe is her idol and her king.

Crusoe's mastery of circumstances.

Crusoe, Polly Flint's father and her mother.

Crusoe, the unchanging, the faithful.

Crusoe, first met at the cracking of Polly Flint's egg.

Crusoe, the imprint.

Crusoe, her King Charles's head.

Will Polly Flint ever attain Crusoe's magnificent simplicity?

Will Polly Flint ever attain his wonderful exploration of emotion as a means to morality and truth?

Will Polly Flint ever attain his wonderful endeavour to bring things to a divine balance? 'Bringing the years to an end as a tale that is told?'

All these became, after the vanishing of Theo, Polly Flint's whole cry.

Sitting in the yellow house with nothing in the world to do. Polly Flint. Twenty years old. Might there be time?

I became very odd. Oh, really quite odd then.

The officers who had begun to be billetted at the yellow house in 1917, I had, as I told Rebecca, left entirely to Alice, who had had charge of the money we were paid for their keep. Only when they were gone did I realise that without them we should be on the way to starvation.

'There's nothing for it now but lodgers,' said Alice.

'Would we ever get them? Right out here?'

'Yes. If we advertise the ozone. We'd get fifteen shillings a week full board. Each.'

'Perhaps we should try just one.'

'We should try more. We should try three.'

'Could you manage, Alice? You know I couldn't spare time from my book?'

'I could manage if we go shares.'

'Shares? Of course. Oh Alice, don't I pay you enough?'

'Twelve shilling a week is all you can afford to give me. But we've possibility here of a decent living, Miss Polly.'

'Lodgers. It does seem extreme.'

'It's the only hope for us. We'll start getting Miss Frances's room up, then the spare room and then I'll make a clearance of Mrs Woods's.'

'Haven't we done that yet?'

'I never quite cared.'

'Yes, I see. Could I—?'

'No. I'll see to it. We'll sell everything since nobody's emerged to take interest in it and there's no will.'

'Precious little,' she said a week or so later. 'Rags, tatters, bibles. Her cross could go to the nuns and her clothes I've taken as charity down to Fishermen's Square though they didn't look overjoyed at the sight. You can't seem to get rid of bibles. It seems a sin to burn them—'

'Oh, burn them. It's only superstition.'

'The knick-knackery I did sell—a picture or two and a sewing-box. I got two pounds so I bought some whisky. It's wise to have a bit of whisky in a house. For emergencies.'

She put bottles down on my desk. 'These,' she said, 'were fastened into her prayer-book with a band,' and she propped against the bottles twelve fat letters unopened and addressed to me. They were Aunt Frances's adventures after her wedding which Mrs Woods, in her dark queerness, had kept between herself and God—long loving letters which had been seen by no one and each one saying how she was looking forward to my going to India.

'I always thought she'd flitted down into the hall and round about sometimes at the beginning and nobody knew it. Right down to the hall-stand. It's why she had the second stroke I wouldn't wonder,' said Alice, 'And never to open them as well as never to say! That's horrible cruel and unforgiving. That's very bad.'

Perhaps it was unfortunate that the happiness the letters gave me would always be associated with the simultaneous arrival of the medicinal whisky. Or perhaps this was just part of the pattern, too.

'Her room's real bonny now,' said Alice, 'and there's a Miss Gowe come to see it, or rather her sister did. Miss Gowe's arriving tonight.' (It was a month later.) 'She works in the post office. To *live* here,' she added. 'You understand?'

'We'll have a drink to celebrate,' I said.

'Another three are arriving next week,' said Alice, pouring. 'My dad says a bottle holds seven drinks. That looks rather a lot. We'll say nine about. My, it's strong!'

'It's splendid. Who are the three?'

'Two commercial gents and a schoolmaster from The New House School. Insignificant little feller so I've put him above you.'

'But that's your room—Charlotte's old room.'

'I've moved down into Miss Younghusband's.'

'Yes I see. Well, thank you for doing so much, Alice.'.

'We'll be rich by next year. Rich enough to see to the window-sashes on the sea side anyway. And in time to the roof.'

'Is the roof bad?'

'You should see the ceiling in Charlotte's bedroom. I'm only taking six shillings from the schoolmaster.'

And Alice from this moment turned into the White Queen, flying here, flying there about the house from dawn until long after dark with bundles of washing (laundry extra) and bed-clothes and trays of food. They were easy lodgers—or Alice saw to it that they were—the commercial travellers turning out

to be pale washes of men, something to do with office equipment in the Stockton and Darlington railway where they spent
long days. Miss Gowe was a fat, grinning creature, all cardi-
gans and said to be in charge of postal telegrams at
Middlesborough, though it seemed rather unlikely, her powers
of communication being scarcely developed.

The schoolmaster was called Selwyn Benson, a near transparent silver-fish of a man, but Alice said that all the masters at the
new school—bought from the Zeits—were either flotsam from
the trenches or too frail to have gone into them in the first place.
Mr Benson was in the first category presumably, for he shook and
flipped past us in terror, up the stairs and down, and froze if we
spoke. At night I sometimes heard him crying in Charlotte's old
bed and Alice said that when she took up his breakfast tray he
often hid behind his wardrobe door, poor little lad.

There were odd folk everywhere after 1918, for many years.

'You'd not think we'd won this bloody war,' said Alice, 'My
dad says after Mafeking you knew who was the heroes.'

'*What* did you say?'

'Bloody,' said Alice. 'Sorry, Miss. It's all over the buildings.
I can't help it. The marsh is all buildings now. It's to be an
amusement park and that next—and a public rose-garden. It's
to make employment. There's to be a hurdy-gurdy and penny-
on-the-mat. We'll hear it all right even out here. Between us
and the town. Well—it's the only good thing mebbe the
Germans has done to give employment.'

'Daniel Defoe,' I said, 'that's to say Robinson Crusoe, spoke
well of the Spanish even though the War with Spain was
scarcely over.'

'I don't want to hear, Miss. You know my views in that
direction. It's time you finished with that romance. You can't
get another squeeze out of it, I'd think. Can I go now? There's
shopping and the orders. And we need another bottle.'

Often I watched from the study window as Alice set off to the town on these housekeeping expeditions in the following months, prancing on her high heels with her imitation fox-fur around her neck and a fondant pink toque upon her head and wondered where Alice, the tired young mouse, had gone—but blessed both of them.

As time went on I saw that a young man from over the marsh often stepped out from the esplanade shelter to meet her. He held a respectful trilby and after placing it carefully back upon his head, took her arm. There was something familiar about him, but it was a long way off, and I was now most furiously busy with no time at all to brood about love.

For the difficult and miserable outer world had by now receded, and almost disappeared. 'Thus in two years time I had a thick grove; and in five or six years time I had a wood before my dwelling, growing so monstrous thick and strong, that it was indeed perfectly impassable.'

Only my monthly letter from Maitland at Thwaite pierced a ray or two of ordinary daylight through my trees, and a spotlight broke through with the occasional letter from Mr Thwaite and a short radiance on his annual visit to us.

Lady Celia was gone. She had died in the war, and was buried in the family vault in the church at the end of Thwaite's old gardens. Maitland minded. Her letters were sad, and sadder because Barker and Mr Thwaite himself did not seem to mourn her as they should. 'And as for them artists and warblers, for years taking her salt, not a sign from them, though Mrs Woolf and poor little Mr Gertler wrote at the time, Mr Gertler enclosing a very nice drawing of her, showing her good points. "My lady had her place", I wrote back to Mr Gertler, "in a tawdry world."'

I answered all Maitland's letters always at once, even on my bad days, wondering whether I had been right in thinking Lady Celia frightful—vain, cold and full of machinations. She had stopped her brother's marriage to my beloved Aunt Frances who otherwise would not have gone so conspicuously mad on board the ship to India. No—Lady Celia had certainly, I thought, been filled with sin.

But perhaps it was in analysing Maitland's letters and Lady Celia's character that I began at last to come to terms with the idea of sin, though I was, of course, taking a very good general instruction in the subject still, in the great book, *Robinson Crusoe.*

For *Robinson Crusoe* is a study of the reality of sin. All his misfortunes spring from it. It is sin which occasioned his first disaster in the Yarmouth Roads to his last shipwreck on the imprisoning island. He sinned from childhood against his father, leaving the good, quiet middle station of life in which it had pleased God to place him. He had sinned in his yearning for the sea which was always his enemy.

Indeed, all his unhappiness was caused one way and another by the sea, it seemed to me, his persistent need for it. Considering this, at the end of each day I took to pacing our own beach and watching the movement of the waters around my boots as they wandered in the red-rusted barbed wire.

'Young man,' had said the captain of Crusoe's first ship, 'you ought never to go to sea any more. You ought to take this as a plain and visible token that you are not to be a seafaring man.'

And because Crusoe acted against God's decree, venturing on a mission contrary to his duty, like Balaam, like Jonah, like Job, like Ishmael of *Moby Dick,* like St Augustine, he foundered. Until his repentance at last.

But why was it a sin for Robinson Crusoe to yearn for freedom, adventure and traveller's joy? Why was it wrong for him to reject his boring Yorkshire home, the middle-class sensible day-to-day life of Hull? Obey his instinctive longing for the sea?

Because God had said so.

Like Job, when he accepted this, things became better for him, In fact, marvellous. At the end of Book I even more so. And at the end of Book II, Crusoe has achieved nobility.

Oh, I envied him. Oh, I envied Robinson Crusoe not his suffering and his repentance, but his having the powers to put up a fight, and his powers of analysis, his seamanship, for knowing exactly where he was. And his being tempted, proved that he was, at least in God's eye, God thought he was worth testing.

Yet here was I, totally unregarded by God, sitting out my life at the yellow house.

Oh, I envied.

I envied Crusoe his sin, his courage, his ruthlessness in leaving all he had been brought up to respect; his resilience, his wonderful survival after disaster.

I envied him his conversion, his penitence, his beautiful self-assurance won through solitude and despair.

I envied him his unselfconsciousness, his powers of decision, his self-reliance—he never dreamed after any specific creature—I envied him his sensible sexlessness which he seemed so easily to have achieved. But most of all I envied his being in God's eye.

I envied.

Seated at my desk, day after day, with only the click of the lodgers' feet on the tiles, the occasional opening and shutting of a door as Alice went hurrying by; the bottle and the glass in front of me and the shadows of people I had known just over my shoulder out of sight, in the corners of the room, watching me, not greatly concerned for me, I envied him.

'Miss Gowe's sister's here and wants a word with you.'
'Tell her I'm busy.'
'I have. She says she's staying till you come.'
'What's she want?'
'She's up in arms for her sister.'

'What's that to do with me? Alice—can't you—?'

'No. I can't. Miss Polly, come.'

The sister sat with Miss Gowe in Mrs Woods's old room. Miss Gowe nodding nicely, smiling and waving nervously at a chair.

The sister glared. She had a glossy mouth and fine arched eye-brows painted with a pointed brush and her crossed legs showed a yard of cream silk-stocking. Miss Gowe, in her dowdy woollies, had become a part of my home, but the powdery silky sister made sure that I was aware that I was in Aunt Frances's old shawl and somebody else's bedroom slippers and my fingers all ink and that was getting fat.

'This house is not suitable for my sister,' said the sister. 'It is isolated, eccentric and the food inadequate.'

'Yes, I see. Does she want to go?'

'She will have to go,' said the sister.

'Yes, all right.'

'Unless,' she said quickly, 'there is a reduction of terms.'

'Yes, all right.'

Alice had come in behind me and gave me a prod in the back. 'How much?' she asked.

'My sister is paying you fourteen shillings a week,' said the sister. 'Are you not, Winnie?'

Miss Gowe gave a shy little snigger.

'Fourteen shillings a week. I suggest ten shillings and six-pence.'

'Yes, all right.'

'Twelve shillings,' said Alice loudly.

They settled for twelve shillings. The sister swept away down the stairs and turned to us at the front door. 'I have to say this!' Alice held the door wide for her. 'There is a certain stigma attached to my sister, living in your house.'

'Stigma?'

'Stigma. I hear what I hear. Perhaps I should tell you that

the Gowes are Scarborough people. I, myself, now live at
Harrogate. In Valley Drive.'

'Yes, I see.'

'Alice,' I asked, 'bring yourself a glass. Why are we inferior
to Valley Drive? And why must we keep Miss Gowe?'

'We need the twelve shillings if the roof's to hold up. And
as to Valley Drive—Miss Polly, look at you. Look in the glass.'

I looked at my whisky.

'No, Miss Polly, in the glass.'

But of course I did not. Metaphorically I covered every
glass like Paul Treece's mother when the telegram came so that
the spirit should not confront itself.

I returned to the manuscript—I was busy now, since finish-
ing the French and German translations of *Robinson Crusoe* a
year before, in 1930, on an analysis of the book as Spiritual
Biography, seeing it in relation to other spiritual biographies of
the seventeenth and eighteenth centuries, busy with the red
ink, busy with the green, and Mr Thwaite brought me beautiful notebooks to write in every year.

Mr Thwaite's placing of the brown-paper-parcel of notebooks on the hall table was the first act of his annual visit to
us every August 1st. It is quite difficult to describe the pleasure of these visits of Mr Thwaite because of any man in the
world he must have been the quietest and some might say the
most colourless. Yet he had authority of a subtle kind—never
once asking if he might come, simply arriving each year at
four o'clock on whichever day of the week August 1st might
be, and remaining for three weeks. He never rang the bell but
was all at once in our midst in knickerbockers and Norfolk
jacket looking mildly at us from his light blue eyes, Box-
Boagey's taxis (Mr Box himself and an assistant) waiting
patiently behind him on the step with two portmanteaux and

a cabin-trunk with brass bands around it. Mr Thwaite loved clothes so long as they were very old. He always changed for dinner and brought a smoking jacket and a great supply of garments for his walks by the sea and his excursions mackerel-fishing or casting for whiting from the pier. He had, after great deliberation, of late years bought outfits suitable for the new boating-lake, though he had not yet embarked on the costume for the penny-on-the-mat at the amusement park. For a motorbus outing to Hinderwell-for-Runswick Bay or Filey he wore deer-stalker or sou-wester depending on the weather. When Alice said, 'It's not the old landau, Mr Thwaite. The motorbus has a roof to it,' he said that he never felt roofed in a motor.

He was the most peaceful of presences. You never heard him move about the house, yet when you opened a door you could always tell if he were in the room by the pleasantness that breathed out of it. At meal-times he ate with small bites and great enjoyment, looking long at Aunt Mary's lovely spoons, sometimes holding them up to the light, looking out of the window and after clearing his throat a few times, remarking on the weather and the direction of the wind. He needed no conversation and made little. And never once did he criticise a thing about us—the decaying house, the funny lodgers, the plain, plain food, my whisky bottle which now accompanied me to table. Seldom did he praise us, yet we knew that his visits were a precious part of his life.

'And how is the book coming along, Polly?'

'Oh coming along. There's a great deal of work.'

'Oh, I expect there is.'

Never asked for details, never suggested it might surely soon be finished, never queried its vital importance. I suspected that he might know that in the end no book might materialise at all, that I was clothing myself in armour, hiding in a lair, hiding from pain. He never hinted it though.

'Tremendous work in a book,' he would say. 'We had a great deal of that sort of thing at Thwaite.'

I went out every single day when he was with us, arm in arm with him along the beach, the sea casting down lace shawls before us, then dragging them away. The wind was always cold—even in August it was usually from the North-East—and I would be wrapped up in anything that came my way from the back-kitchen hooks—waddly boots on feet, my hair dragged up in a bun with the filling falling out, sometimes a hat from ages long ago stuck on my head.

Yet I always felt carefree and pretty, walking with Mr Thwaite. On fine days I removed the boots and paddled and he watched me. Once he said, clearing his throat, 'Polly you are but a child.'

'I'm over thirty. Nearly forty. I'm just behaving myself unseemly as the nuns used to do.'

'Nuns,' he said. 'Ah. I remember those nuns. Poor Frances. They were after her once I believe.'

'Oh I'm sure they weren't. It was Aunt Mary. They just about got her.'

'No, no. It was her own decision, that holy nursing.'

'Well, they've gone now. All of them. The nuns have moved right up into the slums in the Iron-Works now.'

'Mysterious women,' he said. 'But all women are mysterious.'

'I'm not mysterious.'

'No, no. You're not mysterious, Polly. You're a very straightforward sort of girl.'

'Yes. I can't think why they all go on at me.'

'Do they?'

'Alice says I'm wasting my life.'

'Oh, I'd not say that. You have to get your book done. You have to keep the yellow house—the family home. That must be a great strain. Very glad you know—assist—At any time.'

'Oh we can manage. Thank you *very* much though. When the book's done, of course, I shall have to think—'

He said nothing. Sniffed the breeze, watched the ships along the horizon waiting for the tide, the chimneys belching flames across the sand-hills. 'Very beautiful place this,' he said. 'Part of my youth. You are of course—you know—always welcome to live at Thwaite.'

'Thank you.' (Old age, emptiness, even Mr Barker now dead.)

'Thought maybe of travelling? Cruising?'

'Travelling!'

'Just an idea. India, I've often thought. West Indies. Should be glad to take you. Good for Maitland, too. Since she's been widowed and Celia gone she's finding things a little slow.'

'I can't think. I'm so busy. Shall we go home?'

That night the manuscript of the spiritual biography blossomed more wonderfully than ever with coloured inks and various scripts. When Mr Thwaite and I met before bedtime for hot milk we did not speak of cruises but as usual sat hardly speaking at all, listening to the clock tick under its glass dome on the drawing-room chimney-piece between the glass prisms and the photograph of my droll dead father. 'D'you hear of the Zeits?' he asked suddenly. 'I miss old Zeit. I still miss him.'

'No. I hear nothing.'

'They went off to Germany. Curious idea. Very—positive—lot, except for the boy. The boy married—not much of a success, I gather. Delphi Vipont. She stayed once—or maybe it was her mother. Couldn't get on with her, one way and another. Beautiful, of course. Life's hard on very beautiful people.'

'Yes. Maybe.'

'Heard she'd left him. Went off with some German. Something in the German government—or the German army. Not dear. It's a pity the Zeits chose that sorry country.'

'Beccy said they felt it was their own country after all.'

'Poor Zeits. Very mistaken.'

'Why?'

'Jews. Not good at present. For Jews in Dusseldorf.'

'Yes, I see.'

'I liked the boy. Quiet feller like his father. The sister was a bright spark. The mother was a bit of a—challenge. There were grandchildren, I gather. Theo's children and the wife, Delphi. Had some children.'

'Oh?'

'Two girls. Born after a long time. Delphi hadn't been very keen. They're with the father. Well—we're not likely to see any of them again.'

'No.'

This was the longest conversation Mr Thwaite ever had with me which he himself had initiated.

How dull he sounds.

'No letters between you and that family then?' he said as we switched off the lights (Miss Gowe and the rest had resulted in electricity for the yellow house) and made our way up the stairs. I was clutching the banisters, gripping them every third or fourth step, walking like an ancient. I only needed spoons.

'Something there I always thought,' he said, astonishingly keeping on, gazing intently at the belly of the green flowerpot on the landing.

'Where?' I examined the pot.

'Between you and the boy.'

When I said nothing he made his way to his bedroom, turning at his door to say, 'Talked about you to me once or twice. "Good-looking girl. A stunner," he said. 'Appears he once saw you by some river.' Shutting his door quietly behind him he said, 'One always somehow hoped it might not be over.'

The next day, the next week, until the end of Mr Thwaite's

visit that year I did no more work upon the book; and I joined him on the motorbus outing to Filey, dressed clean and neat, Aunt Frances's niece again.

It was the lightening of my heart caused by this particular visit that probably marked the beginning of the great change.

For a long time Alice had been asking me if I would see the silver-fish schoolmaster, Mr Benson, to have a little talk. I knew that she must sometimes discuss me with him. He had been with us for four years now and once when they were helping me upstairs I remember them acting towards each other with more than the intimacy that occurs between sober people dealing with a drunk. Mr Benson had had quite a brisk way with him on that occasion, not at all as in his sliding, apologetic days. Often nowadays I would sit upon the bottom stair, sometimes with my whisky-glass, sometimes when I had decided to drink no more, but having had to pause for a while to take stock of things on my way to bed. 'Good evening,' Mr Benson would always say, flipping past me. Miss Gowe and the businessmen—they were not always the same businessmen and had lately changed into more schoolmasters from The New House School, though I never could tell one from another—Miss Gowe and the other lodgers never spoke to me on these occasions, passing tactfully by.

At last, however, there were no other lodgers but Mr Benson. The businessmen or schoolmasters were gone. Not even Miss Gowe, for she had been taken away on a tempestuous wind of disgust one Saturday afternoon, to a terrace house called Boagey's Guest House for Business Women, Separate Tables. It had hot and cold in the bedrooms and, according to Alice, doilies and bits of parsley. And no doubt a landlady acceptable to Valley Drive.

Miss Gowe didn't want to leave us. She had seemed to like the crashing sea outside her bedroom window and the three-handed

Bridge with the businessmen and dominies with whom a glass of sherry had not been unknown. I don't think she even disapproved totally of her landlady, for once or twice I saw a gleam in her eye of what might have been envy as I examined my bare feet on the stairs, my hair loose for the night. Sometimes I sang a bit.

Plod, plod, Miss Gowe's feet had gone upon the turkey stair-carpets—faded now, beginning to wear thin on the treads, and the brass rods without their lustre, for Alice could not do everything. Once I had tried to help her by polishing these rods and unfastened every one of them and, with Brasso and cloths, set about them on the hall floor. But then I had gone away to look for sustenance and shrieks and hollow cries had assailed my ears. Miss Gowe had fallen heavily on the loose stair-runner and lay in a bulgy heap upon the tiles. She accepted gladly the inch and a half I gave her to pull herself together and we sat for a time pleasantly discussing this and that until Alice came in from shopping and helped us both to bed.

When Miss Gowe had been removed from us into respectability—with a broken arm—Alice said 'All right then. I'm speaking.'

'You're speaking, Alice.'

'I'm speaking. I've seen it coming. You've seen it coming. It stops, or I go.'

'What stops.'

'The drinking stops. You don't drink when Mr Thwaite's here. Nor for maybe a week after you get a letter from him or from that Maitland. So you don't have to have it. It's not essential yet. I know. I remember my father.'

'It helps my work.'

'Rubbish it helps your work. You sit there sozzled at your so-called work. You're a show, Miss Polly, and a disgrace. Everyone's talking.'

'Who is everyone? Everyone's no one to me.' This struck me as a fine epigram, brilliant and sad.

'Look at you—hair in a tatter, face blubbered out, stockings in drapes. Ashamed. I'm *ashamed* of you. Ashamed to say I know you.'

'You drink, too.'

'That I do not. Not no more. I did and I don't, having pride and sense—and proper work. Do you ever think of your aunts?'

'No.'

'Or your friends of bygone days?'

'No.'

'That lovely soldier dead and gone, God rest him, who thought so much of you. Wrote those lovely poems about you.'

'They weren't about me. How d'you know that?'

'I can read.'

'Help me up.'

'I've read them. As I've read that colouring game you play at. And I'm ashamed.'

'Be quiet. Call me what you like. I dare say I do drink, and much I care. But don't call my work or—'

'What?'

'Well, you can go. I'll dismiss you. Help me off with my dress. I'm going to bed. If you say anything about my work—'

'Always in bed. When did you wash your hair? When did you take a bath? You never hardly leave the house. No—the time's come. Oh, Miss Polly, you were a *pretty* girl, and clever. Where's your will?'

'It never grew. I'm in a mess, Alice. I missed education.'

'Now you're telling the truth. A mess. But you haven't missed education. And stop crying. There's Mr Benson wants to talk to you. There now—Will you do this one thing for me, Miss Polly, and see Mr Benson?'

'What about? I don't see Mr Benson doing much for me. Let me get some sleep.'

'Will you see him tomorrow?'

'Tomorrow, tomorrow—'

'Right. Tomorrow. I'll keep you to that then.'

'You take a lot upon yourself, Alice.'

'Just as well,' she said, 'or God help you.'

'He doesn't.'

'I'm scarcely surprised.'

God only helps the strong, I thought, holding my head the next day. Crusoe, so much stronger than I was, helped with visions bringing certainty and joy—Crusoe, who husbanded his supply of brandy for twenty-five years, so that there was even some left for Friday's father when he was recovering from nearly being eaten by cannibals. Crusoe, the controlled, the respected, the beloved of God.

Selwyn Benson, when he knocked at the book-room door, did not seem as eager to see me as Alice had led me to expect. He hung his face only a little way round the green curtain that was there to preserve silence from the house for me at my desk. I had combed my hair that morning, my headache was abating, for there had been a letter from Thwaite and I felt, seeing his hesitance, rather in the ascendant.

'Oh come in, Mr Benson. I hope everything is all right?'

'Oh thank you. Yes, Miss Flint.'

'Do sit down.'

He was a very small man. In among Grandfather Younghusband's furniture he seemed a pigmy.

'Would you like—?' The decanter seemed to be missing. 'Coffee?' (I could hang on a bit.)

Silence fell. I felt a sort of emanation behind the book-room door, the waves of Alice beating. He was no more wishing to see me than I him, but she wasn't going to let him out yet. I wondered if Alice were trying to make some sort of a match.

'We are rather in trouble at the school,' said Mr Benson eventually.

'Oh dear. I hope it isn't going to close. I heard it was doing rather well.'

'Oh yes. Very well. A great many boys. It's mainly boys unable to be accepted by the better-known schools and it's not expensive. It will survive.'

'Oh, good.'

'We are, however, rather—er—short of staff. I understand you have academic qualifications?'

'None.'

'Mr Thwaite and Alice have spoken of Modern Languages?'

'I'm not a man. It's a boy's school.'

'Since the war men have been hard to find. We wondered if, perhaps—a little French?'

'My German's better.'

'Alice tells me that your mother was a teacher. She has the idea that you would be good with children.'

'I don't see how she knows. I've never met any.'

'Alice knows,' he said. We looked at each other. We warmed to each other.

'Perhaps one English lesson a week as well? For pleasure?'

'Yes, I see. I'd like—But is it legal? I thought you had to have qualifications?'

'No.' I could see that he thought this fact appalling. So whyever was he doing this for me?

'Perhaps you might just come to the school to see us? Have a try? Perhaps just tell them a little about your—er special subject.'

'That is *Robinson Crusoe*.'

'Yes.' (He did look doleful, now.) 'Of course, if you feel—' Outside the door I felt Alice planning to wring his delicate neck. He sat very still in the carved oak chair, looking as if he were never going to move.

'I shall have to get on with my work now, Mr Benson.'

'Yes, of course.' He picked his way across the clutter of the room and gazed round it. 'I might be able to help you as well as your helping me,' he said, 'I might teach you something of indexing—filing.'

'Well now—will you go?'

'I think I'm too busy.'

'You're frightened that if you leave that desk you'll find there's been no cause to sit at it, and then you'll have nothing.'

'You're cruel.'

'Aye, I am. And need to be. It's time.'

'I've not had a drink today.'

'Well, that's a start. But you'll be drunk again by bedtime. Drunk with fear—and cowardice and dissolution.'

'I can't go teaching boys, Alice. Look at me.'

'It could be set right still. Just. Out with Mr Thwaite, you looked a girl again. Come on—let me get at your hair.'

'Certainly not.'

'What are those scissors?'

'Cutting contrivances. Now—'

'Alice—stop. Whatever are you doing? You've cut off a yard!'

'Put your chin down. Shut your eyes. Now then.'

'Alice!'

'Hold still.'

'Alice.'

On the floor fell dreadful black lumps, heavy as felt. The scissors crunched and crunched.

'Alice.'

'Now here—mind the kettle. I've a sachet of camomile shampoo. Great Heaven, look at the water!'

'Alice—all this has happened to me before.'

'Pray God it won't have to happen again.'

'And here's a good washing cotton.'

'Wherever from?'

'The new emporium. In the High Street. The Bon Marsh.'

'Who on earth is Bon Marsh? The marsh is nearly gone.'

'It's French—you ought to know if you're going teaching. It means cheap. Not that it was. Nothing's Bon Marsh now we've lost the lodgers. Here get in to it. My—you're thin. Well I never, you do look nice. New shoes—I've got you ankle-straps with bucket backs.'

'They sound awful.'

'Well you can't wear your galoshes on the bus.'

'The bus. To The New House? It's scarcely a mile. I'll go in my old lace-ups.'

'There's these of Mrs Woods. I kept them as curios—I think they're African.'

'I like those.'

And so with bobbed hair with streaks of grey in it and savage slippers and a cotton frock of the very latest design and Mrs Woods's knowledge stored within me, I set forth to become a school mistress.

As I walked the well-known mile, waves of cold fright passed through me followed by surges of excitement of a new kind connected with my coming exposition of the great book, *Robinson Crusoe,* to a room full of children—for Mr Benson suggested that I begin with the subject in which I felt most at home.

The fear rose from the fact that the book, being so much more than a book to me, might lie so deep in the bone that it would be difficult to lay bare. The solitary work I had done upon it as spiritual biography, my later studies in the examination of it, not as fiction but as metaphysical landscape, had been written in the precious quiet of a study—a room I had made as remote from outsiders and as unknown to them as the texture and colour of the brain within the skull.

As one piece of work upon the book had been completed I had begun the next, placing the first carefully on a shelf. All my years had given the lie to the writer's lust for fame. I was too deep down, too separate, too simple, too mad even to trouble myself with the distractions of publication or communication and I did not even think, 'Perhaps when I am dead—'

Now I was to communicate some of my immense knowledge, and to children, when I had known no child since I was one myself and that one Stanley, who had responded by throwing hot coals at my face.

Yet I remembered his large eyes, his 'it's grand, it's right grand', and the feeling that he stirred in me before the cinder and the burning of the book that I had taught. Some small flame had spurted and sparked. And the book's curling pages, the shoots and sparkles and the flap of its flames had not stayed in my mind as a destruction but as a triumph, the completion of an act. I only knew now, and it rose out of an unconscious place, from some deep water-table, as I crossed the stile and on to the tarmac road and through the iron gates and up the familiar drive, weedless, rude cement—I only knew now that as I read and translated the French to Stanley, I had recognised an inherited power. 'Your mother was a wonderful teacher, I'll say that,' all of them had said. 'Oh, it was a loss to the teaching profession when she had you.'

And so today I willed as I walked that the power would return. I should tell the boys, these new Stanleys, receptive, rich, already well educated, things that they would not forget.

I would begin by discussing the concept of the novel: the English Novel, how it had emerged from jumbled and simplistic sources some three hundred years ago into the literary form we now recognise, its purpose to give solace and simultaneously to disturb; though its true genesis lies deep within man himself, in his urge to tell a tale. I would describe how, as blobs of jelly and the flat ribbons in the sea became fish, became birds, became mammals and intricate man, so the grunts and the snuffles of the cave became anecdote, joke, tale, tale set to music, saga, song-cycle and glorious traveller's tale. And then arose Defoe from the smelly streets of London, honest man (and criminal) prolific genius (and hack) to produce the great curiosity, the extraordinary masterpiece, the paradigm, *Robinson Crusoe* itself, the novel elect, fully realised and complete like the child Athene springing from the head of the rough god Zeus.

Having said a little of this I would continue in an analysis of the novel along the following lines (someone sloped by me along The New House School drive—it was the sexton, with his sideways look and I greeted him heartily):

1. Development of narrative during C18. Particular influence of Defoe on English and European fiction. *RC* and its roots—current journalism. The subtle transcendence of these sources. Brilliant manipulation of the reader. We read with the pleasure gained from the best dramatic journalism, unaware at first that we are reading more.

2. Imitators of, then reactors against Defoe, esp. ref. Fielding, Richardson. Outline gulf-stream imitators, sports, curiosities; C18 pattern of novel, its waves sweeping wider: and riding these waves (sub-section) original, unrelated wks. of genius: es. Swift (note Swift's opinion of Defoe!)

3. Rise of the women as novelists: Fanny Burney, Bluestocking writers, Lady Mary Wortley Montagu. 'Embassy Letters as Fiction.' The only book Dr Johnson read entirely for pleasure.

3(b). Interesting developments: horror novel, sickly childhood of the thriller. Dexterity, passion, brilliance at Haworth Parsonage etc.; the five miracles at Alton, Hampshire by a lady beset by domesticity and a querulous mother.

Final Point Every serious novel must in some degree and *unnoticeably* carry the form further. Novel must be 'novel'. To survive—like the blob in the ocean, the seed, it must hold in itself some fibrous strength, some seemingly preposterous new quality, catch some unnoticed angle of light—and unselfconsciously. It may fail—but better to sorry than safe. All the time it must entertain. No polemics. No camouflaged sermons.

The novel in the later nineteenth century, I thought I might leave perhaps until the second lesson.

There was no reply at the peeling front door of The New School House so I walked round to the back and saw the tennis-court scarcely more in trim than when the army had taken it to pieces in 1914. A net sagged, big plants grew, there were holes in the rusty wire. The orangery the Zeits had not quite completed was still beautiful in outline, but—I opened the door and walked in—the stone flags were dirty and covered with splintery dining-tables and cheap old chairs. All smelled of mince.

A boy roamed about. He told me that the Headmaster's room was upstairs. I said, 'Will you run up and tell him I'm here? Miss Flint,' and he went. While I was still thinking about my voice speaking to him as if it knew some of the rules, and wondering why my fluttering stomach wouldn't behave likewise, the boy returned and said, 'You're to take 1c. I'm to show you.'

'What a terrible noise,' I said as we approached Mrs Zeit's old morning-room where she had set up The Depot for the relief of the trenches.

'Mr Benson's not here,' said the boy. 'It's in there.' Without opening the door he went off and I walked in.

There were about twenty little boys. I knew nothing of ages but their hair was still floss or fledgling down. They showed great gaps of gum or the stubs of new frilly-edged teeth coming through gums. They had stick-legs with heartbreaking dents in the backs of the knees. Sagging socks. Most of them were rolling in combat on the floor.

Of those who were not, two were on window-ledges being the Royal Air Force and two more banging their desk-lid with a steady and hypnotic rhythm. Others were gathered at the teacher's tall desk and tall stool, scrabbling and kicking each other to get at what was inside, which didn't seem to be much. The blackboard was covered with faces and words beginning with 'b'.

The noise slowly faded as I stood at the door—the desk lids, mercifully, being the first things to die down, like a thunderstorm receding. Boys on the floor began to recline, then to sit up, those at the teacher's desk laughed less, and fought their way self-consciously back into the body of the room. Two last parachute descents were achieved from the window-ledge a little nonchalantly. A white china ink-well flew, smashed, trickled. I sat on an empty desk by the door.

In the moment of something like silence, the fuzzy photograph of the firm young woman with fat me on her lap in Grandfather Younghusband's study said decidedly, 'Now Polly! Before they start again.'

'Before you start again,' said I, 'pick up that ink-well. Thank you. You—with the torn shirt—go and clean off the board those filthy words. Yes—and stay there. The rest of you sit at your desks if they are not piles of firewood. Shut all the lids. Thank you. Now—take a deep breath.'

'Go on. All of you. Go on.'

'That's better.'

'Now then—I am Miss Flint. I am like SHEET STEEL. Write that on the board and I want your names every one of you. STOP THAT,' as a foot snaked from under a desk and hooked itself round the rail of the chair in front and jerked. 'Get up there beside the board, too, and write your name. *S*s don't go that way round. Write me twenty.'

'Now then, I'm your new teacher and you'd better be careful because I'm a terrible woman. I know a great deal about cannibals. On desert islands. I eat boys far lunch. Who can spell cannibal? Quite wrong. Go back. Someone else have a try—oh, *very* good. It's a difficult one. What's your name? Gegg? Well I never.'

'How dare the rest of you laugh! What's wrong with being called Gegg? He can spell cannibal. I won't eat him, ever.'

(How very delightful! How utterly delightful this was being!)

'Now then, I'll tell you something to stop you sniggering at things people can't help like their names, unless they're ladies and they can sometimes improve things by getting married, though not always—'

'There was a little boy once in a London school called Tim Crusoe and it was a very unusual, queer name and I expect he got laughed at for it. But one of the other boys in the class when he grew up, remembered it and wrote a story about it, and who can tell me what it was?'

'What's the dead silence? What? Gegg—Gegg knows— *"Robinson Crusoe."* That's right! What was the story about? Who was he?'

'He had a wooden leg, miss.'

'He had a wooden leg, Miss Flint. No, he hadn't. Yes?'

'Please Miss—Flint—he had a parrot and a hook for a hand.'

'One point for parrot. No point for hook. You're mixing up sailors. You'll be saying Flint next.'

'He saw a foot-print. On a Friday.'

'One point for foot-print but Friday was a person. Why was he Friday?'

'Please Miss—'

'Please Miss Flint.'

'Please Miss Flint, he was another boy at Mr Crusoe's school.'

'Mr Defoe's school. Daniel Defoe wrote *Robinson Crusoe.* Over two hundred years ago and we're still reading it today. Why?'

'Because you make us.'

'"Because you make us, Miss Flint." I do not. If you don't

want to read it, you needn't. I'll find you something else, you silly young nut. Stop laughing. If you don't want to read it you'll miss a lovely story. I'm going to tell you it first though— it's too long for you to read by yourselves yet. What's thar awful noise?'

'It's the bell, Miss Flint.'

'Bell?'

'It's the end. What have we to do for prep?'

'Prep?—Oh—'

(Prep?) 'Oh. write me a story. Even if it's only two lines long. I promise I'll read every single word. Stand up. Say good morning. Put your tie straight, Biggles. And don't all write about Gegg. It'll make him conceited. Goodbye.'

'Please Miss Flint, when're you coming back?'

'As soon as possible.'

'Yippeee!'

And then—again—alas.

'Please,' said the dispirited boy still hanging Smike-like in the hall of The New House School—and I wouldn't have been surprised to have seen him trailing a broom—'Please, you're to go up to see the Headmaster.' 'Very well,' said I, flushed with power. 'Show me up, please. Come *back*. Show me *up* please. Oughtn't you to be in class by the way?' (Wherever were these words coming from?)

'Mr Benson's not in today,' he said again.

'Things are different when he's here?' I asked.

'Oh yes, miss, very.'

And there, in Mrs Zeit's bedroom, the room in which I had been cossetted and pitied for Paul Treece's death, where still some slight ghost of Paul Treece lingered, where I had expected soon to be embraced as a daughter, sat the owner of The New House School, freckly, porridgy, flaccid, wan.

'One pound', he said, 'per term, per boy, per class. One class, twenty boy maximum.' He heaved a sigh. 'Five mornings a week all subjects. Supervision of football. Dinner duty on occasion, secretarial duties here for me. Cleaning of this study and the landing outside. Light shopping. Position to be surrendered when suitable male teacher available.'

Down through the mince-smelling orangery, over the cemented terrace, along the empty drive again and not a boy in sight. Silence like an old people's home with the inmates shovelled away, silent as the old nunnery, but none of the nunnery's confidence, happiness or life.

And home.

Mr Benson and Alice waited, and Alice became a whirlwind of anger and Mr Benson turned and thumped a mantelpiece so hard that glass prisms jangled and a clock under its dome gave a twang of surprise. 'I can't do it. Oh and I want to do it,' I said. 'But it's too much. I'd fail.'

I went off to my desk. There was a whisky-bottle in the drawer. I poured two inches and then another inch, and after a while an inch again.

Oh the humiliation. But they would be indulgent to me now. It was a relief to be here—in my own setting again, safe behind my own hand-built stockade. Oh, Robinson Crusoe, 'ship-wrecked often, though more by land than by sea'. I drooped above the whisky. Soon they would come with my tea. They would be good to me. Dear Alice, so kind to me.

But tea did not come.

Nor yet did supper, which Alice usually brought on a tray. I poured more whisky and went to the kitchen, but no one was there. The house seemed empty. We were without lodgers until the regular summer visitors arrived to see our housekeeping expenses through the winter. I called about the house. No answer.

I walked out on to the sand-hills and there I saw Alice and

Mr Benson in very determined conversation, Mr Benson with clasped hands and hung head, nodding occasionally, rather sharply. They had seen me. They looked at me. They looked away. They went on talking.

After a time they got up and came over to me, still talking, and Alice said, 'We'll go in. Come along,' and though Mr Benson drew back to let me pass in front of him, Alice marched in front of us both straight into the house and up to the drawing room. I followed, feeling carefully from one chair to the next, on account of my exposure to the brisk fresh air. Mr Benson stood by Aunt Frances's piano in the middle of the room, looking to the left and to the right.

'Shall I leave you then?' said Alice.

'No, no.'

'I think I'd better. It's your place, not mine.'

'Oh sit down Mr Benson, for goodness sake,' I said and sat down myself, hard on Mrs Woods's chair. Dust puffed out. I could not remember anyone sitting in thar chair for years.

Then slowly Mr Benson sat and looked seriously into the grate and I began to feel rather frightened.

Time went by and I began to feel greatly frightened, for Alice sat down, too. She sat down with me in my drawing-room. Alice, the maid.

'Miss Polly,' she said, 'Mr Benson has something to tell you. He has bought The New House School and is to be the next Headmaster.'

'*Mr Benson!* But I met the Headmaster this afternoon. He said nothing—Well, you know what he said.'

'He's a very sad fellow. I don't think he knows what's hap-pening. I was hoping—'

'But then, you're rich Mr Benson! You must have been rich all the time.' I was totally sober.

'No. The school was on the rocks. I borrowed the money. I am quite happy—'

'But—oh, good. Well done. Well, I do congratul—'

'I have something to ask you.'

'There,' said Alice. 'Now I can go away while you get on with it. As is only right.'

I looked at Mr Benson who smiled showing very square determined teeth I had not before noticed and for a moment his face allowed itself to go full rip. He looked joyous. A lunatic thought came to me. He was about to propose.

'I want to ask you', he said, 'to let me have Alice.'

'Oh, I can't possibly spare Alice.'

'I have asked her to be my wife. I asked her a great time ago. I have asked her often. She has always said no, until this afternoon.'

'Oh. Yes, I see. That is wonderful for Alice.'

'It's wonderful for me. Miss Flint, I think you knew. I think you guessed. You are pleased. I always said you would be pleased.'

Alice. A headmaster's wife.

'Oh of course—'

'We shan't be far away.'

'Far away? Alice won't go? You won't leave Oversands?'

'We shall of course live at the school. Of course,' and the square teeth were revealed again.

'Yes, I see.'

'I take up my position next term. We shall have the summer holidays to set the new regime going. I shall be interviewing staff and engaging building contractors. Getting out the new time-table usually takes a week. I have done this for some years already. There will be new boys and new parents to alert and see. A great deal to do and of course the wedding and honeymoon.'

'Oh, honeymoon.'

'We shall be married from Alice's home in Skinningrove.'

'Alice's home? But Alice's home is—'

'Yes. Her mother is determined to give the reception.'

'I didn't know. Of course she goes home at Christmas, but—'

'Her father is a miner, as of course you know.'

'Oh yes. Is he?'

'You will be guest of honour of course.'

'When—?' I saw my fingers slowly rubbing and pleating together the skirt of my dress—the first sign it is said of old age in a woman. 'When do you? When have you—?'

'In one month,' said Mr Benson. 'That gives you time to find Alice's replacement. Now, shall we bring Alice back? I shall find glasses and lemon barley-water for us all to drink to future days.'

'Oh Alice!'

'Oh Miss Polly!'

'It had better be Polly.'

'Oh never. Oh, who'll you get next to replace—?'

'I can never replace you.'

'Oh Miss Polly, whatever will you do? It was do or die. I had to do it. After today it was kill or cure. It's your only chance.'

I wanted to say, 'But can you stand this man, Alice? His time-tables and talk!'

'And oh, Miss Polly, the price of whisky!'

'Hem, heremmm,' said Mr Benson, 'You will of course be able to start your classes next term Miss—Polly. I can assure you there'll be no cleaning of the landings.'

'It wasn't that,' I said, 'it was the—well, I think as much as anything the shopping. And the uncertainty—I should have had to leave, he said, when a male teacher became available.'

'The nerve!' cried Alice.

'That will not be so. Please take more potatoes, Miss—er— Polly—Flint.' (We were sitting all together to three chops round the kitchen table.) 'One morning a week to start with, the proper scale of pay, with increments as time passes. French and German, but also a little general work which we shall call English.'

'You can do it, Miss Polly.'

'I wonder why you think so?' I felt so tired. 'I loved it this afternoon but—'

'There, then!'

'But I was probably just showing off. Acting. I've had no training—I've never been to school.'

'Some can, some can't—isn't it so, Selwyn? Miss Polly—'

'Alice tends', said Mr Benson, 'almost invariably to be right—though neither she nor I was right this afternoon. We mismanaged that. You should not have gone to the school alone.'

Later, as Alice and I washed up together—I dropping the last good plate—she said, 'You see, Miss Polly, Selwyn's scared. He's a right mix, Selwyn. Don't listen to the bombast. He's just whistling in the dark. He's still a scared man, though I've done a lot for him. France and that could still come back. I'm scared, too, but that's between ourselves—coming only from Skinningrove and no airs and graces. Headmaster's wife—Alice! Miss Polly, we'll need you bad.'

'He didn't say that.'

'He's proud. But he knows it. The school's going to need you for tone. They'll be right vulgar common folk sending their little lads at first, just so they can say they sent them to a private school.'

'I don't think I'll impress them. I don't see me adding any tone. I've noticed people think me very funny.'

'You've got something, though, Miss Polly. There's something to you. It's being brought up by people not usual. Not caring what's thought of them. And brains. That great book you're writing. I tell everyone.'

'Colouring game is what you called it last.'

'I only said it after years. I got so frightened for you. I saw you disappearing. All washed up and marooned and far away. But you won't be now. I know it. I know, I truly know. This is to be the right thing for us all.'

So they were married. I gave them Aunt Mary's spoons and my Chinese work-box. Under Alice's care the school flourished and filled and Mr Benson strutted forth in university gown and mortar-board with fierce glances and a kind heart and people began to love them both. Boys spilled about the grounds, swiped balls across the tennis-courts of neat mown green, began to be allowed about the town in smart black blazers and black-and-white caps—and their fathers gave enormous pots and cups of heavy silver for prizes on Sports Days, when Mr Benson wore his blazer of sunset-stripes and a panama hat so large and silky cream it would have graced even Mr Woods of Africa.

Mr Thwaite often attended the Sports Days, and Maitland came, too, dressed in brown tussore and a picture hat and carrying a reticule. Mr Thwaite looked very frail now, his old legs wrapped in rugs against the sandy wind which tossed the names of events and competitors, cried down hand-held megaphones, about the sky. Once Mr Thwaite gave the prizes and a speech which was all about the weather, but the wind took the speech away, too, so that nobody heard it, though they all clapped enthusiastically at the end and told each other how lucky the school was to have him there as he was some sort of lord.

And I, Polly Flint, was always there—at the Sports Days and at the Speech Days and every ordinary day—the weekdays and week-ends, early and late, and 'the yellow home' became 'The Yellow House'—a school boarding-house, and I moved into the front two rooms of it. The dining-room table was covered with red felt and then a white cloth on top and ten boys ate round it noisily and enormously. Upstairs in Mrs Woods's room six boys slept with lockers and photographs of home beside them and as many books and toys as they liked. When I walked home after school at the end of each day, the smallest school-house boys always accompanied me as far as the gates, talking hard and prancing. And when I turned back at the stile to wave to them, they were always there. And so passed some beautiful years.

For Alice's marriage had saved me, had shown me my course. 'I saw my deliverance indeed visibly put into my hands, all things easy, and a large ship ready to carry me any whither I pleased to go.'

And so, how happy now I had become at the yellow house; and one Saturday afternoon, two and a half years later, there came the most miraculous day in my life. For years of our lives the days pass waywardly, featureless, without meaning, without particular happiness or unhappiness. Then, like turning over a tapestry when you have only known the back of it, there is spread the pattern.

It was the early summer of 1939. I was walking home from school where I had been teaching in the morning, then sorting Selwyn Benson's letters for he was busy with a cricket match and Alice supervising visitors' teas—the maids all terrified of her—and it had grown thundery and hot. I walked slowly. I was thinking of my strange madness of long ago, my obsession with my paradigm, *Robinson Crusoe,* now quite gone, fled like the end of a love-affair, the bird flown from the shoulder. The fever over.

Oh such a great many years.

I decided to go home by the church and look at the graves of Aunt Mary and Mrs Woods for I had taken lately—like an old church lady—to visiting the church on Saturday afternoon. I passed the sexton's grave and thought that there should be a black but comic poem about a sexton's grave. I looked at the lonely, meaningless sick-beds of the other graves, pulled weeds out, thanked God that from my purgatory with the works of old Defoe I had emerged with a sense of God and resurrection; and I went into church and sat myself down in a pew at the back.

Women were working in the church for Sunday. Funny old birds. They sounded like birds, too, calling about from one part of the church to another. One was fluttering about the altar and another buffing about at the inside of the holocaustian windows polishing them even brighter, one was tightening up screws in the leading, some twittered round the brasses. Two ostrich-like ladies moved heavily-weighted sticks about over red tiles. Their talk was scarcely words. They spoke in the up and down conversational notes of birds in the evening in quiet woods.

I had grown, the past year, to love this music. To love the church, to begin to take part in this particular kind of song. 'Oh dear, oh dear,' said the lady at the altar, 'everyone's oh-dearing today.' 'Sand everywhere, sand everywhere!' called another, sweeping a lot of it down a grating. 'Sand, sand,' and Christ looked down from beneath the thorns of Jerusalem.

'Here's Miss Flint to help us. Now then, Miss Flint, it's a beautiful day.'

'It's hot,' I said, 'it's hot.'

'There—I've fastened that window,' said the lady with the screwdriver. 'It's been loose since the bombardment of nineteen-fourteen. Oh this church is a show! Miss Flint—if you'd known it once.'

'I've known it from the start,' I said, 'since I was six. But I wouldn't come to it. I was a rebel.'

'Oh, but I remember your Aunt Mary. What a saint. We always said she should have been a nun. And Miss Frances. We all loved Miss Frances. That wasn't much of a marriage—' And the birds began to sing like mad and louder with excitement when the parson arrived.

He was a new parson, said to have been a local lad, he was hungry-looking, with a Grangetown accent and frayed cuffs to his suit. He put his arm round some of the women and called out greetings. I thought of Mrs Woods who had said you shouldn't talk in church. All the ladies warmed and turned to him, like chickens running at feeding time. I saw Mrs Woods's dark, outraged face—and found I loved that, too.

'Hello, Miss Flint,' said the priest. 'Sheltering from the thunder?'

'Just calling.'

'We're in for some dramatics. You ought to get home. Can I give you a lift over the marsh?'

'Over the marsh? There isn't a marsh any more. It's two steps. I'm all right thank you.'

'In your wonderful house,' he said. 'Have you thought of that, by the way?'

'Thought of the yellow house?'

'If there's war they'll have you out of it. You're nearly in the sea.'

'That's what they said last time, but it came to nothing. We stayed put.'

'It'll be different this time.'

'Will there be a war, Father?' asked an old lady.

'Yes,' he said, 'there'll be a war. Very soon now.'

We stood together in the porch the priest and I. I said, 'Look—on the top of the tower on the school. D'you see the telescope? When I was a small child—well about twelve—I saw that telescope for the first time on the way to church and thought it was an angel.'

"Did they sort you out?"

'I didn't tell. Well, only our poor Charlotte. The maid. But look—it's back. The old telescope. Selwyn Benson found it in the cellar.'

'It'll be back down the cellar again when the war starts'.'

We walked together across the marsh field. He said, 'Polly Flint. Do you know, I asked you once for a kiss?'

'What!'

'I was the milk boy. The milkman's lad. I wish I knew you well,' he said.

'There's little to know.' A surging ridiculous blush, and a stumbling over my feet. (And past forty!)

'You live alone, don't you, except for the school? No family? You never come to services.'

'I think I shall soon. Why don't you come and see me at the yellow house?'

'You're always somewhere else. Always working they say at the school.'

'Well, it was time I worked. I must go now. I've books to mark.' I put out my hand and laid it upon his arm. Triumphant.

'How very hot it is,' he said, and I blushed again as he watched me.

'Goodbye, beautiful Miss Flint.'

So I walked home, having been called beautiful, and had to unlock the door of the yellow house, for this evening it was— very unusually—quite empty, the boarders being still at the Match and the housekeeper having the day off this particular Saturday.

I liked the house empty, now that it was so seldom.

I walked through the light and shadow of the hall with its rows of pegs and children's clothes and lockers and muddle of shoes and smell of boys and into the kitchen to boil a kettle for tea, thinking of vestal virgins, the dying face of Christ, of Jews, of the beautiful happiness in the world, all seen so sharp now, before the new war.

I thought of the shabby young priest; and the blush came again, surging up from my waist this time and spreading all about me, and I stopped what I was doing and stood still and thought—I'd suspected it before. Blood again. Disturbance in the blood.

Ah well, so it's over. No children now. A thousand years since the Sunday of the sheepskin rug. Yet only a moment. The blush came yet again.

And I watched the kettle boil and said, 'It's over.'

I cut myself three slices of bread and butter. Thin. I thought of the days of whisky, when food didn't matter. I went to the sink to wash the butter off my hands and looked out of the window and saw Stanley standing watching me out in the yard.

He was sharp-edged and clear.

He wore the clothes in which I had last seen him, over thirty years ago, the week he died.

His trousers were old-fashioned and long, over the knee, and his tie—which I had quite forgotten—was a string of slippery yellow and green stripes. The row of pencils was there, the ruler in the sock. His eyes were blue and attentive and very clear. He had been watching me for some time.

Then the ghost was gone.

It did not fade away. As I looked up, there it was—established. A sharp and definite boy. Then it flicked out and the yard was empty.

But there had been some command—a direction it would have been impossible to describe and which might have been lost had I stopped to think about it. I dried my hands and put the towel beside the sink. Without a word or a gasp or even a glance out of the window again, I walked from the kitchen to the front door.

On the mat were letters left by the afternoon postman and I picked them up. One was inscribed with a red cross in the top left-hand corner and seemed to be an appeal for sponsoring Jewish children being brought out of Germany. A circular.

I would look at it later. It was rather odd that it had been addressed to me in person. Miss Flint.

Then I turned to the other letter but needed my glasses. They were in the study and I found them and sat in the window there among all the fat dead files and the dusty books I seldom looked at now.

The second letter was postmarked Germany. Dusseldorf. And it was from Theo Zeit.

But I couldn't read it. His writing, always so small and odd, was here indecipherable. I couldn't believe it at first—stood up with the letter, pulled the paper tight, peered and peered at it up near my face, paced the room with it, held it to every light.

It was in German. Here and there I could make out a phrase. 'Almost ready', 'lost, no chance—', 'sudden departure', 'planned so long', 'unable to say'. Near the end I read, written quite clearly, 'Soon I shall follow them', and then, 'With my gratitude, blessings, love always—Theo.'

I found the strongest magnifying glass in the house and put the letter on the window sill in the last of the sun, but the calligraphy, always so minute and tense, was now so small as to seem scarcely formed. I went for a torch and blazed it on the paper, then put the paper under a bright light bulb in the desk-lamp. It made no difference.

I put on a jacket to run to the school, but stopped on the step. For all her importance to me I could not take Theo to Alice for interpretation. I turned instead to the other letter.

Hepzibah and Rebecca Zeit, the daughters of Dr Theo Zeit of Dusseldorf, are expected on the refugee train from Dusseldorf on Wednesday, May 8, 1939. Their sponsors—cousins who escaped from Germany a year ago—have waited as long as possible, but have had, at last, to leave for America where there will be work. They have run out of money. Dr Zeit has been contacted with the greatest difficulty and he has given the name of Miss Polly Flint of Oversands as temporary sponsor. He will follow the children with the rest of his family as soon as possible. He is only waiting for his last documents. It is thought wise for the children to leave as planned and very quickly. Their train leaves Dusseldorf on Tuesday, May 7 and will carry several hundred Jewish children. Will Miss Flint please be at Liverpool Street Station in London to meet this train and send word at once on receipt of this letter, also sending a guarantee of sponsorship.

I went out then, not to the school, but along the esplanade. And along and along it until it turned inland. I came to The Hall Estate to find the postmaster. His wife opened the door—she was one of the church ladies of the afternoon and I remembered that she'd asked me if I'd like to come to a get-together that evening. 'Well, I never! She's come,' she cried.

'Now, what about this? Miss Flint's here. She's come to have a sing. Now come inside, Miss Flint. The kettle's just this minute boiled.'

'It's the telephone,' I said, 'I need the telephone. Very quickly. Could you put a call through for me?'

She looked so disappointed that I said, 'Of course I'd love to come to the get-together afterwards.'

'Well, of course you can use the telephone. Dickie will see to the number.'

'It's two numbers. One near York and the other one in Germany.'

'Germany? Well, I don't know that we've done a Germany. We could manage a York. Dickie, we've done calls to York?'

'Well of course we have. What's this then? Sit down and we'll have a look. Well, the Thwaite's possible all right—that's a Pilmoor Junction number, reached through Trunks at York. It'll maybe take an hour. The Germany, we'll have to enquire. Is that the number?'

Theo's address and telephone number were printed on his letter-paper. The postmaster departed.

I sat in his tiny front room with the get-together, knee to knee, twelve of us on hugely-stuffed chairs and a sofa. It was extremely hot. In the corner sat the post-master's daughter who wasn't right in the head. Her mouth was open. She nodded and gaped and her hands tried to stroke me. Her hands were very cold. She seemed another mystery of this haunted day.

'We were just singing hymns,' said the postmistress, 'verse by verse, passing the book. Shall we go on until the call comes through?' Someone gave a note and the mad girl became even more excited and two old men began to sing,

'Old folk, young folk, everybody come
Join the donkey Sunday School and make yourselves
at home'

and I thought: 'This is enough,' and got up and made for the door where the postmaster was suddenly standing to say with quiet pride that Thwaite was on the line.

'Mr Thwaite? It's Polly. No—everything is very well. I think. Mr Thwaite—there has been a letter. I am to take Theo Zeit's children. He has asked me. To live with me. Yes. They are coming on a train full of Jewish refugees from Dusseldorf. On May 8th.'

'The connections should be quite easy,' said Mr Thwaite. 'I have the International Bradshaw beside me.'

'Mr Thwaite. Of course it's going to be absolutely marvelous to have them, but—'

'I liked old Zeit,' said the faint thread of voice, 'I enjoyed it when old Zeit was still about. I liked the boy too. Indeterminate for a Jew—but a good boy.'

'It's just—Mr Thwaite—I have never been to London.'

'Oh, I shall come with you.' The thread vibrated and crackled in the thundery night. 'I shall join you at York. You can get to York safely?'

'Certainly not. I mean, yes, of course I can get to York safely. But you mustn't think—'

'I shall be there. The Tuesday. We shall catch the eleven forty-three from platform four, which means you take the eight forty-five from the marsh to be safe for your Darlington connection. King's Cross six-fifty as I remember. I shall arrange accommodation.'

'Mr Thwaite you are too—You aren't strong enough.'

'I should like to see London again,' said the thin voice; 'it may soon be greatly changed.'

'Dusseldorf', said the post-master, 'is, alas, a different matter. Calls to Germany are not easy just at present. I have booked it in for you tomorrow morning—tentatively. And I fear that it will cost a great deal.'

'That's all right. I'll pay for York now. May I come and wait here tomorrow?'

'As long as ever you like, Miss Flint.'

The get-together was watching me with interest. 'We could go on with the hymns,' said somebody, 'if Miss Flint would like?'

'I've some Jewish children coming from Germany,' I said. 'They're coming to me. It's sudden. To live at Oversands. They're refugees.'

They had all heard the telephone conversation in the back of the shop but put up a fine show of surprise. 'The more the better, the more the better,' said the postmistress; and her dotty daughter nodded her head. 'Poor souls, poor little homeless objects. There's none of us knows here one thing about what's going on out there. None of us. You're a lesson to us, Miss Flint. I suppose you don't play the harmonium?'

So I ended the day when you needed me, my love, playing a harmonium and singing hymns in the street that had grown over Delphi's stable yard and the mausoleum of long ago.

*

'I sat three days in the back of the post office,' I said to Mr Thwaite and Maitland as the train rocked out of York station, 'but I never got through to Germany.'

The three of us sat in a first-class carriage on bluebell and grey plush, our heads against little lace-edged cloths with L.N.E.R. intertwined in satin stitch, but rather less starched somehow than the ones from Wales when I was six. Mr Thwaite's ancient Don Quixote figure gave the carriage a patrician look. No one would divide a meat pie in it.

Maitland sat very straight in black, on her head a shiny straw-hat with a feather held on by a golden pin. Mr Thwaite was in button-boots and a silvery herring-bone coat, rather long for a hot day; a tall coke-hat sat on the rack above his head and his yellow gloves and silver-topped stick lay on the smaller rack below it. Holiday people in shorts and knapsacks looked in with interest at us as they passed along the corridor. I was probably looking rather queer, too, for I have never quite understood about clothes. They are always wrong. But my stockings were silk.

Mr Thwaite gazed about him with enormous composure and Maitland's mouth was tweaked up very tight which signified emotion, her fingers clutched up on a pouchy portmanteau which she kept on her knee.

We trooped to the dining-car for coffee and chocolate biscuits; we trooped to it again for luncheon and drank 'a bottle of bone' which turned out to be wine. We ate roast beef and ginger pudding and custard. Maitland said that the railways always made a nice ginger, and how she was not sure, for a ginger took a good hour or two to steam. The custard she thought passable, though boiled up and not baked. But we were thinking of the children on the other train, starting and stopping, clanking towards Holland.

Mr Thwaite, watching the weather above Selby, pointing out the Abbey as an afterthought, said that a boiled railway pudding eaten in Doncaster could have been initiated in Edinburgh where the train started. He added with pleasure that we should still be on board for tea.

We drank our after-luncheon coffee, poured by a magician who didn't spill a drop as we flew through flat Lincolnshire. Quiet fields, quiet villages. 'They should be over the frontier now,' said Mr Thwaite, 'if they left Dusseldorf on time.' We all saw faces of parents left behind. 'Safe now in Holland,' he said.

Giants made of cardboard walked in the fields of Rutland. They were decorators carrying a ladder between them and on the ladder the name of some sort of paint. 'Miss Polly's still a child,' said Maitland, 'looking and looking.' Mazawattee Tea seemed to be the name of all the stations, or Oxo-Bovril-Oxo, and sometimes a gold-and-pink girl would spring out at us from a huge frame box set up beside the line, great sheaves of corn painted all around her and a steaming cup and saucer at her feet. 'What a lot of beverages we have to choose from these days,' said Mr Thwaite. 'We are really very fortunate.'

The countryside slid quietly by, quicker and quicker. Newark was anonymous, Peterborough invisible. Tea-time was scones and jam, tea in pots with rose-buds round the lid, cups squat and wide like chamberpots. They sat deep in their saucers, unrockable in the pleasant afternoon. Outside basked the bland and peacetime South, with three months remaining. Hertfordshire: cows and large trees.

'What huge trees, Mr Thwaite.'

'Ah yes. You will find the trees huge. It's a pity you can't see a southern spring. I should like you to see a spring in Italy one day, Polly.'

'I hope they will have warm clothes,' said Maitland; 'it's very cold with us in winter.'

'They ought to be getting well through now. Almost to The

Hook,' said Mr Thwaite, looking at his silvery-gold pocket watch.

Eight wild tunnels. We screamed through them, then slid and settled into booming, hissing King's Cross. The porter couldn't hear our voices. They were lost in the echoing great arc above us and I couldn't understand him. He sounded like a foreigner. But he found us a fat taxi like a coach or a pram in which we sat in a row once more and from which we were bowed to Brown's Hotel.

Mr Thwaite went quickly to bed and Maitland and I were asleep soon too, and at seven the next morning were again in a taxi to meet the German train. 'If we are first there,' said Maitland, 'we shall be first away. The poor things—oh, they will be so exhausted.'

'It will be a four-hour wait,' said Mr Thwaite, 'from seven until eleven. Before they even arrive.'

'But if we can sign the papers or whatever we do—there'll be some sort of desk set up, I suppose—in, say, half an hour,— we might just get a train home this afternoon.'

'It would be too much in one day for Mr Thwaite,' said Maitland.

'Oh, not at all. Not at all.'

'Shall we take all our luggage with us to the station?' I asked them. 'And leave directly from Liverpool Street to save time?'

'I shall have a word with the Hotel Manager,' said Mr Thwaite and reported that the Manager felt that we ought perhaps to reserve rooms for one more night, just in case—and a further room for our guests.

'Guests?'

It suddenly dawned that the children to be collected would be guests. People.

Children.

Distraught children, perhaps sick children, and certainly wretched.

'We'll get them quick home,' said Maitland, 'quick as we can. Get them in their beds by midnight and journeying done. That's my feeling—home to-day.'

But Liverpool Street Station, at seven in the morning, was very quiet when we arrived and there was a blackboard covered with copperplate writing saying that the train from Dusseldorf would be arriving twenty-four hours late.

'We ought to look at things,' said Maitland, 'Miss Polly's never been to London.' But we were reluctant to look at anything, reluctant to leave the station.

'What if they come and we're not here?'

Vociferous Jews were talking in clumps. 'Certainly not today,' said a man with a long floaty beard and a round black hat, which I thought must be a joke. 'We should all go home.'

'Perhaps at least we should go and look at Westminster Abbey for Polly,' said Maitland, so we all took a taxi to Parliament Square and there were sandbags piled about in fortress walls all along the buildings, about the cathedral itself. It looked dusty inside, subdued, disappointing. There were a great many people praying. Everyone quiet. We walked a little way down Victoria Street and saw the noble doorways of The Army and Navy Stores. 'Oh, it's where Aunt Frances went,' I said, 'to get her missionary things for India. I wonder if they still sell things like that?'

'I'd think not very many at present. But we might have luncheon there, and see,' said Mr Thwaite.

We made our way after luncheon to the department of missionary equipment and it was very empty indeed. On display was a fortress of cabin trunks with brass ribs, a skyscraper of pigskin camp-stools, tiger-proof tents, chromium and crocodile water-bottles and gleaming elephant-guns.

'Poor Frances,' said Mr Thwaite. 'Elephant-guns. So unlike her.' He took a solar topee and stroked it and set it on his head.

'I have always rather desired one of these things,' he said, standing to willowy attention.

'Twelve shillings and sixpence, sir,' said an assistant.

'Ah—Alas—'

'Mr Thwaite,' I said, 'I want to buy you the solar topee.'

'I don't expect I'd wear it much. It's rather a waste of money. In Yorkshire. In view of the coming war.'

'But still, you shall have it,' said I.

Then, as the assistant went to see to the wrapping of the box, Mr Thwaite said what seemed to be a very frightening thing.

'I am going to leave for Thwaite,' he said.

'What? Oh, of course you're not. You can't leave for Thwaite *now*. You can't possibly travel alone—and Maitland and I can't possibly do without you. We need you to be notice-able. With taxi-drivers and everywhere. We need you—to get the children home.'

'No, no,' he said, and cleared his throat so that the safari fire-irons jingled. 'I am—her—um, going to leave—er—Thwaite.'

'Leave *Thwaite*! You are going to leave *Thwaite*?'

'No,' he said. 'I am—er—trying to say, Polly, that I am—in fact, in my will I have already done so—I am leaving you Thwaite, Polly. When I die.'

'Will you be wanting anything more?' asked the assistant, approaching with the tall box.

The next day we were at Liverpool Street at seven once again, but again there was no train. The blackboard was wiped clean.

No one to ask. No Jewish relatives. Nobody. There had obviously been some vital announcement that we had missed by visiting The Army and Navy Stores the day before. We walked about Moorgate and the City Road and London Wall and went to look at the Bank or England for a time, and up and down. 'How do they stand it?' asked Maitland. 'The noise of it all? Look at all the white faces. And what are they all running for? Miss Polly, I'm sorry—I must sit.'

'Oh yes. So must I.'

'I'd thought we might look over a few of the city churches,' said Mr Thwaite, who was growing more and more vigorous as the days went by and we grew weaker. 'And there's the Mansion House and Smithfield Market. Oh yes, and several excellent stations I believe. For instance, none of us may see Fenchurch Street in our lives if we don't see it now.'

'Well, see it you may but it'll be alone,' said imperious Maitland, who had confessed in the hotel the evening before that since the butler's death and Lady Celia's, she and Mr Thwaite had become very close: 'Miss Polly and I need a cup of coffee.'

'Or Bovril, Oxo, Ovaltine or even Mazawattee Tea,' said I.

'Perhaps one sherry,' said Mr Thwaite. 'If we can stop Polly from being an utter abstainer.'

'No thank you. Look—it's awful here. Maitland's quite right. Listen to us shouting in this traffic. Let's go back to see if there's some news and if there's not—well, we could go to a park somewhere or go and look at the river.'

'It's the river through Thwaite meadows I'll be glad to see again,' said Maitland. 'If ever we do. We're stuck with this Liverpool Street, it seems to me, for life.'

But at the station there was now a great change. Crowds were pushing, yelling, shoving and being issued with identity tags; and in a moment we were among them and being whisked up into the gallery of some sort of railway building. Below us streams of children were flowing in, and Red Cross ladies. Wild-looking government and railway officials ran among them, clutching armfuls of notes and the air was salty and sour with the smell of dirty hot children and cries in German and

English together, and there was quarrelling and weeping. The children poured steadily, slowly into the hall below us as if the tide of them would never cease.

We sat in a row and Mr Thwaite dozed. Maitland and I were now electrically wide-awake. 'He's old,' said Maitland. 'He is old now. Tiredness hits him sudden. He's over eighty. One forgets.'

'I never think of him as any special age.'

'And he has left you Thwaite,' she said, her eyes on the confusion of the world below.

'Oh Maitland—did we dream it? Has he?'

'Yes. I knew already. He's talked about it. After all, you know Polly, he is your grandfather.'

The family next to us were called by a ferocious Red Cross captain with a fine, permanent wave, and bulged and pushed past us wildly, treading on feet.

'*What!*'

'Your grandfather, of course.'

'D'you mean—'

'Emma—your mother—was his daughter.'

'But how could—Maitland! D'you mean—? Aunt Frances?'

'No, no. Mr Thwaite never cared for your Aunt Frances very much except as a sister. It was Miss Younghusband he was in love with, your Aunt Mary. She was a raving beauty when she was young—or so I understand.'

'But you can't mean—' The world tipped and reeled as the uniting families tipped and reeled about us. *'Aunt Mary!'*

'No—your Aunt Mary wasn't your grandmother either, though she was old enough—twenty years older than your mother. Your Aunt Mary wanted to marry him but unfortunately—or fortunately since the result has been you, Polly dear—he then fell in love with her mother.'

'What, the—? The battle-axe bosom? Grandmother Younghusband? The one who had *Fanny Hill?*'

'I know nothing of any Fanny Hill. I don't think she had more children still, though from all accounts the Archdeacon might not have noticed—'

'But she couldn't. She couldn't! Mr Thwaite must have been so young. And Grandmother so very old.'

'He was twenty. She was forty. I am told.'

'But it's terrible.'

'A little strange,' said Maitland, 'but Victorian life is full of surprises. And the Archdeacon, you know, was almost obsessed with stones—and God, of course. I think I'll just pop out on to the station and see about some more sandwiches.'

I sat looking at Mr Thwaite. Mr Thwaite at twenty, the lover of the warrior mother of Aunt Mary, the ice-maiden. I thought of Aunt Mary in the taxi on the way to Aunt Frances's wedding, her face growing whiter and whiter under the wonderful ancient hat. And Mr Thwaite clearing his throat all the time and looking at the rain. And the tension mounting, mounting, so that at last it broke in the storm of my crying. And how I had been unable to stop the crying because of the awful confusion in the air.

Poor Mr Thwaite—conceiving my mother in some fit of pubic madness (I looked at his face—a long brown map, the eyes closed in their deep sockets just like—well, yes: the photograph of my mother in the cardboard mountains with the crease down the middle, tired out in Liverpool.) Had he loved her—his daughter? Had he even been to see her? He must have had to stop coming to the yellow house quite suddenly after it happened. And no explanation to Aunt Mary.

I mean—how *could* he have explained? How tell a girl he had wanted to marry that he had conceived a child by her mother? Well—but it was Borgian!

Poor Aunt Mary—her spoons and her prie-dieu.

Well then, and what a frightful, frightful man, this Arthur Thwaite. What a villain. And yet—oh no.

But what a grandmother I had had! What a terrible woman. And yet—the loneliness, the husband, quietly turning pages, singing hymns as he bounded into the sea. Gazing at stones. Poor woman.

So much never to be known.

And all that church!

Mr Thwaite stirred and woke and looked at me with blue eyes—oh heavens, mine again—and smiled.

'No progress?'

'No progress. Maitland's gone for sandwiches. It's all going awfully slowly.'

'I'll just nod off again then.'

I could not stop looking at him—dropping again easily into sleep, his hands (Oh Lord! My thumb!) crossed on the head of the silver-headed walking-stick.

Oh Lord God—men!

What men I'd known—cautious, inadequate, shadowy, grasping, dull. Maybe it was just bad luck. At any rate Mr Thwaite on one occasion had been none of these things. My grandmother on one astounding night (though maybe more? Maybe dozens? Maybe not even at night?) on at least one astounding occasion had admitted to some forgotten bed at Thwaite or the yellow house or even Danby Wiske—springs squeaking, feathers heaving—oh Lord!—one gloriously incautious man.

'Egg and cress,' said Maitland. 'He's dropped off again. Did I shock you, Polly? Are you sorry to know?'

'No, no—of course not. Did—what did Lady Celia know?'

'Everything of course. She and Mr Thwaite were very close. Always close.'

'You were saying—' I looked at the egg and cress, the taut

dried-out upward curve of the railway sandwich—'You were saying that you and Mr Thwaite are very close, too?'

'Oh yes.'

'He's been quite a—successful sort of man with women hasn't he? I mean, I always adored him as a girl. It's interesting to know that there are such men. Usually they're only in novels.'

'Oh, he's very successful,' said Maitland comfortably. 'He's always needed quite a full-blooded life you know. Those arty, bohemian people at Thwaite—he found them very milk-and-water.'

We sat in our rows in the gallery. The children's names were called out, oh so slowly; and the children in the morass below us thinned out, oh so slowly—talkative children, tired children, very young children—babies really—numbed grey children, fierce tough children and children who looked older than Abraham. All were beautifully dressed in clothes far too hot for the weather and rather too big. Each had a big luggage label round its neck. Some carried parcels, some carried dolls and bears, some leaned against each other on the benches with fingers in their mouths. As time passed, some slept.

At four o'clock in the afternoon there were still sixty or so children left below us. The benches around us full of relations were emptying. We had been brought tea, and something to eat. I ate and drank nothing. I looked. Two children were mine? Which, which, which?

'Why are we so near the end? Haven't they come? I can't see properly. They all have their backs to us now.'

'It is administered alphabetically,' said Mr Thwaite, awaking from the present nap. 'We shall be near the end.'

'A great many Jews are zeds,' said Maitland. 'Let's hope these of Polly's are top of the zeds.'

But they were not. By six o'clock the great mass of children had thinned to a scatter, but ours were still not called.

Which, which, which.

Theo's children. Theo's and mine.

Seven o'clock. They had thinned to half a dozen, and the half a dozen didn't look very special ones. Six times at least my heart had thumped when I thought I saw Theo's turn of the head, Theo's smile—or Rebecca's red hair, long legs. Very quiet, wan children these last ones, crumpled on the benches now, and I allowed myself to think, in order to prepare myself for disappointment: mine may be resentful, sullen, ugly-minded children. Think what has been happening to them. Worse—I tried to think very rationally—they might look or be like Delphi Vipont—the Delphi who had looked at me forty years ago and at whom I had looked back and our dislike had bitten into both of us.

If two small Delphis awaited me?

But, 'Zeit? Flint?' nodded the Red Cross captain in my ear and I went down alone to the hall and saw two thin girls standing by the desk. One was curly and one was straight. They had the wooden faces of people blotched with tiredness but refusing to cry. The taller girl was clutching a book, she had kept her finger in the place she had reached when she had been called away to me. The little one held a doll, a bear, a china horse, and a lop-eared rabbit and had Theo's eyes.

We said goodbye to Maitland and Mr Thwaite at York, Maitland most anxious and reluctant to go, Mr Thwaite, with a porter behind him pushing the luggage and the topee box, clearly relieved that all was done.

I was totally confident, rattling along in flowing German and as comfortable as if I had visited London every week of my life.

Hepzibah, Rebecca and I.

We changed trains at Darlington into the little train that ran down through the steel-works and out on to the marsh—or where the marsh had been. The great flames and plumes of fire still rose from where they were smelting the iron bars, the same long crocodiles of trucks, long puddles in the mud, long clanking pipes and rough old machines, and on the hills opposite, the woods still grew sparse so that the light shone through them like knitting-loops when you draw the needle out.

But the marsh was almost invisible now. So small.

It was afternoon—the afternoon of the next day and of course, since we were getting near the yellow house, it had begun to rain. 'I did so want you to see it sunny,' I said. 'Look Hepzibah—do look out of the window even if it's dreary. It's where Daddy lived. Leave the book for ten seconds.'

'Oh pretty,' said Hepzibah, looking at The New House as the train clattered by. 'What's that thing on the roof?' and then back to the book—which as far as I could see was rubbish.

'A telescope.'

'They're doing something to it,' said Beccy.

'It was your father's. I'm afraid they're taking it down. They keep doing that. It's because of the—'

'The War,' said Beccy looking at the lop-eared rabbit.

'Daddy'll get here,' said Hepzibah firmly. Beccy leaned her head against my side.

'It's quite near,' I said, when we reached our station, 'we can walk if you like. Mr Boagey will bring the luggage on later for us. Would you like that?'

'I won't leave my things,' said Hepzibah, 'I'm not moving without my things.' She was thirteen. There was trouble coming.

'I'm staying with Tante Polly,' said Beccy. 'You go in the taxi, Hep, with the luggage.'

So Beccy and I came striding over the tarmac road and across the last tail-end of marsh to the yellow house.

'Is that ours?' she said.

'Yes. Ours. It's a funny old house.'

'It's wonderful,' she said, 'like a big ship.'

And so we blew in through the great front door, held open for us by Alice, with Hepzibah and the luggage alongside her in the hall. The doors slammed and the sea crashed and the windows shook, and we were all safe home.

THE END

A Victorian study. Shelves floor to ceiling, almost empty of books, but a few objects: a sewing box, a sherry decanter, a framed drawing.

A large sash window shows an expanse of moving sky—big, seagoing, creamy clouds. The furniture is contemporary (1986) sparse but pleasant. A gigantic television set has its back to the audience. One corner of the room is shadowy.

Beside the door an answerphone and an old woman—still tall, her hair still thick and brown and swept up on to the top of her head in a frisky twirl. Ankles rather swollen. Her cheeks, once round and rosy, have dropped a bit, pinching up the mouth. She wears a flamboyant shawl.

She speaks into the answerphone:

POLLY FLINT: Could you speak louder? The traffic—
Could you speak louder? The door is very thick.
Oh dear me, yes. The memoirs.
I'd forgotten the memoirs.
Oh dear, oh dear—I should be locked up.
Well I suppose I am locked up. I've locked myself up. Just a moment. Just a moment. Will you wait till I find the key?

She flicks down the switch, walks vaguely here and there, dabbing about on the shelves, on the chimney piece.

In the shadowy corner a shadowy figure begins to become appar-

ent. It sits facing the television set. After a time POLLY FLINT eases her old self down into a chair also facing the set. Outside the yellow house the traffic zips past continually. At its gates there is a busy roundabout. Beyond them the old Iron-Works stand, dwarfed by the huge chemical city which has grown round them, its chimneys like silver pencils, its cooling towers like vast Christmas puddings decorated with a spaghetti of pipes. They are beautiful and weird. The yellow house sitting in the middle of them is bizarre.

At the back of the house the great front door is little changed but a journalist is sitting on the steps. She has cock's-comb hair, all-in-one leather hose, is knitting a fluffy sweater and smoking a cigarette.

Round the corner after a time a car comes bumping and a black-eyed, dumpy, talkative woman gets out.

BECCY BOAGEY   The traffic's frightful. I can never park outside. Some day I'll sink in this sand. Good morning. I'm Beccy Boagey. I'm the parson's wife.

JOURNALIST   I'm Charlotte Box. *North-Eastern Gazette.*

BECCY   Well, there's no point waiting, dear, I'm afraid. She won't see you. She won't see reporters. She's very old.

JOURNALIST   It's an appointment. She'll see me. I'm not on about this nuclear thing. I was in her Confirmation Class. She knows me. I'm after her memoirs.

BECCY   You'll be lucky.

JOURNALIST   Yes, I will. I am. She likes me. She has a laugh at me. Being called Charlotte Box. I don't know why.

BECCY   She's had a time lately.

The vicar's wife, Beccy Zeit, rings the bell, screams into an answerphone that she's Beccy and please let me in Tante Polly. The metal grille crackles but there is no reply.

She does this I'm afraid. Locks herself in. Then when she comes to look for the key she forgets what she's looking for.

She gives another great peal on the bell and then sits by Journalist.

JOURNALIST   I don't blame her, do you? Not moving. I wouldn't move. Not to make way for nuclear waste I wouldn't. Making way for rubbish. It's a lovely house. It ought to be preserved or something.

BECCY   I believe it was once, but then there was a compulsory purchase. She dug herself in. With the nuns. The house is let to some nuns. They've dug themselves in, too. They live round at the back.

JOURNALIST   Oh, they'll never do it—The Government. The nuclear waste. The dumping of nuclear waste. They'd never dare.

BECCY   There's plenty of room for it, you know. There always has been. Under the Hall Estate there are great salt caves you can run lorries round. They've been used for years as store rooms though nobody seems to have known about it.

JOURNALIST   They catch on slow round here.

BECCY   I never saw the salt caves. For this nuclear waste. But we weren't here for very long, when I was young. The war came and we were evacuated to Thwaite School.

JOURNALIST   That started here, didn't it? Thwaite School? You're Miss Flint's some sort of daughter, aren't you?

BECCY   She adopted me. She adopted me and my sister. We were Jewish refugees. My father sent us from Germany. They'd been lovers of some

	sort. I never exactly heard. I never saw my family of course again.
JOURNALIST	I heard. Weren't they—?
BECCY	Yes, Auschwitz. All of them. My sister and I came out of Germany on the second from last train. My father hesitated. He was a great hesitater. Though usually he was lucky.
JOURNALIST	You must have been little. Coming all that way to England. Did you only know Miss Flint?
BECCY	We didn't even know Miss Flint. We thought she was a bit mad at first. But she spoke German. We felt safe with her. Soon we loved her. We'd had no mother for a long time you see. She'd gone off when we were babies. She died at Dresden.
JOURNALIST	And your father at Auschwitz. Oh my God!
BECCY	Oh no. My father didn't die in Auschwitz. The rest of the family, not my father. Don't ask me how he survived. I asked him and he said, 'All that I can say is that I do not know.' He had the number across his wrist. He used to cover it with his other hand gripped tight. It's all I can remember of him really, though I was seventeen by then. That and the look of him on the white seat by the privet hedge.
JOURNALIST	Here? He didn't come back here?
BECCY	Yes. Oh dear me—where is Tante Polly? We'll have to go round to the back. The nuns keep a key for when this happens.
JOURNALIST	I didn't know your father came back. They all say Miss Flint's a—well—
BECCY	An old virgin? So indecent. Yes. She is. It was a terrible shock his coming back. It was one morning in the summer and my sister Hep—

you know her? Yes. It is that one. The international lawyer. She runs Europe. Hep had got up early to work. She was taking the Scholarship to Oxford—which she won of course with twenty stars—and while she was dressing she looked out of the window, and then she came upstairs to me. I had the little attic bedroom—the crow's nest where the poor maids used to sleep in the bad old days. I liked it. Tante had made it lovely. So then Hepzibah and I both looked out of the window. And then—it was odd. Hepzibah being so bossy and always trying to be in charge. She simply said, 'Come on,' and we went down into Tante's room and stood there, looking down at her in bed. She's rather large you know—or she was. She was lying there asleep, rather splendid. And she opened her eyes on us in the early light, and looked. Then she got out of bed and went to the window and said, 'Stay here,' and put on her slippers and a queer old coat—but she looked beautiful.

And we saw her walk in to the garden to the awful-looking thing on the seat. And they stood looking at each other, and the wind blew Tante's nightdress about. Then she brought him in to us.

JOURNALIST   And he stayed?

BECCY   Yes. He died soon.

JOURNALIST   They didn't marry?

BECCY   I think it had gone beyond that.

JOURNALIST   They were old?

BECCY   No, no. It was not important. Let's get the key from the nuns.

In the book-room inside the yellow house POLLY FLINT is

seated looking on a television screen which does not seem to be switched on. The bright window is behind her, the clouds soaring along. In the shadow the other shadowy figure is now rather more defined.

POLLY FLINT	I was looking—what was I looking for? I don't know—losing things, forgetting things. The key. And I knew she was coming, the journalist. Dear Charlotte Box. For my memoirs.
CRUSOE	My creator was a great believer in memoirs.
POLLY FLINT	So impossible, so false. Talking about memories.
CRUSOE	Oh, I don't know. My creator had quite a facility. Stood him in very good stead. Memoirs.
POLLY FLINT	Nonsense—he made it all up. Fiction isn't memory.
CRUSOE	But memory is fiction. I tell you my creator had no compunction—well, here I am, for a start.
POLLY FLINT	Making things up from nothing is another matter. An easier matter.
CRUSOE	He didn't quite do that. I'm not sure that I was easy, exactly. I believe I quite tired him. Even God had to rest on the Seventh Day.
POLLY FLINT	Your creator must have been ready for a rest by the end of Book Three. I'll concede that.
CRUSOE	He said something of the sort. He said that I tended to take charge.
POLLY FLINT	You are apt to do that.
CRUSOE	Can't think why. I'm very ordinary.
POLLY FLINT	Yes—Dickens thought so.
CRUSOE	Never met him.
POLLY FLINT	I never thought so, though. You've lasted me out, Crusoe.

CRUSOE	You're not dead yet. You may find another yet, Pol Flint.
POLLY FLINT	Not at eighty-seven.
CRUSOE	You never know. Your mind may begin to wander.
POLLY FLINT	It has never done anything else. But you're the only—You have been my great love.
CRUSOE	That was your misfortune. Your heart was never thoroughly in it, Pol. Loving real men. You were after the moon.
POLLY FLINT	One ought to be after the moon. And what do you know? My heart was in nothing else but love for years and years. Like a dumpling in broth.
CRUSOE	My creator liked a homely phrase. Pol Flint— your men were all duds or shadows.
POLLY FLINT	The men one meets are matters of luck. I was properly kissed once. On Darlington Station. I can remember that.
CRUSOE	I know nothing of it. Pol Flint—you know that I never loved you?
POLLY FLINT	Yes.
CRUSOE	I have made you happy. But I have never loved you.
POLLY FLINT	Yes.
CRUSOE	Characters in fiction cannot make new departures. We are eunuchs. Frozen eunuchs.
POLLY FLINT	Maybe we are all just fiction.
CRUSOE	Don't be ridiculous. You are talking like a satirist. Like that fool, Swift.
POLLY FLINT	He thought nothing of you, either. Maybe your creator, maybe Defoe himself, was only a character in fiction. Nobody really knows. He had a lot of disguises—very queer. All those warts,

	and the stoop. And in the pillory and prison. He sired you at sixty. An unlikely man.
CRUSOE	A perfectly ordinary journalist. Bit of genius. In a minute you'll be on about what is fiction.
POLLY FLINT	No I won't. I'm over fiction. As I'm over drink. I keep cream sherry for the nuns and watch them sip, all nods and smiles. As I nod and smile when people talk about the importance of art. I cleared the shelves after all. That gave you a shock Crusoe, didn't it? When I sent all the books to Thwaite School? Marooned all over again.
CRUSOE	Well, you kept me.
POLLY FLINT	Of course. And a few others. A few since your day, too, dear Crusoe. But on the whole, it's all over now.
CRUSOE	What, fiction? Or you having affairs with novels?
POLLY FLINT	Both.
CRUSOE	Fiction'll fade out?
POLLY FLINT	It won't fade out, but it will have to change. It's become quite canonically boring—all about politics or marital discord. The minutiae. You should see the fiction they have thought up about you and Friday.
CRUSOE	Yes, well, he could be very trying.
POLLY FLINT	We don't have heroes now. We shan't see your like again.
CRUSOE	You didn't see my like before. I was an innovation. Though I was but a plain man.
POLLY FLINT	Yes. But you became immortal. There are no immortals now.
CRUSOE	No, no. I was just a man. I can't think why I still hang about. I do hang about, don't I? It's not just you?

POLLY FLINT   Oh yes you're still here. They put you in films and song-and-dance acts. They've had you On Ice.

CRUSOE   However did they do the footprint? My setting of course was good. He knew all the best sites. And very exciting. He knew about excitement, my creator.

POLLY FLINT   Novels aren't exciting now. Just writers rambling on.

CRUSOE   How curious. In my creator's day writers hated one another.

POLLY FLINT   Oh they do now. Great haters.

CRUSOE   Ah yes. Knew very few.

(*Pause for thought.*)

I did think it was all rather moving of course. My battle. My courage. The way I dealt with things, all those years.

POLLY FLINT   Let's not boast.

CRUSOE   Our weaknesses begin to show in old age.

POLLY FLINT   But you're ageless, Crusoe. You were new and yet eternal. You were 'novel'. Dramatic. Poetic. You could tell the tale. You nourish us.

CRUSOE   Like bread.

POLLY FLINT   You were my bread. You are my bread.

CRUSOE   That sounds like blasphemy.

POLLY FLINT   Quite a few people see an affinity between you and Jesus Christ. They are given grants for theses on the subject.

CRUSOE   These are blasphemers.

POLLY FLINT   Oh, quite often people confuse their fictional heroes with God. As they confuse their human lovers. Or themselves. It is a great hindrance to a happy life. Emily Brontë did it. So did Proust.

CRUSOE   I don't know them. Should I care for them?

POLLY FLINT   You'd find conversation difficult with Proust.

CRUSOE   Pol—I think you should find that key. The journalist's been on the step for quite twenty minutes. It is a great profession. You should remember my creator and treat it with respect.

POLLY FLINT   I'll look in a moment.

She sits back in the button-back chair. The sky outside darkens. The CRUSOE-shape grows clearer—shaggy beard, tattery garments, great hairy-mushroom umbrella, suspicion of parrot on shoulder. As this figure grows grander and bolder, POLLY FLINT's figure begins to fade. Now she looks old. Her cheeks sag. Old, knobbed hands drop down, slide off her lap. Her head rests sideways at a gentle angle. Her mouth hangs open a bit. CRUSOE has become a Titan.

CRUSOE   (*rambling. Even Crusoe grows old*)
              You've been a good and faithful woman, Pol Flint, and children love you. A room of empty shelves, but still half in love with books. Is it enough? A quiet life. But Godly—and some of that because of me. As a life, not bad. Marooned of course. But there's something to be said for islands.

POLLY FLINT   Good night.

CRUSOE   You know, when my wife died, there were children. There was a daughter. We don't hear about the daughter. What became of her?

POLLY FLINT   Goodbye, Crusoe, Robin Crusoe.

CRUSOE   Goodbye, Pol Flint.

ABOUT THE AUTHOR

Jane Gardam is the only writer to have been twice awarded the Whitbread Prize for Best Novel of the Year (for *The Queen of the Tambourine* and *The Hollow Land*). She also holds a Heywood Hill Literary Prize for a lifetime's contribution to the enjoyment of literature.

She has published four volumes of acclaimed stories: *Black Faces, White Faces* (David Higham Prize and the Royal Society for Literature's Winifred Holtby Prize); *The Pangs of Love* (Katherine Mansfield Prize); *Going into a Dark House* (Silver Pen Award from PEN); and most recently, *Missing the Midnight*.

Her novels include *God on the Rocks* (shortlisted for the Booker Prize), *Faith Fox*, *The Flight of the Maidens* and *Old Filth*, a *New York Times* Notable Book of the Year.

Jane Gardam lives with her husband in England.